P9-DEI-385

St. George & the Dragon

It was a shame to let this man fight the beast. Even with that broken pitchfork and stubble on his chin, he was passing handsome. She was thankful for her concealing hood, that oh-so-necessary fabric that kept him from knowing how often her eyes strayed over the revealed *V* of his chest and down to that silver-coated bulge, so wrongly exposed by the slit in the bottom half of his surcoat.

The man was indecent. She ought to have a proper tunic made for him.

Ought to.

Did not want to.

Not only did she like his chest, she would be happy if his surcoat blew away entirely, and left her with an unobstructed view. She understood now the powerful forces that had moved Osbert so long ago to his leering, slobbering behavior. It had taken her twelve years to reach the stage of a fifteen-year-old boy, but she was there now, and by St. Stephen she did not know what the hungers of her body might make her do.

It was a pity she could not chain him to a wall and keep him like a pet, to do with as she would. He had the look of someone who might know how to properly deflower a virgin, if he did not get himself killed first.

She looked at him, standing there with his pitchfork and an expectant look on his face. Sadly, his demise was more likely than not.

Other *Love Spell* and *Leisure* books
by Lisa Cach:

A MOTHER'S WAY ROMANCE ANTHOLOGY
WISH LIST
THE WILDEST SHORE
THE MERMAID OF PENPERRO
OF MIDNIGHT BORN
BEWITCHING THE BARON
THE CHANGELING BRIDE

Critics Praise *Romantic Times* Readers' Choice Award Nominee Lisa Cach!

The Wildest Shore

"Cach's descriptive writing is brilliant. . . .
A book that's romantic, sexy, and a lot of fun!"
—*All About Romance*

"Cast aside civilization and allow yourself
to be swept away into a new kind of women's fantasy."
—*Romantic Times*

The Mermaid of Penperro

"Cach's beautifully crafted, erotically charged scenes
and light humorous touch will please fans."
—*Booklist*

"A wonderful and engaging tale with unique twists that
offer happy surprises . . . [Cach's] ability to create toe-
curling sexual tension makes for a must-stay-up-and-read-
till-dawn story."
—*Romantic Times*

Of Midnight Born

"*Of Midnight Born* passes my CODPIECE test . . .
Creative, rather Original, Dramatic, Poetic, Intensely
Emotional, Comedic, and best of all, Entertaining."
—Mrs. Giggles from *Everything Romantic*

"A mix of magic, romance, and humor, *Of Midnight Born*
delights the reader's imagination. . . . [It] kept me glued to
my seat, turning pages, till the very end."
—*Romance Reviews Today*

Bewitching the Baron

"With complex and colorful characters, lush detail
and a compelling story, Ms. Cach weaves a story rich
in humanity and emotional intensity."
—*Romantic Times*

LISA CACH

George & the Virgin

LOVE SPELL   NEW YORK CITY

To Tyler, who is not afraid of sharp-tooths.

LOVE SPELL®

June 2002

Published by

Dorchester Publishing Co., Inc.
276 Fifth Avenue
New York, NY 10001

If you purchased this book without a cover you should be aware that this book is stolen property. It was reported as "unsold and destroyed" to the publisher and neither the author nor the publisher has received any payment for this "stripped book."

Copyright © 2002 by Lisa Cach

All rights reserved. No part of this book may be reproduced or transmitted in any form or by any electronic or mechanical means, including photocopying, recording or by any information storage and retrieval system, without the written permission of the publisher, except where permitted by law.

ISBN 0-505-52489-9

The name "Love Spell" and its logo are trademarks of Dorchester Publishing Co., Inc.

Printed in the United States of America.

Visit us on the web at www.dorchesterpub.com.

George & the Virgin

And though that he was valiant, he was wise,
And of his bearing as meek as is a maid.
He never let no villainy be said
In all his life unto no matter whom:
He was a true, perfect, gentle knight.
                                    —"The General Prologue"

"Then have I got of you mastery," quod she,
"Since I may choose and govern as I wish?"
"Yes, certain, wife," quod he. "I hold it best."
                                    —"The Wife of Bath's Tale"

                                    —Canterbury Tales
                                    Geoffrey Chaucer

Chapter One

The southwest coast of England
Medieval times

"Hurry up, Osbert! It will be morning soon."

"Don't rush me, Alizon. I cannot do it if you rush me."

She held his pizzle in her hand and jerked on it as he had shown her. "Why aren't you getting hard?"

"You're not doing it right," he whined. "I am not a cow to be milked."

"You certainly *feel* spongy as a cow's teat. You'll never get it in me if it stays like this."

"Devil take you! If I don't, it won't be my fault. You're the one who doesn't know what you're doing. You're the *virgin.*" He said it with a taunt in

1

his voice, and she was glad of the dark of the shed, which saved her from seeing his face and being tempted to slap it.

"I wouldn't be here if I wasn't a virgin and well you know it. Sheep would speak Latin before I would let you touch me."

"Be nice to me. It's a favor I'm doing you."

She bit off the retort that came to her tongue, knowing that she should not alienate Osbert, however much she loathed him, loathed touching his damp and floppy pizzle, and loathed being here in this dark shed, fuggy with the stink of sheep and cow.

She had to be nice, at least until she had gotten what she wanted. Even as she reminded herself of that, her hand betrayed her, giving his cock a jerk that made him yelp.

"Christ's blood, Alizon! It will be of no use if you tear it off!"

She took the protest as an excuse to give up the task of arousing him. "You do it, then."

"You could suck on it."

The thought made her gorge rise. She would never let him put that filthy thing into her mouth. This time it was her own face she was glad could not be seen; otherwise her grimace of revulsion might have angered him into giving up this foul task. "We've no time. Please, do what you need to and let's be done with it."

"You'd do it wrong, anyway," he grumbled. "You'd probably bite me." And then he was quiet but for the catching of his breath as he worked on himself.

Alizon turned to the shed door, where through the spaces between the rough slats she could see the lightening of the sky. Sick anxiety roiled through her stomach, cold-hot panic pouring down her chest like water, and she had to clench her jaw to keep from urging Osbert yet again to hurry. Morning was almost upon them, and his family would be rousing. Time was almost up.

She *had* to lose her virginity.

The body heat of the livestock took the worst of the chill off the damp spring morning but could not keep her from shivering. For all her urging Osbert on, she dreaded the hurried, clumsy coupling that awaited her. There would be pain, and a humiliation greater than she thought she could bear.

Her fear turned quickly to anger, as it had many times in these past weeks. God's breath, she could not believe this was how she had chosen to lose her virginity. She was fourteen years old, and she should have managed a better deflowering for herself before now.

Like others before her, though, she had been hoping against hope that something would happen to make it unnecessary—maybe she would be married, or have a chance to leave Markesew, or maybe her menses would wait another year to start and she would still be considered a girl, too young to take part in the annual lottery of virgins.

None of that had happened. No one had shown

any interest in taking her to wife. Her menses had begun three months ago. There had been no opportunity to leave Markesew.

She was an orphan, and lucky to have been sponsored by the church for an apprenticeship to the widow Bartlett, who wove tapestries with her sister. It would be suicide to leave her apprenticeship and run away; a young girl alone was too easy prey.

Better Osbert in a shed at her own bidding than unknown men on the road at theirs.

Even knowing this, she had hung on to hope, waiting until the last minute to get the deed done. Osbert had been trailing after her like a hungry dog ever since her breasts had begun to bud two years past, and she had known she had only to whistle and he would drop his braies and be on her.

Only, now that the time was at hand, he was having trouble fulfilling the promise of those two years of leers and unwelcome fondles.

Dawn was coming, it was the summer solstice, and at noon the lottery would be held, just in time for low tide and the march across the exposed causeway to Devil's Mount.

She heard Osbert's grunting breath, his body a hunched wraith in the gloom. "Are you ready?" she asked.

"Almost, almost . . ."

She pulled up her long woolen skirts and leaned against the stone wall. She touched herself, the soft, sparse growth of new hair around her sex, and felt a welling of sadness for what she was about to do.

The feeling took her by surprise; before this, she had spared no time to dwell upon the loss of any girlish dreams of a more tender bedding. But her body had always been her own, her private vessel, and now she was being forced to share it with one who would foul it with his dirty hands and his pizzle, and she would never be the same again.

She let anger burn away the sadness. It was the townsfolk of Markesew who were to blame for this, they who had managed no better solution to their curse than the sacrifice of virgins.

Damn them! Damn them all for their cowardice!

Damn them for making her do this thing, in a shed that stank of wool and droppings, with a boy whose nose ran constantly with snot.

Osbert stumbled nearer, then fell against her, the firmness of his erection against her belly. He kissed her, his tongue plunging inside her mouth. She turned her head away, grimacing against the salty taste of the snotty mucus that had transferred to her lips. He went on slobbering at her neck, his tongue sticky with thick saliva, while his hand fumbled and groped between her legs. She felt him shifting his organ, the tip of it like a thick, hard knob of wood prodding at her.

"Spread your legs. I can't get it in like this."

She did as bid, and Osbert squatted lower, jabbing with his cock against her soft folds, trying to find entry.

"Just get it in!" Her revulsion made her want to retch. Could she truly go through with this?

5

"Do not tell me what to do! Peace, Alizon! You cannot command me in this!"

"I would not need to order you if you did it right!"

"Shut up!" He panted and strained against her, then she felt him softening, his pizzle bending against her. "See what your ordering did? See? I told you to shut up, I told you not to tell me what to do!"

She was torn between relief and desperation, his failure both a deliverance and her sentence of death.

"Lie down; it's this standing that is spoiling it," he said.

"I'm not lying down in here." The floor was made up of matted straw and excrement, and she would not so much as bend her knee to it.

"Then bend over the stall wall."

"What?"

He pulled her to the stall and pressed his hand to her back, making her lean forward until her face was pressed into the warm side of the cow on the other side, the animal shifting its weight away with a soft sigh. Osbert fumbled with Alizon's heavy skirts, then shoved them up past her hips.

She was still confused. "You're going to do it like a sheep?"

"Peace! Unless you want to ruin it again."

The idea of a ewe must have appealed to him, because he was back at her, harder than he had been moments before, albeit no closer to success.

"By all the saints, Osbert, not *that* hole!"

Suddenly she could stand it no longer: the shed, the stink, the cow her face was pressed against, Osbert and his bungling of this simple task. It was too much to bear.

She could not do this. She could not let him enter her with his dirty pizzle, could not let him grunt and groan above her and take his animal pleasure from her body. She suddenly knew that she would rather die than give herself away like this.

"No!" She pushed back from the rail, taking Osbert by surprise and knocking him off balance. Sheep bleated, and he cursed as he fell into the muck.

"I would rather lie with the Devil than let you take me," Alizon screeched. "At least *he* would know what he was doing!"

Osbert sucked in a breath of horror, and his voice came from the shadows of milling sheep. "God hears such blasphemous thoughts, Alizon. He will make you suffer for them."

"It is the innocent girls of Markesew who suffer, and if that is how God cares for the devout, then I will gladly go to the Devil!" Tears in her eyes, she pushed her way out of the cowshed and into the gray morning.

"The Devil take you, then!" Osbert called after her. "He will welcome a slut like you!"

She ignored his words, running across the dewy grass until her breath came in gasps and her sides ached. She stopped and stood, looking down over the misty sloping fields to the town that sat upon the edge of the coast. Her gaze then traveled across the gray water to the black silhouette of Devil's Mount.

The rocky island and what it contained had been a blight upon the coastal village of Markesew for nearly thirty years. There were a few still living who recalled the days when the mount had been home to the de Burroughs, rich and powerful barons who had ruled from their castle atop the island, and who had gathered riches from the trading in their harbor.

And then the dragon had come. Some said the de Burroughs had brought it on themselves by reaching too high, and thinking themselves holy; they said God had sent the dragon to teach the de Burroughs their place.

Others said it was the Devil who had sent the dragon to devour the de Burroughs, that the barons had been born in Hell and were being called home. But once loosed upon the earth the dragon had been impossible to recall, and, its hunger not satisfied with the de Burroughs, it had turned to the shore for its appeasement, laying waste to the innocent.

In truth, no one knew why the dragon had come to the mount. And no one knew how to be rid of it. The only way the villagers could keep it from ravaging their shores was to feed it a steady supply of sheep—and once a year a virgin.

Alizon gazed out at the mountainous island, her

heart wrenched with grief and helpless fury. She wept, the sobs tightening her throat and stealing what breath she had left.

The tears were for herself. They were for the girls who had died over these many years. And they were for the girl who would today be sent to the dragon.

"Will it be me?" Alizon asked, holding Emoni's hands. "Tell me. Have you any sense of who it will be?"

Emoni shook her head, her hazel eyes glazed with tears, the pallor of her face frightening Alizon with the knowledge that it implied. "I do not know."

Alizon squeezed the fingers of her dear friend. Emoni had the gift of sight, a secret she had shared with no one else. "Do not be afraid to tell me. It is my future, and I will see it myself whether you tell me or no. I would rather be prepared."

Alizon's hair was a wild and curling red, her eyes nearly black, her build tall and large-boned. Emoni's hair was straight and brown, her eyes hazel, her build small and delicate. For all their differences of appearance, though, the two girls were as close as sisters. From their first meeting, it had been as if they had known each other a lifetime already—and the bond they shared had only grown stronger through the events of the last year: Emoni's marriage and her discovery two months past that she was pregnant.

"I am not hiding the truth from you—you know

I would not. It is as I said: I do not know. I have had visions, but they are visions that make no sense."

"Tell me!"

It was almost noon, and the whole town was gathered at the seawall, milling and mumbling, the mood halfway between that of tragedy and celebration. A dozen flower-bedecked sheep baa-ed from a temporary pen and tried to nibble the garlands off the necks of their neighbors, unaware that they themselves were soon to be eaten.

The sea had receded past Devil's Mount, revealing the raised stone causeway that glimmered wetly in the cloud-hazed sunlight, curving like a white snake in its path across the gray muck of the sea bed.

"I see you in the lair of the dragon," Emoni said.

Alizon caught her breath, her blood turning cold and draining down her legs. It *was* to be her who would be fed to the beast. Her knees buckled, and she caught herself on the seawall.

"But in my vision, you are unharmed."

"Am I about to be eaten?"

"I do not think so, but there is blood—"

"Blood!"

"Not yours!"

"But blood! Whose, then—"

"I do not know what it means!" Emoni interrupted, in her voice a desperation that matched Alizon's own.

A boy blew a trumpet, startling them. It was the

signal that the lottery was about to be drawn and the virgins must take their places.

"Horrid Tommy," Alizon said, glaring at the youth. "You know he likes calling us to our deaths."

"He wouldn't be so gleeful if it were his little sister in the lottery."

"Wouldn't he?" Alizon asked bitterly.

Emoni hugged her. "May God keep you safe from harm."

"May He keep us *all* safe. It is what He should have been doing these past thirty years." She stepped back from her friend. "There are times I think He does not exist at all."

"Do not abandon faith, Alizon. Never that."

She touched Emoni's cheek and swallowed against the tears that tightened her throat. Worse than being devoured by a dragon would be to never again see her beloved friend's face. "I will never lose my faith in *you.*"

She turned then from Emoni and nodded to the widow Bartlett and her sister, who were standing at the front of the mass of townspeople. The widow's jaw was set, her eyes barely meeting Alizon's own. As Alizon's mistress the woman was demanding, but never had she been cruel. No words of affection had ever been spoken between them, but Alizon thought she saw in the rigidness of the widow's stance the signs of a caring heart. If the widow had felt nothing, she would be chatting with her neighbors or eating a bun like some of the others, not standing as if she were trying to stare down Death himself.

Alizon looked around. The frightened faces in the crowd belonged to the girls who would be in the lottery today, and to their families: the baker and his wife, each with a hand on their daughter's shaking shoulders; a widowed fisherman in gray and tattered clothing, standing stiff beside his wide-eyed girl; a merchant's wife, her rich gown doing nothing to ease the terror in her eyes as she and her daughter's nurse stood sentinel on either side of the silent girl, whose lower lip trembled.

The non-frightened faces were those of the other townsfolk, men or women relieved it was not to be one of their own this time to be devoured. They tried to hide their happiness under solemn expressions, but the brightness of their eyes and the quick smiles that slipped across their lips betrayed their hearts.

The worst of the bunch were the wealthy land-owners. These had come to be certain the sacrifice would be made, and their flocks of sheep safe for another year—but they were never the ones who paid the price.

Alizon stepped up onto a wooden platform with the five other virgins, their ages ranging from twelve to sixteen. The sixteen-year-old, Greta, had been through the same ordeal thrice before, and had become a town joke between her good luck with the lottery and her poor luck at finding a husband. She was a homely girl, with a harelip and a shambling gait. Whenever speculation was made on what would happen if the town ran out of virgins, someone was sure to say, "There will always be Greta." Alizon took a place next to her and slipped her hand into the girl's, giving it a squeeze.

Greta glanced over, and her malformed mouth twisted into a bitter smile that did nothing to vanquish the tears in her eyes, or the knowledge that the only value she had was as a potential meal for a monster. "I wish it *would* be me this time."

"God's breath, Greta, why?"

"It would be a relief, to have it over."

She gave Greta's hand another squeeze, for it was a sentiment against which she could not argue. She herself was worn out from the emotions that had been driving her. Now her gut was cramping, urging her to relieve herself, and sweat with the sour scent of fear had broken out all over her body. Her limbs were weak with exhaustion. The thought of finding herself here year after year, like Greta, made her want to lie down and die.

The village priest began reading off the names of the girls for the lottery, dropping a square of wood for each into a black bag. It was yet another sign of the evil that had come to this town that the priest himself should participate in such a profane ritual. If she had succeeded in getting deflowered, that same priest would have stood beside the midwife as Alizon was examined for evidence of her state, and he would have taken the sworn testimony of her defiler.

From the platform Alizon looked over the crowd, finding no set of eyes that would meet hers. Even Osbert looked away, as if he had not just this morning been pressing himself against her, his tongue in her mouth. She saw the merchant whose daughter was on display beside her. The man was standing beside his richly garbed wife, whispering in her ear. As Alizon watched, the wife's expression showed surprise and then tearful relief. She began to turn toward her husband, but he scolded her, and she faced forward again, her expression glowing.

Suspicion raised the hairs on the back of Alizon's neck. The man's joy could have been due to faith, or to the acceptance of God's will. Or it could be from a certainty that had nothing to do with the divine.

Alizon shifted her gaze to the baker and his wife. Their faces were pale, their eyes fixed upon their daughter. The fisherman was also still plainly fearful, as was Greta's older brother, and the impoverished parents of the last girl. She knew then that the merchant's daughter would not be chosen, no matter that the square with her name was supposed to be in the bag with all the others.

Fiery anger flushed through Alizon where moments before she had been cold. Worse even than the injustice of bribery was her own helplessness in the face of it. There was nothing she could do against this town that tossed its poorest and least comely young women to a dragon for the sake of their precious sheep and houses.

"You're hurting me," Greta said, and she tried to pull her hand free from Alizon's.

"Your pardon." She released Greta's hand, which she had been crushing in her own.

The priest began speaking a blessing in Latin, as if doing so could make this unholiest of acts holy. A chill breeze blew up, pulling at skirts and cotehardies, tugging at hair.

Damn them! Damn them all! Damn every one of them who encouraged these sacrifices year after year!

She and the other girls faced out to sea, the platform upon which they stood giving them a view over the heads of the townsfolk. For a moment the sun broke through and shone down upon Devil's Mount, setting aglow the green grasses and trees of its steep, rocky slopes, and the pale yellow stones of the fortress crouched at the top. For a brief instant the island was beautiful, the hideous evil at its heart unseen.

For a brief instant Alizon could tell herself that there was no dragon, and that, if she were the one to cross that causeway and descend into the dragon's lair, she would find nothing there but an empty cavern.

She met Emoni's eyes, thinking of her friend's vision of her in the dragon's lair, blood all around. Not all of Emoni's visions foretold the future; some, like daydreams, were but wishes played out in the mind. Which would this one be?

She held Emoni's gaze as the priest reached into

the black bag. His high voice fluted out over the suddenly silent crowd.

"She who will honor the dragon this year is named . . . Alizon."

Chapter Two

Present day
The United States

"The monster is going to get you!"

Five-year-old Gabrielle shrieked in delight and ran down the hall. "He can't catch me! I'm too fast!"

"He's going to get you! Do you hear his big feet?" George stomped on the floor with each step, moving as slowly as a brontosaurus. "He's coming! And when he catches you, he'll eat you up!"

Gabrielle shrieked again and dashed through the door to his bedroom. He gave her time to hide and then followed her in, pausing to claw the air and roar. "There's a little girl in here, and when he finds her, he's going to eat her in a hundred bites!"

"No he won't!" came from the closet.

George sniffed and roared and clawed around the room, pretending to look under the bed and behind the curtains, in the bathroom and inside the armoire, and then came to the closet door and lowered his six-foot-four frame to his knees. He growled and was answered by a shriek and giggles from within.

"I know where the little girl is!"

He pulled open the door, and Gabrielle flew out at him. He pretended to fall over backwards, and she leapt atop his chest, bouncing up and down as if riding a Clydesdale.

"I got the monster!" Gabrielle cried. "I got him! And I'm going to eat him all up!"

She started tickling him, her babyish fingers too clumsy to do it well, but he writhed and begged her to stop.

"George! You've got her all wound up and it's past her bedtime!"

George craned his head from the floor to see his sister Athena standing in the doorway, her hands on her hips. Her dark hair was down, and she was wearing a loose dress of green batik. She looked as if she should be leading a group discussion on community recycling, or reading auras at a psychic fair.

"Peace, man," George said, holding up his fingers in the *V* shape. The gesture was a remnant of their childhood, a joke between them long before they were old enough to know anything about the political movement behind the gesture.

"Peace, Mommy," Gabrielle said, imitating him and holding up three fingers.

"There'll be peace when you're in bed, young lady." The words were stern, but both George and Gabrielle knew that she wasn't angry. Athena—née Elizabeth, and called Elizabeth until she had hit her teens and decided otherwise—was and always had been a softie. It had more than once gotten her into trouble.

"I want Uncle George to tuck me in."

"Brush your teeth first."

"Okeydokey, artichokey!" Gabrielle climbed off George's chest and galloped out of the room.

George sat up, his smile fading. With Gabby gone, a familiar sense of weariness settled over him. He tried to distract himself from it by examining his bedroom from this lowered perspective, but he saw nothing but beige blandness.

Why had he not noticed before how empty the room was? Hotel rooms had more warmth, and he spent enough time in them to know; his career kept him on the road for two-thirds of the year.

"How's your leg?" Athena asked, coming over and sitting on the edge of his extra-long mattress, the one item of furniture he had taken the time to have custom-made.

"Good as new. There shouldn't be any trouble with going back into the ring."

He had torn a muscle a few months earlier, during a match for Champions of the Universe Wrestling, where he was one of the top three stars. The injury had kept him out of the ring, but after the surgery he had alternated between being a guest commentator and playing parts in the backstage storylines. Those dramas had become as important a part of the entertainment of professional wrestling as the matches themselves.

The writers at CUW—or "Cow," as those who so profitably milked it for cash called the organization—had put him in a metal leg brace in which he creaked around backstage like a long-haired Frankenstein, ambushing foes with folding chairs and lurking in their dressing rooms, trying to gain the sympathy and betrayal of their girlfriends. It was a male version of the soap opera, with him playing the part of the wounded and misunderstood brute.

"No trouble with the leg, maybe," Athena said. "What about the heart?"

He shrugged, said nothing. He didn't want to talk about it. Talking made it impossible to ignore the hollow feeling that was expanding inside him with each passing day.

"Don't play the Neanderthal with me. I know those television reporters have gotten to you. About the only time I see you smile is when you play with Gabby."

She was right, as usual. He sometimes wondered if Athena had a sixth sense when it came to the emotions of others, or if her intuition was just a refined version of the male-baffling perception that most women possessed.

A few weeks after he had ripped his muscle, right at that point in his recovery when he was getting depressed by the limits on his activity, the national news media had broken the story of a ten-year-old boy in Missouri who had tried to imitate his signature move, the Slayer: leaping off the top turnbuckle in the corner of the ring, doing a forward flip through the air, landing sitting on the shoulders of his opponent, then with his legs wrapped around the man's neck arching into a back flip through the man's parted legs. The flip dragged his opponent along for the ride in an echoing somersault, both of them ending up lying flat in the ring, he on his stomach and his opponent on his back.

It had taken intense training to be able to perform the Slayer safely, and he never did it without previously working with the other wrestler to be sure that neither would be hurt when it came time for the match.

Wrestlers who could perform such aerobatics were known as "high-flyers," and George had worked hard to be able to fly higher than any other. He weighed 235 pounds, which made him slender for his sleekly muscled height; but then, you couldn't be heavy and fly.

The boy in Missouri—who was indeed heavy and had little hope of flying—had had no training beyond tumbling in his grade-school P.E. class, and had decided that the roof of his ranch house would make an adequate substitute for the top turnbuckle of the ring. Luckily or unluckily, he had partially missed his landing on his unfortunate friend. Both had ended up in the hospital, the novice high-flyer with a bruised spinal cord and his landing-pad buddy with a broken leg.

Professional wrestling was sports entertainment, but that didn't mean you didn't get hurt. Wrestlers were in an almost constant state of injury, and continued putting on shows despite the pain. By the time they reached age thirty most were forced to change their moves to suit a permanently damaged body. In the ring they pretended agony when attacked by an opponent, but the real pain and harm usually came from moves they did themselves. A truly *professional* wrestler put the safety of his opponent far above his own.

The Missouri boys' mothers, when they heard who and what had inspired the roof-jump stunt, had gone to the local news in outrage. The story had spread through the national media like a summer wildfire, and was just as impossible to stop. Anything George said on camera only served to fan the flames, his words taken out of context and twisted.

News magazines did exposés on backyard wrestling and aired clips of him executing the Slayer over and over, and every expert and organization who had ever debated the link between violence on television and violence in children focused on him— George Arlington, known in the ring as the Saint— as their poster villain for all that was wrong in today's entertainment industry.

"He Ain't No Saint" went from being the cheer of fans, painted on posterboards they held above their heads during matches, to the mocking headline in tabloids.

After a while, being reviled coast to coast had a way of getting to a guy.

Every time it seemed the story would die down, there would be a fresh injury in a backyard in some other state, and the story would revive, coming back to life like a smoldering hot spot touched by the wind.

He had tried to visit the Missouri boys, had tried to call them, but their mothers refused. He felt obscurely guilty about their injuries, as if he owed the two youngsters an apology and a lecture both.

All the publicity had done nothing to hurt sales of the Saint merchandise, though, and cable pay-per-view viewership of CUW events had doubled since the story broke—even though George himself wasn't wrestling in any matches because of his surgery.

He had been rich before the brouhaha, his place in the CUW secure for the time being, but now he was worth tens of millions to the company in publicity. His name and that of the CUW were spoken in households that had previously known nothing about professional wrestling: an unforeseen effect that he was sure chapped the hides of those mothers in Missouri.

Still, however much his career had been helped, however strongly he argued that professional wrestling was family entertainment where fathers and sons—and some daughters, too—came to cheer and boo at comic-book heroes and villains, there was a small part of him that wondered if, maybe, all the pundits and angry mothers had a point.

All he had ever wanted to do was put on a good show with the flash and daring of a circus act and the Good vs. Evil themes of Superman. He loved the physicality of wrestling, loved the theatricality, and loved the interaction with the crowd. He even loved his fellow wrestlers, who were for the most part a bunch of pansies once they dried their hair and took out their wallets full of baby photos. Some even knew how to chew with their mouths closed and could spell big words.

But now there was doubt within him about his chosen profession, and that doubt festered like a cyst, threatening to burst and spread its infection throughout his system.

Maybe it wasn't a hero that kids were tacking to their bedroom walls when they bought a poster of the Saint. Maybe it was a real-life villain—appealing in his silver Lycra pants and his white surcoat with the red cross of St. George, but a force of evil all the same.

Maybe he was what in the world of wrestling was called a "heel": one of the bad guys.

He looked at his sister with her compassionate eyes, who, whatever foolish choices she had made, had always made them with a loving heart. She was, and always had been, part of the light.

"I worry I might be in the wrong," he admitted to her. "Maybe I really am doing more harm than good. How can I continue wrestling if that's true? What if . . ." He widened his eyes and lowered his voice to Darth Vader pitch, playing at melodrama to hide a fear he didn't want to admit was real, "What if I've gone to the Dark Side?"

"George, you silly lug. No one who knows you could ever think you were a bad person."

"But what if all along I've been doing wrong, and I just didn't recognize it? Saint George is supposed to slay the dragon. He's supposed to defeat evil, not be a part of it."

Athena gave a growl of frustration. "I could just kick those women in Missouri for doing this to you. Making a person doubt himself: *that* is an evil thing. *They* are the monsters, not you."

"But what if . . ." It pained him to voice the thought. "What if they're right?"

Athena stared at him for a long moment, her hazel eyes focused with an intensity that made him uneasy. At times like this she seemed to have the ability to see into his soul.

"All right, that's it," she said, blinking and releasing him from her gaze. "After you've tucked in Gabby, come down to the great room."

His uneasiness increased. "What are you going to do?"

"Fix you, of course. We can't have the Saint thinking he's a devil, now can we?"

Chapter Three

As a child, George had once stayed home from school with the chickenpox and spent his days on the couch, watching television and sipping 7-Up. Somewhere between *Days of our Lives* and black-and-white reruns of *Perry Mason*, he'd found the 1938 Errol Flynn movie *The Adventures of Robin Hood*. For two hours of bliss he'd forgotten that he was covered with maddening, itchy spots and lost himself in Sherwood Forest.

Since that day, he had been a lover of all things medieval. He had a library full of books and movies set in the middle ages, and used to think he would give his left nut to live back then. He'd since grown more protective of the family jewels, but when he'd built his house, he'd built it on his childhood fantasies. The result was 8000 square feet of pseudo-

English manor, with towers at each end and a drawbridge, planted in the middle of fifty acres of field and forest land.

The local papers had poked fun at the house when it was built, but George had never had a problem accepting the cheesiness of his own taste. *I'll take the cheese, you can have the whine* was his motto. He had figured what the hell, let the public giggle about the fake wrestler in his fake castle. At least it would give them something to talk about over their morning bran flakes and coffee.

Eight thousand square feet was too much house for one man who was rarely home, though. He had turned over a suite of rooms to his parents, to use when they were not heeding the call of the open road in their Winnebago or wintering in the house he had bought them in Hawaii. Another suite went to Athena and Gabrielle.

Athena, who was a single mother, supervised the maintenance of the house and grounds, and volunteered at Gabby's kindergarten. They were two activities he thought inarguably useful to all concerned.

She also practiced hypno- and aromatherapy.

He was considerably less convinced of the usefulness of either of those two activities, but Athena had a growing circle of clients who were happy to pay for her services, so who was he, a man who shaved his chest as a part of his job, to make smart-ass comments about her chosen profession?

"Christ, Athena, what's that smell?"

He had tucked in Gabrielle and read her *Goodnight, Moon,* a book he loved almost as much as she did. Now he had come down to the great room to find the lights off, logs crackling in the oversized fireplace, and the dim flickerings of a dozen squat candles scattered on the floor around the two wingback chairs in front of the fire.

And then there was the stink.

"I'm burning sage to ward off malevolent influences."

"You aren't going to try putting me in a trance again, are you? My butt goes numb and I fall asleep." He went and sat in the chair facing her. On the coffee table between them was a quartz crystal six inches high, set upright in a wrought-gold base of fluid lines and swirls.

Athena blew on the embers of sage burning in a bowl in her hands, then set the bowl on the hearth to her right. "I sometimes think it's an elaborate scam you've pulled on the family, convincing us that you graduated from college. You're too good at playing the muscle-headed moron when it suits you."

"You gotta problem wid morons?" he asked in his best New Jersey tough-guy voice.

She made a face. "Dad was right: You should have majored in business instead of theater."

"So speaks the women's-studies major, the voice of practicality." He picked up the crystal, turning it to catch the firelight, the flames reflecting off its facets. "What's this for?"

"Isn't it amazing? I found it at that antique mall in McMinnville, of all places. The dealer said she bought it from a deeply religious woman, whose husband had inherited it from his Hungarian grandmother. The grandmother had used it for fortune-telling, and the lady didn't want such trappings of witchcraft in her house."

He snorted. "Or the dealer ordered it from a wholesaler's New Age catalog."

She took the crystal back from him, holding it cradled in her hands. "No, it's old. Very old."

"All rocks are."

"But not all rocks have a history. I can feel the past when I hold this. This crystal has been used by sensitives for centuries, I'm sure of it."

And George was sure that his sister had a spectacular imagination.

Still, he had nothing else to do tonight, so he might as well humor her and let her try whatever mumbo jumbo she had in mind. Sometimes, in the midst of the rest of the nonsense, Athena came up with words that made a person stop and think about his situation in a new way. It was those rare gems of wisdom, and her personal warmth, that he thought accounted for her popularity with her clients.

"So, how is that crystal going to help me?"

"You're going to focus on it while I guide you through a creative visualization exercise."

"I knew it! You're going to try to hypnotize me again. Get me an extra cushion for my butt."

She set the crystal back on the coffee table, gave him a considering look, then reached down and took a plastic spray bottle from a compartmented tray beside her chair. She leaned forward and spritzed him.

He coughed as the scent of lavender filled the air.

"That's to calm you," Athena said. "As I've told you before, all hypnosis is actually self-hypnosis. It's a focused state of concentration, that's all."

"Hell, I can concentrate. So, why is it that you can never hypnotize me?"

"Because it's *self*-hypnosis, as I said. Look, you're in a state akin to hypnosis a half-dozen times a day and you don't even notice it. When you're driving and suddenly realize you've gone ten miles and can't remember a single one of them; when you're engrossed in your reading and don't hear someone speaking to you; when you're in the ring, for heaven's sake, and can shut out the noise and flashing lights well enough to focus on what you're doing, that's all self-hypnosis. Focused concentration. You've got to get rid of the idea that I'm taking control of you, and then you can do it."

"And doing so is supposed to help me how?"

"I'm going to guide you into a waking dream where everything seems real, however strange, and yet where you are able to direct your own actions. During this visualization you will confront the issues that are troubling you, and will work through them. When you 'wake up,' you'll have perfect recall of the experience."

30

Athena had once given him a copy of Carl Jung's *Man and His Symbols* for his birthday. He had put it in his bathroom to read during contemplative moments, and to his surprise he had been fascinated by Jung's theories. His legs had fallen asleep on several thoughtful occasions as he had become engrossed in the book.

Jung had suggested, among other things, that people and events in dreams are symbolic of aspects of the dreamer, both good and bad, known and unacknowledged. To understand a dream was to understand oneself, and the issues with which one was struggling.

Or so Jung would have one believe.

"So if I do this, then I'll wake up happy and sure of what's right?"

"The answers to all our questions are already inside us. Sometimes we just need a little help in finding them." His sister took out another bottle and spritzed him again. "Rosemary. For concentration."

He wiped a bit of mist off his cheek. "You're not going to do that while I'm in a trance, are you? I don't want to wake up smelling like one of those froufrou soap shops you like so much."

"I'm done for the moment." She folded her hands in her lap, smiling with gentle innocence.

He eyed the tray. There were many more bottles.

He sighed, acting put-upon, although he was actually growing curious about the experiment. "Let's get going, then. I don't want to miss Letterman."

31

"Heaven forbid! Now put your feet flat on the floor and let your hands rest palms up at your sides."

He obeyed, then shifted in the chair a few times until he was sure he was comfortable, and as free as he could be from the threat of butt-numbness.

"Look into the crystal, into the center of it. Let the rest of the room fade away." Her voice took on the low monotone of television hypnotists, and a laugh choked in his throat. He took a deep breath and tried to relax the grin that was pulling at his cheeks. This was serious.

"The room is fading away. The candles are fading away. Keep your eyes focused on the heart of the crystal, and hear only my voice."

His smirk relaxed as the darkness of the room, the warmth of the fire, and the scents of lavender and rosemary soothed him along with her voice. He focused on the heart of the crystal, where the stone held traces of milky flaws and the deep flames of refracted firelight.

Athena went through a standard hypnotic induction, repeatedly suggesting that he was going deeper and deeper into his trance. He had heard it all from her before, but this time his mind didn't shy away from the commands. He didn't hold tight to the control of his thoughts, but instead, gazing at the crystal, allowed Athena to guide him.

The room faded away, and the crystal on which he focused became a screen for the images of his mind.

"You are standing on the ground," Athena said. "Look down at your feet. Do you see them?"

"Yes," he answered, the single word an effort to push past his lips.

"Tell me what you see."

"My silver boots." They were the ones he wore while in the ring, as part of his costume. He could feel now the soft embrace of his Lycra pants and the tighter pressure of his black knee and elbow pads. Across his bare shoulders he felt the coolness of his silk surcoat—a loose, sleeveless garment like that which knights of the past had worn over their armor to proclaim their colors. His reached to mid-thigh and had a slit center front and center back, as if to allow him to ride a horse. He usually tore it off over his head shortly after entering the ring.

"Look at the ground. What type is it?"

"Dirt. And straw," he said, surprised. "Like a barn." Why would his mind choose such a place? He must think of himself as an animal, as less than human.

"Now I want you to raise your eyes, slowly, and tell me what you see."

He obeyed. Instead of the emptiness he expected, he saw a small rough wooden table, melting candles set in a neat circle around the same crystal he had been staring at all along. A slight movement behind the table caught his attention, and he raised his eyes farther.

He met the hazel gaze of a woman whom he had never seen before.

"Christ!" he cried out, startled. She looked real enough to touch. She was wearing a dark, featureless dress and her hair was completely concealed by a white, wimplelike cloth.

"What do you see?" he heard Athena ask, faintly, as if from a great distance.

The woman's eyes were wide with terror, her lips moving rapidly, and then it wasn't Athena's voice he heard, but this woman's, frantically chanting words he couldn't understand.

Suddenly he could smell the barn: the sweet, dusty scent of hay; the fuggy odor of animals; the mustiness of mice and pigeons.

Athena must have spritzed him again.

He felt a chill draft on his bare arms, and the weight of his body on the soles of his feet. He lifted his hand and stared at it, rubbing his fingers together, then touching them to his face. The illusion stayed with him, and he was no longer aware of sitting in his house or staring at the crystal.

The sense of hypnotized lethargy was gone, and if Athena was still talking, he couldn't hear her.

He had disappeared into his own mind.

Chapter Four

He had never expected the visualization to work so well. Who needed movies or amusement parks when you could do this inside your own head? This was a degree of authenticity that virtual-reality developers could only dream of.

"Un-be-*frickin'*-liev-able!"

The woman made the sign of the cross and stopped chanting. She gaped up at him, her lips parted with an incredulity to match his own.

He stared back.

Seconds passed.

Now what?

This was his visualization, so the first move must be up to him. He decided to do what he always did when making an entrance as the Saint.

He spread his legs and planted his fists on his

hips in the classic Superman pose. "The Saint has come!" he bellowed. "And he shall deliver you from evil!"

The crowd usually roared its approval at this point.

The woman flinched and trembled. Animals gave frightened bleats from the shadows.

He held his pose a moment longer, chin raised and head turned to the side to show off his profile; then, when the woman continued to cower, he grimaced and relaxed, feeling like a clod. "Sorry." He smiled sheepishly and stepped forward, holding out his hand to her. "I'm George."

"George?" she asked in a whisper. "Artou Saint George? Verily?"

She had a heavy accent, and he could barely make out what she was saying, but his own name and the questioning tone were clear enough. "Yes, George."

She sank into a low curtsy, head bowed, her plain dark dress pooling in the straw and dirt.

"Hey, no need for that!"

She peeped up at him from under her white headcloth, and he gestured with his hands for her to get up. This was embarrassing, seeing played out his unconscious need for adoration. Athena would laugh her ass off when he told her.

The woman rose, and a smile started to tremble on her lips. She came slowly toward him, her hand slightly reaching out, as if she wanted to touch him but was afraid to try.

"I won't bite. Here," he said, holding out his hand as he might to an unfamiliar dog.

Her glance went from his hand to his eyes, then back and forth again, then suddenly her hand flashed forward and retreated, withdrawn almost before he had felt the featherlike touch of her fingertips on his skin.

They stood and stared at each other, and then she giggled and started patting her hands together in front of her like a pleased child. "Saint George. *Ich trow Ich haav dewn mahgic!*"

He screwed up his face and tilted his head to one side, as if either action could help him to decipher her words. He had heard his name again, and perhaps the word *magic*. She seemed to be speaking English, and if he could only listen closely enough he was sure he could understand what she was saying.

It was a sensation he often had while talking with women. He rarely figured out what they really meant, so it was no wonder his unconscious had chosen to make this female all but unintelligible.

"Who are you?" he asked, enunciating carefully.

She squinted, as he had. *"Yewr pahrdewn?"*

"Who? You?" he said, pointing at her.

"Ahh. Emoni."

"Eh-moe-nee?"

She nodded. It was hard to tell in the flickering candlelight, but she looked to be a few years older than him, her face showing the wear of a hard life.

He pointed to the crystal. "Magic?"

Lisa Cach

She clasped her hands together and smiled, nodding. *"Yea, mahgic! Ich cahlled you toe kill thay drahgahn."*

"To kill the dragon?" He crouched, with claws out. *"Drahgahn?"*

"Yea!"

Now this was just too cool. He was going to get to play out his one major fantasy since childhood: to truly *be* St. George the Dragonslayer!

It made perfect sense. If he could kill the dastardly dragon and rescue the virgin—there was always a virgin fainting in terror somewhere, wearing a filmy white dress and flowers in her hair—then he would wake up without any doubts about either himself or his career. That seeping blackness in his heart would be gone, and life could go on exactly as it had for the past eight years.

This was going to be a blast. He wished he had a way of recording it all for someone else to see. What a pay-per-view special *this* would make! Maybe he could write a movie script based on it. Maybe star in the film himself.

Too *frickin'* cool!

"I will kill the dragon," he confirmed for her, standing straight, then thumping his fist upon his chest, over the red cross of St. George on its white field. "I am St. George!"

She nodded, probably more at the tone of his voice than the words, and then, as she looked him over, a tiny creeping frown of doubt creased between her eyes. Her worried gaze met his; then she

38

ducked her head in apology and sidled past to the door behind him. She opened it and peered out into darkness, then closed it again and frowned some more.

"*Sswear-d? Ahrse?*"

"*Sswear-d?* Oh, sword?" He did a Jedi master impression, swinging his imaginary blade.

She nodded.

"No *sswear-d.*"

"*Ahrse?*" She feigned holding reins and bouncing along.

"No *ahrse* either."

She made the soft, tongue-clicking sound of disapproval unique to women. Then, with one hand on her hip and the other alternately gesturing in the air and resting fingertips in contemplation on her chin, she embarked upon an extended monologue, clearly trying to work out how he was going to kill the dragon with no *ahrse* and no *sswear-d.*

He listened, and as he did he caught more and more of her words. It *was* English she was speaking, only her vowels were sometimes pronounced differently. She also used those archaic *thou* and *art* words, and ended her verbs as if she was reading from the Bible.

During his hungry years as a wrestler he had traveled to Africa and Asia for matches in towns both big and small. He had learned to make sense of whatever fragments of English a speaker offered, and to use the context of the conversation to fill in the blanks. His college theater training had helped perfect his natural talent for mimicry, and he could speak back to foreigners in their own accents. They were skills that served him well now.

Emoni's words gradually came more and more clearly to him, without the need to make translations in his head.

". . . smith make . . . *something something something* . . . no . . . *something something* . . . we have nothing that . . . *something* . . . they would try to stop . . . *something* . . . you will have to make do for now with this." She stepped into the shadows, then came back into the candlelight holding a wooden pitchfork.

He gave it a doubtful look. One of the carved tines was broken. "Do you think I can kill a dragon with that?" he asked, speaking slowly and mimicking her way of speech.

She shrugged and spoke with equal care. "You are Saint George."

"Er, yes."

"If you gain the castle, you might find a sword and armor there."

"Castle?" All right! A castle!

This was like a video game. Invade the castle. Find the sword. Kill the dragon. And if he got killed, he would just reset and start over.

Then again, he had heard that it was impossible to die in a dream, so maybe the same thing was true of being in a creative visualization.

But what if he imagined the dragon biting him—after he annoyed it by sticking that sorry pitchfork

40

in its ass—and then his hypnotized brain convinced his body to die in real life?

He dismissed the thought. Wouldn't happen. That was the stuff of cheesy late-night television, of which he was a connoisseur.

"The castle of the de Burroughs, on Devil's Mount," Emoni was explaining. "There is an entrance from it into the lair of the dragon. There is also an entrance through a cave on the shore."

"The dragon lives under the castle?"

"Yes."

"Who must I fight to get to the castle?"

"Milo, who tends the sheep. And the crone."

What kind of matchup was that, a shepherd and a crone? Surely not one worthy of St. George. "I cannot fight an old woman."

"You must get past her—it is not for me to say how."

"But who is she?"

"She was once a nun. When the first sacrifice was made, over forty years past, she was the one who brought the virgin to the dragon. She has remained at the castle ever since, to give the dragon its yearly tribute."

The woman sounded like a real sweetie—probably a jealous, bitter old witch who *liked* throwing nubile young beauties to their deaths. "Who is the virgin I must rescue?"

Emoni cocked her head, brows raised in question.

"There *is* a virgin to rescue, yes?" The way the

story usually went, the hero was offered the virgin's hand in marriage after he saved her from a hideous death. A creative visualization of wedding-night action might be fun. And since this was *his* dream . . .

Emoni's face grew sad. "There are only bones. In three weeks the lottery of virgins will be held, and a new one will be chosen to feed to the dragon. You must kill the beast before then."

He took the pitchfork from her. It was as light as a garden rake, and he couldn't imagine killing an iguana with it, much less a dragon. "I will do my best."

Emoni shook her head. "No. You *must* kill it." She pressed her lips tight together against the trembling that had suddenly started there. "You *must.*"

He reached out and touched her shoulder. "Emoni?"

She gave a choked sob and took a shuddering breath. The eyes she raised to his were bright with pain and passion. "Twelve years ago my closest friend was given to the dragon. I have fought the town ever since, to end the sacrifices. They would not do so, so I turned to studying the old ways— magic—to end them myself. And they *must* be ended. This year, my daughter . . ." She choked once more in misery, and it was several moments before she could again speak. "This year my daughter will be in the lottery. She is only twelve years old."

"Ah, crap," he said by way of consolation, and

wrapped his arms around her in a hug. She stiffened in his embrace, and it belatedly occurred to him that such might be a faux pas in this world where women wore cloths on their heads. He released her, and she scooted away.

"What is your daughter's name?" he asked. If someone tried to feed Gabby to a lizard, George would have stomped their sorry ass into the ground. This poor woman had a whole town to fight, though. No wonder she was frightened.

"Alisoun. I named her after my friend."

"I swear to you, Emoni, that Alisoun will not go to the dragon." And at twelve years old, she would not be going to his visualized marriage bed, either.

Emoni clasped her hands together. "Then blessed be the name of Saint George, and may you deliver this town from the evil that has come to live in its heart!"

The solemnity of her words were like a prayer, but the godlike feeling he expected to come when paid such reverence was nowhere to be found. Instead, he felt a twinge of anxiety. What if he failed?

There was no advantage in letting Emoni see that trickle of doubt, though. "Rest easy. You have nothing more to fear."

While he himself had everything to worry about. He had better be able to find a real sword in that castle. Or a spear. Even a big knife, for God's sake, would be better than attacking the dragon with a pointy stick that looked better suited to roasting marshmallows.

He hefted the pitchfork as if it had substance and was a weapon to be feared in the mighty hand of St. George. "So, which way do I go?"

Chapter Five

Alizon lay in bed in her dark chamber, gazing at the sky visible through her narrow windows. It was the charcoal blue of the pre-dawn hour, telling her that she had once again lost a night's sleep to the fitful wanderings of her imagination.

They were of no use, these half-waking dreams she played with through the black hours: dreams of dark men ravishing her body, thrusting deep within her, accepting no refusal as they took her again and again.

In her dreams, the men found her irresistible in the way that Osbert had not. She needed to do nothing to please or to arouse, for her beauty and her spirit had charmed her phantom lovers, and they could never get enough of her.

In her dreams, no one had her pretending to be a sheep.

Several times a month she found herself unable to sleep, her mind restless and her body even more so, and it was then that the fantasies invaded her thoughts and stole the peace from her soul.

She was twenty-six, and as virgin still as the day she had gone to the dragon.

During the daylight hours she thought nothing of that, her mind occupied elsewhere. During the night and its solitude, there was nothing to fill her mind *but* her untouched state. These castle walls that in the sunlight seemed protection from the evils of man and beast, at night felt cold and thick around her, cutting her off from the life she might have led.

On nights such as this she felt herself slowly petrifying, turning into a stone effigy of virginal youth, as if lying coldly carved above the crypt of a noblewoman.

Sometimes, when she looked into her silver mirror, she was startled by the stillness of her features. She would wonder if she had lost the ability to smile or cry, and if her heart, too, had turned to stone.

There were times she wondered if the only emotion left was hatred for the townsfolk of Markesew.

"*Mistress!* Mistress!"

Alizon bolted upright, pulling high the blankets to cover her bare breasts as Milo burst through her doorway. "What is it? What is wrong?"

Milo was a hulking shadow in the dark, stumbling up to her bed. He was usually a quiet man, solitary, with simple wishes and simple tastes, preferring his small cottage at the base of Devil's Mount to the majesty of the castle. He was rarely frightened or worried, for he had the imagination for neither, and that he had invaded Alizon's chamber at such an hour and in such distress spoke of something gone dreadfully amiss.

"A man! A giant of a man, and half naked!"

The reality of an intruder had no kin in her mind with her fantasies of the night. A stranger could only mean danger—to all that she had built. "Where?" The word came out terse and fierce, her mind skimming through courses of action.

"On the path. He said strange words, and then he hit me!"

"He attacked you?" She reached for the chemise she had left at the foot of the bed and pulled it on over her head as she kicked back the covers and rose. Milo turned half away, giving her privacy, although she was as much a shadow as he in the dark.

"He hit me, with a weak arm like a little girl. I almost could not feel the blows, although they cost him great effort to give. He grunted and stomped his foot with each one."

Alizon fumbled in the dark for her clothes, stepping into her leather shoes even as her hand found the soft wool of her gown. She must be more asleep than she thought, and it was addling her brain: the naked giant had the strength of a little girl?

47

"I tripped and fell to my hands and knees, and he dropped to the ground and grabbed one of my feet, lifting it like a man shoeing a horse. He made more grunting noises, and I kicked him away and stood up. And then"—Milo's voice rose, taking on an edge of hysterical disbelief—"then he jumped onto my shoulders! Like a demon he was, leaping from the ground!"

Alizon paused in donning her gown. Milo was a huge man himself, and if this man could jump onto his shoulders . . . "But why would he do such a thing?" she puzzled aloud. She could imagine no reason for such a fighting technique.

"He wrapped his legs around my neck as I staggered under his weight, and then we both fell over. He hit his head on a rock, and now he lies on the path."

"Is he dead?"

"I do not think so."

"Then he might wake at any moment." She grabbed her brown hooded robe off its peg on the wall.

She needed no light to guide her through the castle, but stopped anyway to gather a lantern and light its candle in the embers of the fire in the great hall. She wanted to see this intruder's face before she decided what to do with him. She might recognize him as one of the villagers, although none before had ever dared to come to this mount.

There was only one main path from the castle down to where the seabed causeway came ashore, and she led the way down it as Milo followed.

"How did you happen to see him?" she asked. The threat of the dragon was all the guard Alizon had ever felt the mount needed. Milo's work was with livestock and heavy chores, not as a sentry.

"I went out to piss, and thank Saint Stephen I did. He wears a white surcoat, and was easy to see under the moon."

Alizon shook her head in wonder. Who was this man, who had not even the sense to wear a dark color while creeping up a mountain? He sounded an uncommon manner of fool.

They hurried through the grove of evergreens beneath the castle, then followed the switchbacks of the path two more turns and came upon an open slope. They found him, lying where Milo had left him, limbs sprawling and the split panels of his white surcoat shimmering like broken angel wings upon the ground.

She gaped at the unconscious man. He was huge! Not huge as Milo was, with a barrel chest and heavy arms, but long—unbelievably long—and well-formed, muscled yet slender, with broad shoulders and a trim waist. His legs looked as if they might reach to her chin when he stood.

She squatted down and moved the lantern up to his face.

"Jesu mercy!" she whispered. A flicker of faint recognition lit within her, and then as quickly died.

No, she did not know him. She would have remembered, even had he been a mere child when she left Markesew. Such clean features—a high-bridged, straight nose; square jaw; dark, arching brows—were not to be forgotten. His long, dark brown hair was swirled to one side, and without thinking she reached out to touch it.

Soft. Silky.

The familiar, nighttime erotic hunger stirred to life inside her, rising beneath her caution and apprehension. Her sensitive nose caught a trace of scents both spicy and sweet, not at all like the odors she associated with Milo, or those she remembered from men on shore.

She glanced down at what little clothing he wore; then, with a cautious look to be sure he was still unconscious, lightly touched his hose. They shone like silver and were molded to his body, reaching up past where his braies should have been. The bulge of his sex was indecently visible, drawing her gaze. Alizon took a pinch of the strange silver material above his hip and pulled gently. It stretched, and she released it in surprise, the material snapping back into place.

Marry! She had never seen such stuff!

The man was plainly foreign, which brought yet more questions about why he had come sneaking onto Devil's Mount in the dead of night. She decided she had better find out what that reason was, and who *he* was, before finding a way to be rid of him.

She stood and realized she was shaking. Not for many years had she been so unnerved. She was mistress of her world here on the mount, and had remained so by letting surprises come to others, never to herself. "We must lock him up until he awakes."

"Where, mistress?"

Milo's cottage would be too easy from which to escape for such a giant, even one with the strength of a girl. "The guard room. We will have to carry him up to the castle." She looked again at the huge sprawled body. He looked heavy. "Or drag him, if we must."

Jesu mercy, how would she control him once he woke?

George woke cold and sore. His head throbbed, his butt felt like someone had used it for a doormat, and his feet were chilled and damp.

He was lying on the hard floor of a small room, a thin blanket doing nothing to keep him warm. Weak sunlight sifted sickly through narrow, unglazed windows in three walls, and in the fourth wall a closed wooden door stared blankly back at him.

Jumbled memories of trying to wrestle a barrel of a man came back to him. Unfortunately.

He had assumed that any human opponent in this visualization would act like a professional wrestler, knowing his role in a match and the correct moves to answer his own. This fellow, presumably the shepherd Milo that Emoni had warned him about, had had no such notions of how to behave.

He didn't remember anything after jumping on Milo's shoulders, but the lump George felt on the back of his head was a clear enough indication of what had happened.

He wasn't getting off to a heroic start in this adventure. He had even lost his pitchfork.

He sat up, groaning at the stiffness in his muscles and the sorry state of his buttocks.

Giggling came from behind the door, faint but audible, and the whispering movement of cloth. George jumped up and bounded to the door, pulling at the iron ring that served as its knob.

Locked.

Many light footsteps ran away, the giggling fading with them. He bent down and put his eye to the keyhole, and saw an empty, stone-flagged hallway and a flicker of shadow at the end that was there for an instant, then gone.

The flesh crept on the back of his neck. Spooky.

His head throbbing, he turned to the windows, with their promise of sunlight and a view. Through the one on the wall to his left he could see down over a patch of stunted evergreens and far beyond and below them the blue of open water. Stretching off into the distance was the shoreline of the mainland.

The window opposite the door faced the mainland straight on, and the village through which Emoni had led him last night. The tide was in now, but George could see beneath its rough turquoise surface the paler S of the stone causeway that he had crossed in the dead of night.

He looked down at his silver lace-up boots. They

were stained in blossoms of water and salt, still dark in patches of dampness.

The tide had turned while he was only halfway across, the waves splashing at the sides of the causeway, spitting up their warnings at him. Emoni had made clear he should hurry, and had illustrated the importance with an old tale of a de Burrough heir. The young nobleman had spent the evening drinking in Markesew and lost track of the time. The tide was coming in when, drunk and reckless, he decided to ignore caution and ride his horse home across the causeway.

Emoni said that on some nights you could still hear the scream of the horse as it was swept away. The heir was never found.

Emoni hadn't warned him that the causeway would be slippery and slimed with seaweed, or the stones of its uneven surface impossible to distinguish in the dark. Hurrying had meant mistakes, and he had cause to be grateful for his elbow and knee pads when he fell on the slick stones—once halfway off into the water. The second fall, he'd nearly impaled himself on his pitchfork.

When he came to shore he climbed a few steps up the slope and dropped onto the rough grass, to rest and to wonder at the murky world of the unconscious. The night around him had been eerily beautiful, dark and silent but for the light of the moon and the sloshing of the water, and he had pulled his arms inside his thin silk surcoat for warmth and sat to soak it in.

He had tried to find the symbolic meaning of the night journey across the seabed. Was it to do with the dark night of the soul? The muck at the bottom of everything? Was it something about the errors made and the price paid when living a rushed life?

Or maybe it meant nothing and was a long-forgotten scene from a movie he had viewed as a child. One he'd chosen to replay in this cinema of the mind for no other reason than that it fit his idea of the proper perils in approaching a dragon's lair.

As he had sat there, the breeze picked up and he caught a low, bellowing sound, like some great creature howling from the bowels of the earth. He had felt the hairs on the back of his neck rise, his skin going cold.

He had decided right then that there was no need to overthink the question of symbolism; he could figure it all out when he woke up. Getting into the castle was his first concern—that and avoiding being eaten like an hors d'oeuvre off a buffet table.

The third window of his prison looked out over a terrace, with tufts of grass and weeds growing in the cracks between the stones. A parapet was to the left, and the yellow stone walls of a castle to the right. He could see the arched doors that must lead into the hall, and felt a quickening of excitement. Escaping from this locked room and finding his way through the castle was all part of the puzzle.

He had met Milo and, sadly, been vanquished. What that meant, he didn't know. He still had a second opponent to confront, however, one perhaps against whom he could prove himself a more worthy adversary.

It was time for the crone to appear.

A soft knocking came at the door.

Chapter Six

"We want to see him!" Pippa insisted. Her hair stood out like a black sunburst around her head. She was thirteen years old and had no patience for long tresses, regularly hacking hers into shapes of her pleasing. "Please, mistress, just a peep."

"We'll watch him through the keyhole, and he'll never know we were there." Flur was the baby at twelve—fair and fine-boned, and so innocent it almost hurt to look at her.

The girls were standing around Alizon in the immense kitchen as she prepared a tray of porridge and beer for the foreign giant. It had occurred to her that feeding the man might encourage him to answer her questions. She would even apologize for leaving him to sleep on the bare floor, if she must, although any man who attacked in the middle of the night should be thankful for even that small hospitality.

"I will not risk his waking while you two are gaping at him."

"He's already awake," Ysmay said, from where she was stirring a cauldron of steaming dye. She was seventeen, dark, thin, and prone to black moods and imaginary passions.

Joye, standing nearby with a skein of wool in her hand, elbowed her friend, widening her eyes in a warning that came much too late. Joye was eighteen, with wavy light brown hair, a lush body, and a quick wit.

"And how would you know *that?*" Alizon asked, turning to the girl who'd spoken.

Ysmay's lips parted, and her cheeks colored as she realized what she had given away. "We only—" she started to say, and got elbowed again.

"I won't ask how many of you went to spy on him, despite my instructions to the contrary," Alizon said coldly, letting them feel the chill of her disapproval. She gave both Ysmay and Joye her most quelling look, holding it long enough that they began to fidget. "Have you any notion of what could happen were he to return to Markesew with tales of us all? Must Reyne tell her story yet again?"

Ysmay's lips pulled down, her eyes sheening with tears. Joye frowned, chastised and yet clearly not entirely sorry for her misdeed.

There was plenty that Alizon *did* let slip by, recognizing the relief that bouts of mischief could provide from the sameness of their days and the constant, rarely acknowledged undercurrent of fear that was companion to them all. Actions that endangered those who lived on the mount, however, were not to be tolerated.

Whatever squabbles and differences there might be between the twelve women and girls who lived upon Devil's Mount, they were united with bonds stronger than sisterhood by the events that had brought them here. Each had gone through the terror of anticipating her own death, and each had felt the deep hurt of being given to the dragon by the people who had known her since birth.

Year after year, Alizon had stood on the shore of the mount in a hooded robe, playing the role of crone. "Do not fear," had been her first words to each girl as she arrived. "You shall not go to the dragon."

When understood and believed, those words formed a bond of loyalty that could not be broken. Even those near to her in age looked upon her as their Mother Superior. It was she who had saved them, and she who had built the world that protected them now.

The responsibility set her apart from them. She had to be strong when she wanted to weep, had to be cold and impartial in her decisions when she would have rather gone by her own likes and dislikes. She knew the virgins trusted her with their lives, though perhaps they would not always trust her with the secrets of their hearts.

Only Reyne, desperately missing her mother, had once tried to return to Markesew. The villagers had stoned her half to death, forcing her back along the causeway and disfiguring her for life. What had happened to Reyne was proof to them all that they had only each other on whom to rely.

Not even naughty Pippa would knowingly do anything that would risk harm to the others; the price was too dear, the sense of responsibility toward each other too great.

"You could take the stranger out onto the south terrace," Reyne said. She was the peacemaker of them all, with her small voice and timid mien. She was washing the spoons from breakfast, strands of her light-brown hair brushing her pale, scarred cheeks. "We could all see him from the windows then, and he would be none the wiser. Even Braya is curious about him, though she will not admit it."

Pippa and Flur giggled at the mention of the absent Braya. Twenty years old, Braya was built like a brewer and had the mannish gestures to match. She tried to order the younger girls around but succeeded only in annoying them. They knew that the one true voice of authority was Alizon's.

Alizon sighed. The stranger's presence was too great a curiosity to be resisted, and she should have anticipated as much. It might be best to give them a look under circumstances that she controlled, rather than risk their going behind her back and perhaps giving themselves away.

"Let me first discover his purpose in coming. If

I then think it safe, I will consider taking him out to the south terrace." She raised a brow. "I make no promises, though. Do not set your hearts upon seeing him."

"May we tell the others? They will be so pleased," Pippa said.

"I said no promises. Do not think you can pressure me by making the others as eager as you."

"But they *will* be happy to think upon it," Pippa said with an angelic smile.

"Well I know it," Alizon muttered. The only new faces came once a year at midsummer, and never were they male. Even if the foreign giant were to leave within the hour, he would be the subject of talk and speculation among them for the next decade at least.

She had only seen him unconscious, and already she was certain that he would remain painted in her memory for the rest of her days. He must leave, the sooner the better for them all, but she could wish that she had a day in which to sit and gaze upon him. She might never see his like again.

His tray of food arranged, she went to one of the small hearths that was not in use and rubbed ashes on her hands, turning the skin an aged, unhealthy gray. She donned her robe, pulled its deep hood over her head, and arranged the long strands of white wool that were sewn inside its edge to screen her face and mimic the wispy hair of a crone.

"I do not like you in that," little Flur said and shuddered.

"I don't like it, either," Alizon agreed. She knew that Flur was remembering the same vision that she herself had had twelve years ago, coming across the causeway to the waiting hooded figure. That faceless woman had been more frightening than even the thought of the dragon.

She picked up the tray. "No one goes out. Keep the doors barred and your voices down. He might get past Milo and try to find his way inside."

"Could he hurt you?" Flur asked, her voice quavering.

Alizon paused and looked around the kitchen at the others. They were suddenly staring at her with the same wide-eyed, worried look on their faces. Spying on an unconscious man was one thing, but clearly none of them liked the idea of seeing him face-to-face with no heavy door between them. It was like the dancing bear that a man had once brought to a fair in Markesew: All had laughed and poked sticks at the beast—until he had gotten loose of his chains. Then all to be heard were screams of fright.

"Milo says his arm is not half as strong as yours, Flur. No, he cannot hurt me. I only worry that he may be fast and run past us." Which was a little bit of a lie. She could not believe that the man was truly as weak as Milo had said. Milo was not one to exaggerate, but perhaps in this instance pride had tempted him to paint himself immensely stronger than his fallen foe.

"He would run all the way to London if we set

Braya after him," Joye said, breaking the tension.

"Hush, Joye. That is not kind." Braya enjoyed a certain amount of teasing, Alizon knew, but even she could have her feelings hurt, and it was too easy in the castle for words meant for one set of ears to be overheard by another.

She carried out the tray into the great hall, where the others were already at work at the tapestries she had trained them to weave, and repeated the warning to keep the doors barred. Milo was waiting for her, as was Greta, whose luck had finally run out in the lottery two years after Alizon herself had been chosen. Together they exited through a door into a foyer, off of which were the rooms where the soldiers of times past had lodged. A staircase led upward to the family living quarters of the de Burroughs, now inhabited by twelve aging virgins.

She and Milo passed through another door, leaving Greta on the other side to bar it. They were now in the small, open, stone-flagged entrance hall. This passageway ended in the guardroom, with the gateway out of the castle on the left and on the right an archway to the north terrace.

Alizon took a deep breath and tried to still the shaking of her hands. The beer in its cup showed concentric ripples on its surface, and the bowl of porridge was jittering sideways, testament to her nervousness.

Jesu, this was nearly as bad as facing the dragon! Thank the saints she had been able to hide her uncertainty from the others.

Except for Milo, who had become like an uncle, it had been twelve years since she had spoken to a man. It had been twelve years since she had met anyone other than a frightened young girl, whose fears and thoughts and moods were easily predicted. She might as well be preparing to speak to a lion, the giant was such an unknown and potentially dangerous creature.

A shiver ran through her as she pictured him as she had last seen him, bare skin under the thin surcoat and with those otherworldly breeches clinging to every contour.

Faint, unwelcome excitement tingled over her skin, an echo of the fantasies that had filled many a long and lonely night. Whatever her mind said to the contrary, her body suspected that the answer to years of secret desires lay behind that door.

God's breath. She had better watch herself, and watch the others, who might be feeling much the same. They had none of them freely chosen to live chaste lives, and all wondered—sometimes freely and at length, especially if the wine had flowed heavily that night—what it would be like to lie in the arms of a man.

A man such as women dreamt of, that was, not a creature like Osbert, all clumsy hands and ignorance and filth. A few of the others had stories like hers, of unbearable fumblings in the dark, and in contrast they liked to entertain each other by making up stories of knights and ladies and a love that was true.

This man was real, though, and thus a danger. However beautiful his body, the passions of her flesh were the least of her concerns, and she had best remember that.

She approached the door. Balancing the tray on one hip, she knocked lightly, then slid the heavy iron key into the lock. Milo stood behind her, ready to catch the man should he bolt out like a hare.

"Come in," the stranger said pleasantly enough, his voice accented but comprehensible. So he *did* speak English. That would make this easier.

She pushed open the door, keeping her head down and her shoulders hunched as if they were those of an old lady. She held the shaking tray in two hands again, her fingers hurting from their tight grip. The beer was sloshing out of its cup, the bowl of porridge in danger of bouncing off the edge of the tray.

The stranger was standing halfway across the room, in a wary pose.

Good. Let him be uncertain.

She needed no lantern now to see his bare chest and that bulge in his silver breeches, which drew her eyes as if it possessed a magical power of its own. She had to force herself to raise her gaze from it to his elegantly featured face, now stubbled with dark whiskers. The screen of wool in front of her eyes was suddenly a torturous annoyance, keeping her from seeing him as clearly as she wished.

"Good morrow," she said, pitching her voice high and trying to speak in the quavering tones of an old woman. "I have brought you food to break your fast." More beer sloshed onto the tray. Maybe he would think it was her age that made her shake so.

"Thank you," he said, and slowly came toward her.

She could feel a mist of sweat dampening her brow, but she stood her ground as the giant approached.

God's breath, but he was huge! Her head reached only to his shoulders, and she was a tall woman!

When he was directly in front of her, he reached out and gently took the tray from her hands. He stepped back, holding it, and she tilted her head back far enough that she could see his face.

There was nothing threatening in the stranger's expression, just wary curiosity and, of all things, a trace of humor—as if he was savoring a private joke at her expense. That thought, and his lack of fear, gave irritation a chance to wear away her nervousness. He looked as if he thought he was more in control of the situation than she, although the opposite was clearly the case.

"Eat," she ordered.

"May I sit?"

She waved her hand, gesturing to the floor. He grinned with astonishingly perfect white teeth and lowered himself cross-legged, then grimaced when his buttocks took his weight.

Last night she had held his legs, and Milo his

shoulders, as they hauled him up the path. Her strength had not been equal to the task, and several times she had accidentally let the stranger's buttocks drag on the ground or dropped him completely as she struggled to catch her breath. His behind was likely three shades of blue. The thought gave her pleasure.

Even sitting, he was uncomfortably large. At least the tray in his lap hid his crotch, so she was saved the temptation to stare at it. His white surcoat was soiled now, ripped in places, but she noticed now the red cross of St. George upon it.

Was he a knight, then? A crusader?

He picked up the spoon and shook drops of spilled beer off it, then stirred the porridge. They had honey and butter in the kitchen, but she had decided against giving him any for fear he would wonder how the crone of the castle could live so well. She told herself that he really should count himself fortunate to be getting even bland porridge.

He took a spoonful, sniffed it, glanced at her, then put it in his mouth. The expression that followed was not one of delight, the corners of his mouth pulling down, although she could see him trying not to let his distaste show. He reached for the beer.

"Who are you?" she asked. Let him talk while he ate the food she had given him, so he would know he owed her answers.

He took a swallow of the beer, and this time he could not hide the grimace of revulsion.

She tucked in her chin, taken aback. It was very fine beer! They had brewed it themselves.

He regained control of his face. "I am Saint George."

"Your pardon?"

"I am Saint George, and I have come to slay the dragon!" he said more loudly, and punched a fist into the air.

She jumped back, startled. "You are not!"

He frowned at her, not looking particularly upset. "Yes, I am."

"You cannot be Saint George."

"Why not?"

Because Saint George would not walk around half naked, with the bulge of his privates for all to see! "You could not best Milo. If you were Saint George, you would have gotten past him." And if he truly *were* St. George, she had much to fear.

"I am a saint. I do not hurt *people*. I wanted to get to the castle, and to the castle I have gotten."

She crossed her arms over her chest. "Where is your horse, and your spear, if you have come to kill the dragon?"

"I thought it was a sword I needed."

"Where is it? And your horse and armor?"

He blinked at her and gazed off up to the right, as if watching a fly on the ceiling. "Stolen?" he asked, looking back at her. "My hope was to borrow a sword from you. I had a pitchfork, but I lost it."

She laughed, shaking her head. The man, for all

67

his size, was nothing more than a child. She had nothing to be afraid of. "I should let you try to kill the dragon, and let it thus free the world from a fool!"

"All I ask is that you let me try."

She narrowed her eyes, her amusement dying away. Was he more clever than he appeared? Perhaps he hid strength and intelligence beneath a harmless demeanor.

She watched him neatly eat his porridge, his back straight and his long fingers delicately holding the spoon. What to make of this man?

"Saint George died centuries past. How do you come to be here, if you are he?"

"I was needed. A woman called for me using a magic crystal, and I came."

She smiled. "It is so simple! I wonder no one else has thought to do the same. This woman must have needed you very badly, to draw you from heaven."

"She does. Her daughter is to be in the next lottery."

Alizon's breath was stolen by that simple explanation. A mix of grief and anger welled up inside her, undiminished since the day she herself had been sent to the mount. Her next words came out hard. "Why does she not take her daughter and flee the town? She seems a foolish sort of woman, to trust in prayers to a saint to save her child when she could save her on her own."

"She did not strike me as foolish. After all, I am here. I came."

"With no horse and no spear. How much did you demand she pay you?"

He set aside the tray and moved to stand up. She backed away. "Stay seated!"

"I am not going to hurt you," he snapped, rising. "But I'll be damned if I will sit on the floor while you, of all people, insult my honor."

"I beg your pardon!"

"As you should, Sister. What manner of nun throws innocent girls to a dragon? Is that not a sin?"

It took her a moment to remember she was supposed to be the crone, who had been a nun. She had not expected confrontation of this nature. "It must be done. If it was not God's will, He would not let it happen. He would not have formed the dragon so that he was appeased by virgin flesh."

"If it wasn't God's will that I come here, then I would not be here. You had best lend me a sword and take me to the dragon." He crossed his arms and smirked at her.

"You speak nonsense!" He had put her on the defensive, and she did not know how it had happened. He was her prisoner! He should be bowing down to her, asking forgiveness for invading her island, not smirking at her like a over-smug child!

He did not look in the least repentant, standing now with one hand on his hip, the other gesturing as he spoke, as if he was carrying on a normal conversation. "I speak no more nonsense than you. If you are going to say that the one is God's will, you must say that all is His will. So, now that that is settled, will you lend me a sword and show me the passage to the dragon?"

"He will kill you."

"Then you will no longer be troubled by my presence."

"You will die a most horrible death. He will tear you to pieces."

"You sound as if you are trying to frighten a child. Why do you bother? My death will be no worse than that you have meted out to dozens of girls."

"It is the dragon who kills them, not I. It is as God wills." She wanted to shout out that she had sent no one to her death, that she had *saved* almost a dozen girls. She wanted this infuriating man to know that he was wrong, wrong, wrong!

But of course she could say nothing of the kind. Everything she had built would be destroyed: the tapestry workshop, their peaceful lives, and most of all the retribution they steadily wrought on the townsfolk of Markesew, by year after year demanding more and more of what they valued most—sheep.

"One might almost think you did not want the dragon killed," he said. "Do you enjoy your work here so much?"

For a moment she thought he had seen into her thoughts, that he knew the reality of Devil's Mount. Then, just as quickly, she realized that such was impossible. He knew nothing.

She tried a different tack. "I fear that you will enrage the dragon. If you wound it before it kills you, it may go out and wreak revenge upon the shore. Many could die. You do not wish that to happen, do you?"

"Then I must be certain to kill it."

"Why do you persist in seeking your own death?"

"I made a promise. I will not leave the lady to fight for her daughter's life alone."

Ah, Jesu mercy, how was she supposed to argue against that? "Who is this lady who holds such sway over you?"

"She called herself Emoni. You sent her dearest friend to the dragon a dozen years past, a girl named Alizon."

"Emoni?" she whispered, stunned.

"Do you remember the girl Alizon?"

"No," she said, her voice hoarse. She felt a tingle in her nose, and the sting of tears in her eyes. Emoni, dear Emoni, had not forgotten her.

A thousand times Alizon had stood on the north terrace and looked to the distant town and fields, asking herself if one of those tiny moving people might be Emoni—and might Emoni know, somewhere in her heart, that her Alizon still lived?

"She named her daughter Alisoun, after her friend."

Alizon could not answer. Tears tightened her throat.

"Would you have so much be taken from this woman, both a friend and a daughter?"

71

The denial squeezed from her throat. "No."

"I am Saint George. It is my duty to kill the dragon."

"You will fail."

"Then I will try again, and again, as long as it takes."

"You will enrage it, and cause it to maraud on shore, and then this Emoni and her daughter will be eaten just the same."

"Then give me three tries. If I cannot kill it in three tries, I will go back to the village and tell the lady I have failed."

Whoever this man truly was, Emoni believed he was her only hope. Alizon could not send him back to her saying he had not so much as seen the dragon's lair.

She would give the man his three tries, would make sure that neither he nor the hidden dragon suffered for them. Then he could return to Emoni and persuade her to take her daughter and leave Markesew. Her friend's daughter would not go to the dragon even if she was chosen in the lottery, but Emoni had no way of knowing that. She would think her child lost to her forever as soon as she set foot on the causeway.

"Three tries," Alizon relented.

The stranger grinned, his unnaturally white teeth shining.

Chapter Seven

George sauntered after Milo, following him down the path from the castle. The "crone" had sent them to fetch a sheep to feed to the dragon, but he got the feeling that it was busywork, meant to get him out of the castle while she did God only knew what.

It was obvious that the "crone" was no such thing; he had seen better costuming on trick-or-treaters, and he himself could do a better impression of an old woman's voice. A bit of false white hair and a deep hood did not a crone make, and when he had first seen her he had almost laughed out loud.

His unconscious mind was seriously messed up. According to that Jung book, women in his dreams represented his feminine side. So what did it mean that this "crone" was a younger woman, pretending to be old?

He wondered what else she was lying about, and why she wasn't happier to see him. He was St. George! She should be overjoyed to have him come to kill the dragon.

At least if she believed him she should be overjoyed, but she apparently didn't. She was the negative aspect of his unconscious feminine self, the part that doubted.

Wasn't she?

And what about those giggles and running footsteps; what were they about? More feminine aspects that he was afraid to see?

He was giving himself a headache trying to figure it out, and the awful beer had done its work upon his system. "Hey, Milo, is there a john somewhere that I can use?"

Milo stopped and stared at him without comprehension.

He flipped through his mind for euphemisms, sorting out the likeliest. "Water closet? Privy? Latrine? Jakes?"

Milo grunted and pointed to some shrubs.

Great. He should have asked up at the castle. He doubted that the "crone" would be content to squat in the bushes like a bear; she probably had a very nice seat in a dark little stone closet somewhere.

As he was about to take care of that basic bodily function, a horrible thought crossed his mind, stopping him before he could release so much as a drop.

He wasn't going to wet himself in the wing-back chair in front of the fire, was he, like a child dreaming of going to the bathroom?

He held himself ready and worried over the question. The pressure built in his bladder. How long could he hold it? Not long enough to kill a dragon, that was for sure. Better to just go for it.

He tried to release, but thoughts of the wing-back chair kept intruding.

Dammit!

"Athena, you are going to be *so* sorry if I pee my pants," he said aloud, and then he forced himself to go.

He felt no warm wetness in his groin. Everything worked as it would if he truly was outside taking a leak in the bushes.

The scent of the evergreens, the chill sea breeze, the crispness of the visual details in the plants and rocks around him suggested that such was the case. Everything looked and felt so real, he could almost believe he had slipped back in time and was physically *here*, wherever *here* was. It would be easy to forget that this was only happening in his mind.

And if he did forget? A shiver passed through his heart, fluttering it to the edge of panic. Might it be possible to be trapped forever in this trance, his unresponsive body shipped off to the hospital and tubes stuck in to feed and drain it? Athena had said nothing of how she would revive him, and she had given him no key with which to revive himself.

But then he remembered Emoni, who had "summoned" him, and who had eyes the same hazel as Athena's. She must be the exit from this mental video game, she and the crystal.

The thought was a small comfort, and he shook and tucked himself back into his pants. He shouldn't freak himself out like that, not when there was a dragon to kill! The goal of the exercise was to work through his issues by action in this dream world, not to sit around wondering at the symbolism of a bowl of porridge.

Although he *did* wonder about it. Why so bland? Why no cream or sugar?

He caught up to Milo, who had been standing waiting for him, his large pie face without expression. "How long have you lived here, Milo?"

"Long enough."

Ah, a conversationalist. "Long enough for what?"

Milo grunted.

George worked among men who could teach Milo a thing or two about grunting, and he wasn't intimidated. "Hey, I'm sorry about attacking you last night. I didn't mean to hurt you."

The heavy brows drew down into a frown. "I was not hurt."

"Good!" He considered giving him a slap on the back, but refrained. One step at a time. "So, the dragon. Have you seen it yourself?"

Another grunt.

"It must be a terrible sight, flying through the air, breathing fire on everything below."

Milo turned his head just enough to give him a strange look, then kept walking, his heavy feet grinding the dirt and gravel of the path.

"Not many men would have the courage to live next door to one, I wouldn't think. You don't worry that it might come eat you in the night?"

They came to a small cottage a hundred yards from the shore, the thatch of the roof green with moss and darkened with rot. The wattle-and-daub walls were splotched with gray and brown, and bits of discarded carts and equipment were scattered over the patchy grass of the yard.

"Mistress would not let it," Milo said, and ducked down to enter the cottage through its low door.

But she would let Milo live in this hovel? George followed Milo inside, bending almost double to keep from hitting his head on the lintel.

Inside it was almost too dark to see, the only light coming from the doorway and the pair of small windows to either side, their shutters hanging open. The place smelled of wood smoke, rotting thatch, and mice, and as his eyes adjusted George saw that there was an open hearth in the center of the dwelling, with no chimney to draw away the smoke.

The poor bastard! What type of life was this?

There was a narrow table shoved up against the wall under one of the windows. George stepped closer and saw that its surface was scattered with small pieces of wood and tools. There was a half-finished box in the corner, its surfaces covered in an intricate geometric pattern of inlaid wood.

"Come," Milo said, ducking back out of the cottage, the loops of a rope dangling from one hand and a wooden bucket of grain from the other.

George followed, saying nothing about the box and its finely done artistry. He felt abashed at his unconscious assumption that Milo was nothing but a slovenly simpleton, a sort of medieval redneck. No one was ever only what they appeared. He of all people should know that.

They trudged up the slope of the mount, eschewing the path for the open meadows. The land was so steep in places, the grazing sheep above would only need to take a small leap to land on his head. Milo gave the bucket a shake, and sheep everywhere raised their heads, ears pivoting like radar dishes to capture the sound. A half dozen trotted toward them, fat white bodies bouncing above thin black legs.

"Poor stupid things," George said. "They have no idea."

"They are sheep," Milo said, in a tone that implied this fact was obvious and explained and excused everything. He let one of the black-faced animals eat from the bucket while he tied the rope around its neck. The leash secured, he took the bucket away and set off back toward the castle, shaking the remainder of the grain every few steps, keeping the chosen sacrifice intrigued enough to follow.

"So, your mistress . . ." George said, following as well. "She has some control over the dragon?"

"It is a dragon."

"So she doesn't have any control?"

"She knows its ways."

He bet she did. She was a bit of a dragon lady herself, and he bet she knew an awful lot more than she would admit to him. There would be little help coming from that quarter. "Has anyone tried to kill the dragon, before?"

"You must ask mistress."

"You don't know?"

"Ask mistress."

"Does she always wear that hood?" he asked, just to see what type of reaction he would get. "She must be old and ugly, to want to hide her face."

Milo said nothing.

"Or maybe she is young and beautiful."

The bucket slipped from Milo's hand, hitting the ground and spilling grain onto the path. The sheep gobbled it up.

"Git, go on now!" Milo grunted, pushing the sheep away and scooping grain back into the bucket, his motions jerky.

Was that an involuntary "yes"? If the mistress wasn't old, then she couldn't be the original nun. Who was she, then?

George's curiosity about the woman behind the fake white hair went up a notch, and at the same time he felt renewed hope for a bit of dreamland nookie. Maybe he would have to "accidentally" pull the hood off her head, and see who this mystery chick was who had Milo in such thrall, and who knew the ways of the dragon.

The breeze picked up, chill against his bare skin, and with it came a faint stink of something unspeakably foul and corrupted.

"What the hell is that smell?"

"Have you never smelled a dragon?"

He caught himself, realizing St. George would have recognized the scent of a dragon. "Of course I have. I just haven't smelled one that stank so bad."

Milo grinned, his chest vibrating in what could only be a chuckle. "You think this is bad? I think life for a saint is too easy." He laughed, tears coming into his eyes, and he ignored the sheep that was nibbling the ground in search of missed grain. "You cannot fight, you make faces at your food, you shiver in the wind, you wrinkle your nose at a bad smell. I think I will not see you again after you meet the dragon."

George gave Milo his best glare, the one he used while awaiting his opponent in the ring. Usually there was a bit of sweat—real or fake—rolling down his temples and dampening his hair as the cameras zoomed in on his heavy-browed gaze of contempt.

Milo bent double, holding his sides, his brays echoing down the slopes.

If the glare didn't do it, maybe some medieval trash-talking would. "That dung-spawned snake of a dragon will see what Hell looks like when I shove his head up his ass!"

"He will tear you apart," Milo gasped and began to hiccup.

"I'll wear his teeth 'round my neck!"

"You will!—hic!—He will bite—hic!—off your head!" Gasping and laughing, Milo tugged on the leash, dragging the sheep with him up the path.

George watched Milo's shoulders continue to shake, the man's hiccups deepening into great rasping caws that jerked his whole body, and he felt a very real desire to pile-drive the bastard.

Dammit. He was St. George in this vision, but he was getting no respect at all!

He spotted his pitchfork under a bush and retrieved it, feinting with the sorry weapon against imaginary dragons as he followed Milo and the sheep. He would show them, Milo and the "mistress," even if he had to kill the dragon with his bare hands, twisting its neck like a dish towel.

The foul breeze rippled through his surcoat and lifted tendrils of his hair, and as it whispered past his ears he heard again that distant, buried rumble. It was so low that it was more felt in his chest than heard, and a primitive part of his animal brain urged him to hide under a rock and poke his stick at anything that came near.

He knew about fear, though: One took note of it, then set it aside and got on with business. He *would* be as pathetic as Milo thought if a mere sound could make him cower like a rodent.

The mistress was waiting for them at the gateway, still hooded. "Where did he get that?" she asked Milo, flicking her fingers toward George.

Milo turned, and the laughter that had died down during the walk returned full force when the man saw the pitchfork.

"A sheet of paper can cut through a tree, if blown by a strong enough wind," George said, and he prided himself on the Oriental-sounding wisdom of the statement.

"Mmm," the mistress said.

George shrugged. "Emoni gave it to me—it was the only weapon she had. I lost it last night on the path."

"That was . . . kind of her. I may be able to find you something better, if after seeing the dragon you are still set upon fighting it."

"Not fighting it; killing it."

"Mmm." She coughed, as if masking a laugh, and then turned and disappeared through the archway.

George and Milo and the sheep followed, crossing through the stone-flagged hall and out onto the terrace he had seen through his window. She led them all down the length of the castle, around the end, and to another terrace beyond whose battlements the sea stretched out to the horizon. There was one short crenellated tower at the corner of the terrace, perhaps once used as a lookout.

George went to lean on the wall, looking down at the cliff that fell away beneath this side of the castle, and then out across the ocean. The water was blinding with sunlight.

The dragon had a damn good eye for real estate, George had to give it that.

He looked back at the castle and saw that they were on the other side of the great hall, and that another wing of the building stretched out toward the sea, giving the building an *L* shape. All the doors were shut, but in the upper story the windows had no coverings. There must be a devil of a draft, what with the wind off the ocean.

The mistress and Milo were waiting for him across the terrace, beside a wooden door in the main part of the castle. George started back toward them, then for no reason looked back over his shoulder at the upper-story windows.

He saw three pale faces that quickly disappeared.

A cold flush ran down his body. The windows were dark now, lifeless, holding no promise of anything beyond. Had he imagined them?

"Is this castle haunted?" he asked, half-joking, as he rejoined them.

The mistress's head turned slightly, as if she was looking back at the other wing. As if she knew exactly what he meant. "Why do you ask?"

"I thought I saw something."

"Many young girls have died here." She hesitated, then continued: "At times I have heard footsteps, and voices, as if in another room, but when I go to look there is no one there."

Ghosts! Just great. Why was his unconscious

throwing this at him, too? Maybe they were symbolic of guilt . . . or maybe of his own lost spirit. Whatever it was, doubtless if he was still here tonight, the ghosts would come make their purpose known, probably in the dark of night when they could scare the crap out of him. In the waking world he didn't believe in ghosts—not really—but this wasn't that world of consciousness and electric lights.

He tried to smile. "I've never slept in a haunted castle."

"I think you have more to worry about than ghosts," she said and opened the wooden door. The iron hinges screeched, and the room beyond was dark. "Are you ready to meet the dragon?"

Chapter Eight

Damn those virgins! They were going to be put on privy-scrubbing duty when she found out who had shown their faces at the window. They had all sworn to stand back in the shadows, to not let so much as a fingertip show to this false St. George. They had said they could be trusted, had vowed to not utter a single word while he was on the terrace, that in no manner would they give away their presence.

Apparently the excitement of a half-naked male was too much for them to handle.

Not that she could blame them. Even with that broken pitchfork and stubble on his chin, the man was passing handsome. She was thankful for her concealing hood, that oh-so-necessary fabric that kept him from knowing how often her eyes strayed over the revealed *V* of his chest and down to that silver-coated bulge, so wrongly exposed by the slit in the bottom half of his surcoat.

The man was indecent. She ought to have a proper tunic made for him.

Ought to.

Did not want to.

Not only did she like his chest, she would be happy if his surcoat blew away entirely and left her with an unobstructed view of his lower body.

She understood now the powerful forces that had moved Osbert to his leering, slobbering behavior. It had taken her twelve years to reach the stage of a fifteen-year-old boy, but she was there now, and by St. Stephen she did not know what the hungers of her body might make her do.

It was a pity she could not chain him to a wall and keep him like a pet, to do with as she would. He had the look of someone who might know how to properly deflower a virgin, if he did not get himself killed first.

She looked at him, standing there with his pitchfork and an expectant look on his face. Sadly, his demise was more likely than not.

"This way," she said and led him into the corridor that ran the width of the castle, separating the kitchen from the great hall. There were doors off it that led down to cool storage cellars carved out of the rock, and a large central archway that opened onto the kitchen. Another archway, directly opposite the kitchen's, led into the great hall, but she had had the virgins close and bar its massive doors.

Windows high up in the lofty-ceilinged kitchen kept the room well-ventilated and filled with warm light reflecting off the yellow stones. The scents of herbs and wood smoke predominated, over traces of wool and dye, steaming mineral water, baked breads, and stewed meats. This room was the heart of the castle, was her favorite chamber, and she turned to see his reaction.

George—she could not think of him as "St. George"; it was impossible to believe that was who he was—looked confused. A tremor of concern passed through her. Had she missed some detail, one that gave away that she was not the only one who lived here?

"Is this the kitchen?" he asked, and stared around him like a gape-jawed lack-wit.

"By the rood, it is not the privy! What else should it be but the kitchen?"

"I meant no offense, mistress. In my homeland, the kitchens are small enough to fit in that corner," he said, pointing. "And the fires are built against the wall, with a pipe above to draw away the smoke."

"And to draw away the warmth as well, I should think. It sounds a backward place, this homeland. Tell me, is it where you lived before you died, or is it the heaven for saints that you speak of?"

"A world beyond this one is all I can say."

She snorted. "Germania, is my guess."

"Farther still," he said, with a crook to his mouth

and a look in his eye that said he knew much more than she ever would.

She would enjoy seeing that smugness wiped away. With unaccustomed pleasure she unlocked and pulled open the heavy oaken door to the staircase that would take them beneath the castle. Dampness and a faint hint of dragon stink welled out of the darkness.

The door was next to the stone basin where steaming mineral water bubbled, and George paused to dip his fingers in, pulling them back with surprise at the heat.

"A hot spring?" he asked.

"The veins of it run through the mount." She lowered her voice. "Sometimes, in the night, I almost think I can hear the heart that pumps it, beating deep beneath the earth."

He stared at her for a moment. "That must keep you awake," he said, and forced a laugh.

"Yes." She lit a torch from the central hearth. "Take the sheep's lead."

"What?" he asked, even as Milo handed him the end of the rope.

"Milo does not go down to the dragon."

George turned to the man. "You said you had seen the dragon."

"Once," Milo said, and nothing more.

"Once is as much as most can bear," Alizon said. Except for Pippa, that was, which was the reason the door had to be kept locked: the mischief-prone girl found the dragon more exciting than frightening.

Alizon stepped through the doorway and descended into the dark dankness of the stairwell. She felt George follow a moment after, dragging the sheep along behind him, its hooves scrabbling against the stone as it bleated in protest.

The walls were raw stone, cracked in places and seeping mineral water that ran in trickling cataracts down the stairs. A rope was threaded through wall brackets, providing a loose handrail.

The air was a blend of drafts: one with the cold scent of buried stone, the other with the warm odor of the mineral water and a hint of something else, something with the fetid breath of feces and rotted flesh. *Belch.* It was the name she had given to the dragon, for the stink that wafted from the lair.

Her heart beat more quickly, and she felt a chill mist of perspiration growing on her brow and down her body. The torch quivered in her grip, and she hoped George, if he noticed, put it down to the flickering of the flames and nothing more.

For the sake of the other virgins she had grown skilled at masking her fear when she descended these stairs, but it was always there. She had never grown used to this passage, or what lay at its end.

Fluttering images of remembered horror came back to her, of her first descent, in the company of the crone. She heard again the nun's rasping breath, close behind, pushing her forward, and her stomach churned with an echo of the sick desperation she had felt.

"How often do you feed the dragon?" George asked.

The question broke the spell of her thoughts, bringing her back to the present. "Once a week. Any longer and he begins to complain."

"In words?"

She paused on the steps to look back at him, and he bumped into her, then steadied her with his enormous hand. His palm swallowed her shoulder, and she had the unsettling feeling that, contrary to what Milo had said of his weakness, George would have only to flick his fingers to toss her against the wall. She wished she *did* have him in chains, and safely within her control.

She used sarcasm to mask her discomfort. "Have you met many dragons that *could* speak?"

"I have heard of such things. Some are said to be wise."

She snorted. "Not this one." She continued back down the stairs, which ended in another door, pads of leather attached around its edges, sealing it as well as could be managed. Even so, tendrils of stink wafted through invisible openings, and she swallowed against the urge to cough.

She gestured for George to open the door.

He cast her an assessing glance, as if he thought the dragon was going to be waiting with an open mouth on the other side but did not want to admit to concern over the possibility. He pulled open the door, releasing a thick stench that blew out at them as if from the dragon's gaseous bowels. The sheep bleated in terror. George started to gag, then glanced at her and shut his mouth, his face going impassive even as his chest muscles clenched in betrayal of his revulsion.

She smiled beneath the cover of her hood. "You will become used to it."

His perfect-toothed grin showed strain at the edges. "I have known men who smelled worse."

"I pity their wives." She stepped into the low-ceilinged passageway beyond, the torch held before her. "Watch your head."

All sounds were drowned out by the baa-ing of the sheep as George dragged it after them, the bleats reverberating off the walls of the tunnel, seeming to increase in volume with every step. The passageway curved, and then up ahead there was a rough rectangle of dim light. Alizon slowed her steps, aware of George bent low immediately behind her.

"There used to be a door," she said over the ringing bleats of the sheep, "but the hinges rusted and it became stuck half open. Then the dragon tried to come through it."

"What happened?" His mouth was so close to her ear, she thought she could feel his warm breath through the wool of her hood.

A shiver ran down her neck that had nothing to do with what awaited them. Sense said to step away, but she stayed where she was. "His head got stuck, and when he tried to pull it back, he wrenched the door away."

"He is free to come in?" He shifted behind her, as if preparing to run.

"He is too big now to do so. That, at least, is not a concern you need have."

"I am not concerned." He sounded offended and moved slightly away from her. "I am here to kill the damned thing, and a tunnel is as good a place as any other."

"Yes, kill it with your pitchfork, I know," she said, turning toward him, her voice quavering with hysterical amusement. Clearly he was going to insist on cockiness to the end, and the end it might very well be.

"You have never seen one of these in the hands of a master." He was holding the pitchfork at an angle across his body, but against the expanse of his chest it looked more like a kitchen implement than a weapon.

The bleating of the sheep was beginning to make her head hurt, the sound ringing in her ears. She ignored George's bravado, wanting only to get this over with. Let him see what he was up against, and then perhaps he would know how foolish his bravery was. "Obey me when we step out onto the platform beyond the doorway. I would not see you die too soon."

"Yes, mistress."

He was like a mocking child. She had forgotten the irritating behaviors of men.

They came to the end of the tunnel and stepped out onto a wooden platform that extended a few feet into a vast cavern, a smooth rock beach and a lake of water thirty feet below. To her left were narrow steps carved into the face of the rock, descending around the side of the cavern to the beach. The lake emptied through a wide crack in the cavern wall, big enough for Belch to depart if he wished, which was also the source of the daylight.

The platform and the stone stairs had been built in the de Burroughs' time, as an easily defended back entrance to the castle. A small boat could be rowed through the passage to the sea.

From an opening halfway down the wall to Alizon's right, hot mineral water poured down the rocks to the water, its heat against the chillier air of the cavern creating a permanent atmosphere of fog. It drifted in layers, sometimes clearing, sometimes swirling from winds blowing in from the sea, and sometimes lying in an impenetrable layer upon beach and water alike.

The dragon was nowhere to be seen.

She took the rope from George and pulled the sheep into a small stall set at the corner of the platform, closing the gate behind it and then removing the rope from its neck. She scooped a handful of grain into the stall from a canister tucked against the wall. The bleats stopped. The sheep's hooves made hollow sounds upon the boards, and in the sudden quiet they could hear it snuffling at the oats and grinding its molars.

"Where's the dragon?" George asked, going like an eager child to the low wooden wall around the platform. He leaned on it and looked down into the swirling fog.

"Do not lean over the rail," Alizon warned, shuddering with remembrance of one other who had stood too close to the edge.

"I don't see it."

"He is there."

"Yoo hoo! Dragon!" The man waved his pitchfork in the air. "Come on, show yourself, you godforsaken lizard! Or are you afraid of St. George?"

"Please," Alizon said, grabbing a handful of surcoat and tugging on it. "Step back."

"Hello!" he shouted, his voice echoing in the cavern. "Hellll-oooooo!"

She laid her hand on George's arm, trying to get his attention. He glanced at her, the light of excitement in his eyes. "We'll be able to see him, won't we?"

"More closely than you wish, if you do not step away from the rail."

He didn't seem to hear her, turning back and looking again for his foe. Nothing moved below but the fog, silent and slow.

"Do you think he went out, over there?" George nodded toward the wide crack in the cavern wall.

"No. He would do so only if I did not feed him. He is too fond of his comfort, I think."

George leaned back on his heels, some of the excitement visibly draining from him. "I don't see him. I'm always the one who doesn't see the deer beside the road, or misses the bear running off into the forest."

"If you shout and swing your arms about as you have here, it is no wonder."

He looked at her, a thoughtful expression on his face. Then it cleared. He grinned and slapped himself on the forehead. "I understand! If I have the courage to face my dragons, I will find that they are nothing but so much mist! Such a simple lesson! There is no dragon. There is nothing here but the smell of my own fear!"

She had no idea what he was talking about, concerned only that in his excitement he was again flinging his arms around. "Please, come away from the rail," she implored.

"You had me frightened in the tunnel, I admit. I really thought there would be a dragon here." He leaned way out over the edge, shaking his pitchfork. "You don't scare me, you beastly Missouri women! Call me what names you will, I am St. George the Dragonslayer, and proud of it!"

She damned modesty and gripped his hips from behind with both her hands and pulled, trying forcibly to drag him away. He was too heavy and too strong. She might as well have been pulling against a tree.

"You don't scare me! Do you hear that?" he shouted.

And then it happened.

The splash of water was the only warning, but

one that came too late. The great green-black body rose from the mist, propelled from the water by Belch's thrusting tail. His pink maw was open wide enough to swallow a cow, and lined with ivory teeth the size of her hand. The massive jaws snapped shut mere inches from George's forward-bent head, and then Belch was falling back into the mist, his body hitting the water below with a slapping boom.

"Jeeee-zus!" George cried, dropping his pitchfork over the railing and falling back, bumping into Alizon and knocking them both to the floor of the platform. "Christ!" And then he started talking in English she could not quite understand but knew from the forceful delivery to be a trail of curses.

A bone-vibrating bellow rose up from the mists below, the sound reverberating off the cavern walls. Water sloshed about as Belch swam, and then there was a moment of silence.

"Back! Back!" Alizon cried, pulling at George's upper arm as she scrambled backward on the wood platform.

George stopped cursing long enough to look at her in confused alarm, and then there was another splash, and up rose the immensity of Belch's head, and the scrabbling claws at the ends of his stubby arms. He landed on the edge of the platform, most of his weight on the narrow stone stairs. Boards splintered, part of the plank wall of the platform giving way.

The great maw opened and bellowed a call of rage and hunger, the stink of his breath blowing through Alizon's clothes and under her hood, coating her skin in foul dragon air.

Belch's weight dragged him down, and even as the great dragon snapped his jaws inches from George's feet, he was sliding back and then falling, his body slamming once again into the water below.

Alizon lunged to the stall with the wildly bleating sheep, the creature rising up on its hind legs to look over the gate and try to scramble free. There was a lever to the side of the gate, and with no more than a quick mental apology to the animal, Alizon pulled it.

The trapdoor beneath the stall fell open, and with a wild squawk the sheep dropped through, its cries lasting only a moment before there was the unmistakable sound of snapping jaws and impacted flesh.

Alizon peered over the edge of the open trap door, staying as far back as she could, and could make out only the swirls of fog where Belch swam beneath. She knew from past experience that he might not eat the sheep all at once, but store it in some rocky crevice underwater, the flesh softening to his preferred consistency.

She turned back to George, who was half-sprawled in the entrance to the tunnel, propped up by his arms. The man's mouth was hanging open, almost as wide as his eyes. His pupils were drawn to pinpricks in the field of his meadow-green irises, the color startling in his now-pale face.

She shook her head. "If you were truly St. George, you would have known: One must never tease a dragon."

Chapter Nine

His hand shook as he raised the spoonful of re-heated mutton stew to his lips. He was beyond tasting, wanting only the warmth of the food as it made its way into his belly, washed down with a mouthful of the beer he had decided was not quite so horrible if it could lessen the quivering of his limbs.

What the hell *was* that thing?

"Belch," the mistress had called it. "Demon from the Black Lagoon," he would name it. In the few terror-stricken glimpses he had gotten, it had looked like a cross between an alligator and a dinosaur, with a bit of horror-film creature thrown in. It was blackish-green, its monstrous paws webbed between the claws, its head that of an alligator but on a longer neck.

It wasn't the pretty dragon he had imagined, with

batlike wings and iridescent scales. There had been no magical wisdom in those yellow reptilian eyes, nothing but the soulless animal imperative to kill and devour.

And he had stood there like a meal on the hoof, his body hanging out over the mist like an invitation. "Come and get me! Here I am! Big doofus for dinner!"

He tried to remind himself that this was all happening in his mind, that he had been in no real danger.

It didn't work.

Just as in a nightmare you could believe yourself pursued to a grisly end, so the shaking of his body told him that he had almost lost his life to that prehistoric lizard. His mind claimed this to be reality. This was real for him, and would be to the end. Until he woke.

He'd even lost his pitchfork, dropping it like a startled child. He saw now it had been a mere toothpick for Belch to use when the beast had finished dining on his flesh.

Aw, Christ. How the hell was he going to kill that thing?

The mistress sat down across from him, settling her hands neatly together on the table. He could detect no shaking in those suspiciously young and smooth fingers. The gray she had smeared upon them had rubbed off in places, revealing healthy skin.

He turned his scrambled emotions upon her.

"Why don't you remove your hood?"

The hands tightened their grip on one another. "I will not. What need have you to see the workings of time upon a woman's face?"

"So, it's vanity that keeps you concealed? That is a deadly sin, Sister, lest you have forgotten."

"And lest you have forgotten, my purpose here is not to play lady of the manor to foolish young men out to prove themselves against dragons. Do not impose upon my hospitality."

He reached across the planks and took one of her hands, gripping it before she could pull back. She tugged, but he pulled it slowly toward him, rubbing his thumb over its back.

"Smooth skin. Your knuckles aren't large with age; there are no brown spots beneath this gray." He dipped a fingertip of his free hand into his beer and rubbed it against her skin. "You look in the very pink of health." Except . . .

He held up her hand, tilting it in the light that came down from the open windows high overhead. She was exerting a constant pull, but it was nothing to him to keep her hand within his grasp. "Except for these bits of green, and blue . . . and red. What have you been doing? Painting pictures?"

She tugged again, and this time he released her. He stared into the darkness beneath her hood, and past the screen of white wool he thought he could make out the dimmest shadows of her nose and mouth, and the curve of her chin as it was caught by light reflected from the table. She was no older than he, of that he was fairly certain.

His eyes slipped down to her chest, covered by the brown robe, but a deep maroon gown showed in a sliver at the opening. Her contours bespoke high and rounded breasts. The line of her shoulders was clean and square, and despite her occasional attempts to move as an old woman, more often she forgot and strode with confidence and her head held high, her limbs limber and strong. He remembered her grip on his waist, trying to pull him from the rail, and the way she had lunged for the lever that had plunged the sheep to its doom. They weren't the movements of the old and frail.

He wanted to see her face. There was no one who could stop him if he were to leap across the table and pull her hood back.

Something inside rebelled against such a thought, though. He had never been one to use his size to force his way. Except for in the ring, he was careful to ease the intimidation others felt standing near him. It was a lesson he had learned in fifth grade, when he had been taller than his teacher, Mrs. Stubbs. He had seen the flash of fear in her eyes when he had become upset about her markings on his homework assignment and argued with her, his voice louder than he realized. His words had stopped the moment he had seen that fear, and the small step backward she had taken. He had silently retreated to his desk and put his head down on his arms, feeling like a creature from *Where the Wild Things Are.*

He would wait, and persuade the mistress to reveal herself. It might even prove entertaining, something to keep his mind off that dragon.

Hell's bells! The dragon. A shudder went through him. How would he ever bring himself to descend into that foggy lair and attack the thing? He needed a rocket launcher, that's what he needed. Anti-tank ordnance. Or a mine to drop into the water, to let Belch swim into it and blow himself up.

He had seen *Jurassic Park.* One didn't kill a dinosaur; one ran like mad and found a plane to escape the damn thing.

Unless you were the woman across the table from him.

"How have you stayed here all these years with that monster living below?" he asked in genuine awe. She had kept her head while Belch was leaping and bellowing and clawing at the platform. If not for her, he would be bathing in stomach acids right now.

"Monsters come in all shapes and sizes," she said. "A dragon's evil is easy to see and understand, and so there is less to fear."

"Less to fear than what?"

She shrugged and did not answer. He guessed he was supposed to figure it out for himself.

"Less to fear than from people?" he asked.

"Perhaps."

"It's no wonder you feel that way, since you have yourself as an example, tossing innocent girls to that . . . thing." He had his doubts that she had ever done such an act, and not just because he had trouble believing ill of anyone without proof. No child-killing hag would have tried to save him from having his head chomped off.

She said nothing, but he thought she was sitting more rigidly. If he put his hand in front of that hood she would probably bite off a finger.

Good. When she lost control she was more likely to speak in her normal voice, her words less closely watched. He *would* figure out exactly who or what she was, and what role she played in this queer adventure.

"If you are finished, I can take you to the armory. That is, if you still have the courage to battle Belch."

"I have courage enough," he lied. "It's a plan I'm lacking."

"A plan? What plan do you need? You take a weapon, go down, and try to kill him."

"It's clear enough that I'm no match for Belch in strength." He tapped his forehead. "But Belch is no match for me in wits."

A sound suspiciously like laughter came from beneath the hood, and the woman's shoulders shook. "Ah, I see."

"I never enter a fight without a plan. Well, except with Milo, and you saw how poorly that turned out."

"Marry! You are a wise and cautious man!"

"And you are a kind and honest woman."

She stood, shoving back the end of the bench upon which she sat. "What mean you by that, sir?"

"What should I mean but what I said? It can be no insult to call you kind and honest."

"It was the tone to which I object. Do not judge that which you do not understand."

He wondered which bothered her more, being thought cruel or being thought a liar, and whether there might be danger for him in the answer. He couldn't make out whether she wished to be friend or foe to him.

Damn that hood!

He stood and picked up his dishes. "Thank you for the meal; it was delicious. Where should I put these?"

She said nothing, and he looked about until he saw the stone scullery sink near the basin with the hot spring water. He took them over there, rinsed them, and set them in the sink. "This all right, then?"

"Verily, this land you come from is far away," she said in stunned tones.

"Hmmm?"

She gestured toward the scullery sink. "Will you scrub them, too?"

"Oh, sorry! Yes, of course!" He turned back and picked up his bowl, looking for whatever passed for a scrubber or soap.

"No, please, leave it!" She was at his side now,

taking the bowl from his hands. "This is no task for a guest, and certainly none for a man who claims to be a saint."

"The women I know would argue otherwise. My mother would clout me on the ear if I didn't at least offer."

She tilted her head back and stared up at him, and for a moment he could see shadowed lips and nose, and a glimpse of dark eyes. "Would she? Your homeland is different from England, then. Tell me, for what else would your mother clout you on the ear?"

"Clouting isn't her usual punishment," he said. He followed as she led him back into the dark hall that would take them onto the terrace. "She has a way of looking at you that makes you sorry you ever disobeyed."

"A look of anger?"

"Disappointment."

"And with this look she has her son cleaning his own dishes. I shall have to learn it."

The sun stung George's eyes, bright after the softer light inside the castle. He used his hand as a visor and squinted up at the windows of the other wing, looking for another pale face but finding nothing but darkness. The only sounds were of the wind gusting and the squawks of a seagull hovering on the air. "More powerful than her look of disappointment was her promise to me that women would love a man who cleaned up after himself and could cook at least five good meals."

She stopped and again stared up at him. He gave her his best smarmy, charming grin. What he could see of her skin was pale, her pursed lips a healthy dark pink. "The men in your land follow such beliefs?" she asked.

"Some do. Some even stay home and tend to the children, while their wives are merchants who travel the world."

She made a rude noise. "You jest with me!"

"I speak truly."

"Then are these men who have been injured in a war and cannot work?"

"A few may be. But there are others who do so by choice, especially if their wives are better at business than they."

She shook her head. "No, you tell a good tale, but this I cannot believe. It would be easier to believe that you are truly St. George."

He shrugged, amused. "Believe what you will. All the same, I shall kill your dragon and wash my dishes, and then you shall pull back your hood and kiss me in thanks."

A choking sound came from beneath the hood, and he grinned, knowing an exaggerated protest when he heard one. So, she wasn't completely uninterested! Maybe there was more to keep him busy here than killing lizards.

"The longer you wear that hood, the more curious I become. I'm spending much more time thinking about your face than I would if you simply showed it to me."

"Better that you think about your plan for Belch."

"There are only so many hours of the day one can think about fighting. What of the sport of loving?"

Her pace picked up, as if trying to escape him. "How dare you speak of such things to me?" she asked, her voice rising to a nervous squeak.

"Better to you than to Milo, I should think."

She came to a sudden stop at a door at the end of the haunted wing and mumbled something. From beneath her robe she took out an oversized keyring.

"I beg your pardon?"

She turned the key in the lock and tossed her head back, nearly unseating her hood. "I was reflecting that you might have better luck discussing such thoughts with a sheep." She pushed open the door and took a step inside, looking back over her shoulder at him. "I hear that they are the only fit companions for some men."

He roared with laughter and pursued her into the castle. "You are no nun, of that I am certain! For shame, Sister, that such thoughts should ever enter your pure head!"

"I have had some experience of the world, sir! I was not born a nun." She scampered ahead of him through a large room scattered with beds and piles of what looked to be narrow, thin mattresses. The sunbeams coming through the windows were filled with motes of dust, stirred by her passage.

"Not born one, nor ever been one, I warrant."

"As if you, a foreigner from a backward land, would have the wit to know one way or the other!"

"There are some things that are the same in every land," he said. He closed the distance between them and raised his hand almost to her chin, as if he would touch it.

"Enough of this nonsense! I insist you stop this line of discourse at once!" She fumbled at the latch to another door.

"You were the one who mentioned the sheep."

She pulled back, turning her head away. "I have no interest in sheep!"

"Neither do I."

He lowered his hand to the latch and, gently brushing her motionless fingers aside, opened it himself.

Chapter Ten

She was not a sheep.

Horrible man! If he only knew what she had been through, and what she had accomplished! She was the mistress of Devil's Mount, and she was not to be trifled with.

Or touched. Or goaded. Or teased, by St. Nicholas! She would not stand for it.

Alizon fumed beneath her hood as George poked through the piles of weapons and armor in what was left of the armory. The de Burroughs had left a fair quantity of it behind when Belch had come and eaten them, but she had with Milo's help secretly sold off the better portion of it. Providing for the care and luxurious comfort of twelve virgins was not inexpensive.

Swords and shields were not the only trade that

went on secretly in the harbor of Devil's Mount, of course. What a surprise St. Bumbles the Overconfident here would have if he knew about the tapestries and the profits they brought!

She scolded herself for the thought. He was tempting her to boast, and then where would she be? All secrets revealed, everything she had built destroyed. And for what? For a moment's surprise on his face, and to hear him say he was wrong?

It was almost worth it.

"Excellent! Look at this!" he said, holding up a dull sword with half its helm broken off.

She was standing with arms crossed, watching him as a mother watches a child playing in the mud. "Yes, splendid. Belch will stand no chance against you."

"And look, a spear! And what is this thing?" He held up a stick with a chain and iron-spiked ball at the end, and gave it a swing. It swung back and hit him in the thigh. "Ow!"

She snickered.

He frowned at her, then with a look of disgust threw the weapon back into the pile. "You could hurt someone with that."

"Is that not the point?"

"Not when that someone is likely to be *me.*"

She shook her head, smirking. "A new and strange sort of warrior you are! How brave! How fearless! How skilled!"

"Hey babe," he snapped. "I know you're just being bratty because you want my body."

She sucked in an offended breath, having understood only half the words but all the meaning. "I beg your pardon!"

He grinned and went back to digging through weapons.

And, horrid as he was, she found her gaze going to his buttocks. The split panels of his surcoat had slid off to either side, and his muscled backside was clear for her to see, his silver hose doing more to reveal than to conceal.

He deserved a good spanking. Alizon's palms tingled with the desire to slap him across those flexing mounds.

She grimaced and clenched her hands into fists, quelling the impulse. Honesty made her admit that any spanking would be but an excuse to touch him.

Just looking at him made her feel that everything was going out of her control. Even as he dug through the dregs of weapons, making his choices more on appearance than on function, she felt that he was a threat.

She should be satisfied he was not, after his expression of utter horror when Belch had all but snipped his head from his neck. Watching his hands shake as he ate—and he, making no move to conceal the weakness!—should have been enough for her. But it wasn't.

She had to keep him in his place.

"How do I look?" he asked, turning toward her with a helmet on his head, his face concealed by a visor.

She smothered a chuckle. It should not be hard to maintain control of him. "Much better."

He turned his head to one side, angling up his chin. He held the pose for a moment, then changed it, standing with legs spread and hands on hips, face-forward. A moment later he changed it again, twisting to the side and lowering one knee to the ground. He raised a fisted hand in front of his downturned face, the muscle in his arm bulging.

She watched in puzzled fascination. "By St. Michael, what are you doing?"

"Just playing," he said, standing again. "You do play, mistress, don't you? Or have you no time for that, alone in your castle?"

"Play?"

"You know. Have fun." He walked slowly toward her.

She checked the urge to step back, forcing herself to hold her ground. She would not let him cow her! She was in control! "You see I have no servants. There is much to do, and little time for playing games."

"Is that so? I could have sworn you were playing one right now."

"What do you mean?" she asked, her voice rising.

"I think you like to pretend." He stepped closer still.

She could smell the hint of sweat on his body, and the trace of spices she had noted the night before. He was close enough that she could feel the

113

heat emanating from his chest. Her breathing quickened, and her thoughts became muddled. She fought against the stirring desires of her body. "Pretend at what?" she asked and looked up at his visored face.

His eyes were hidden in the shadows behind the visor, visible only as a faint glint of reflected light. He was as faceless as she, and silent. The tilt of his head was the only indication that he was looking at her.

As the moment stretched, Alizon was suddenly overcome by a vision of him taking her in his arms and lowering her to the ground, his hand sliding up her leg to touch her most intimate places, it all happening in faceless silence. Her eyes half-closed of their own accord, and she swayed on her feet.

"You pretend at everything," he said.

The spell of his physical closeness was broken by a spurt of fear. She stepped back, ducking her head down as she realized he might have seen more of her face than she had thought. If he did not know for certain she was not the crone, then he at least suspected. "If I do, then I am not the only one present who does so."

He lifted the helmet from his head and ran his fingers through his dark hair, pushing it back from his face. "There is more truth to that than I would like to admit."

She stared at him, startled that he should make such an admission.

He was oblivious to her surprise. "I wish I could

take this home with me," he said, stepping back and holding the helmet out in front of him. He rubbed at a spot with his thumb.

"You may buy it from me."

His eyes lifted to hers, and he grinned. "I should have known you would put a price on it, no matter that it is of no use to you. But alas, my darling, I have no gold or silver, so I must decline your offer." He moved to put it on the pile of discarded junk.

"You may work for it," she blurted, then grimaced at her idiocy. She had just made an offer that might keep him here even longer.

"Will I have to work, too, for the rent of the weapons?"

"The killing of Belch will be payment enough," she said, trying to backtrack.

"And if I fail, as you believe I will?"

"We can talk about it then, if you still live. You look to be a strong man. I will find something for you to do." The thought came to her that she could use this as the leverage to have him take Emoni and her daughter away from Markesew: that could be his payment if he failed—as he would—to kill the dragon. She smiled beneath her hood, pleased with the simple solution.

"I can think of a few things a strong fellow like myself could do for you," he said and waggled his eyebrows at her.

She gaped at him. He could not mean . . . "Like what?"

He dumped the helmet onto the pile and picked

up the sword he had chosen, then with it made chopping motions through the air. "Chopping and hauling wood, perhaps?"

She struggled to keep her voice calm. "You may do that for the helmet, if you wish." The fool had her not knowing if she was coming or going, and it made her want to scream.

"I'll do it for my room and board, the wood chopping and whatever else you would have me do. I can't expect you to continue feeding me for free."

Now he was being considerate. She could not stand it! "Speak with Milo, and he will show you what to do."

"Great! And where should I stay? I assume you don't still think me so dangerous that I need to be locked in a bare cell again."

"You may stay with Milo."

He made a face. "Is there no place here in the castle I could sleep? Milo's cottage is, ah . . . small for two large men."

"There are no rooms fit for guests," she lied. Have him sleeping in the castle, free to roam around? She would not sleep a wink, and she would never be able to keep the virgins from revealing themselves. "The bedding is rotten. Damp got in."

"A pile of blankets by the fire in the kitchen, then?"

"You would be more comfortable with Milo."

He stalked to the open doorway to the old garrison room, where the soldiers of times past had slept and eaten. He braced his hands on the wall to either side and ducked his head down to stare into the room. "I can stay in here."

"There?" she squeaked. Her room, and those that the virgins shared, were directly overhead. They would have to walk on tiptoe and whisper every word.

"I will be out of your way, and those mattresses look usable. It will be a good place to plan my attack, as well, since the armor is right here. I'll know what I have to work with. Do you have any objection?" he asked, looking back over his shoulder at her.

"I cannot let you wander at will. . . ."

"I promise not to creep into your bedroom."

"That was not what I meant! You might come to harm, is what I fear."

"You are worried about my safety?" he asked, laughter in his voice.

"You do not know all the dangers. Belch sometimes stirs at night. I should not like him to find you wandering on the terrace, unarmed."

"And yet you have survived quite well all these years. I should think I would fare no worse."

What argument could she possibly give that he could not counter? A mist of anger fogged her brain. Why did she have to give any argument whatsoever? "Sleep with Milo," she commanded.

"No."

"It is not for you to say 'no'! I say, sleep with Milo!"

"And still, I say 'no.' "

"I am mistress here!" she gasped.

"Mistress of an empty castle. There's no reason I shouldn't stay here rather than in a cramped and, let us say it, filthy cottage."

"It is not your decision!"

"I will not be bound by another's unreasoning demands, especially when that person doesn't own the castle she claims to command! You clearly don't use these rooms, so it will be no invasion of your privacy to have me stay in them. Unless you can give me a sound reason for your refusal, I see no reason to abide by it. I'm not a child who will be forced to make do with an explanation such as 'Because I said so.' "

Alizon pursed her lips together, those very words having been on the verge of spilling out. She fumed silently, anger sucking away any ability to come up with a fitting response.

He came over to her and put his hands on her shoulders, the weight of his palms heavy and warm. She wanted to snap her teeth into his arm, like an angry dog.

"If you are afraid of me, you have no need to be," he said, his voice softening.

"I fear no man."

"I don't wish to be your enemy. I'm here to kill the dragon, not to harm you."

But he would. She suddenly knew that if it was not the world she had built on the mount he destroyed, it would be something within herself. She

118

had spent twelve years building a fortress around her heart, and she would not let him tear it down. She would not be left weak and helpless, and she would not put herself at the mercy of another.

"Sleep here if you must," she ground out, "but give your word that you will not wander from these rooms."

"Done." He grinned and squeezed her shoulders.

She pushed off his hands. She could not trust his word, and she would put her faith in her own plans for keeping him where he belonged.

Chapter Eleven

George caught a whiff of himself and grimaced. Damn that Athena; what was she spritzing him with now? Between his own body odor and the smoke from the central hearth, he could barely stand to breathe.

He stacked the final load of wood against the wall in the kitchen and straightened, then arched his back, stretching it. Chopping and carrying wood was almost better than a circuit on the gym equipment. His muscles felt as if he truly had been exercising, not just imagining it.

He had forgotten for several hours, in fact, that he wasn't really here; that *here* didn't exist except in his mind.

The creeping doubt came back that maybe this was real. He played for a moment with the idea that somehow he really had slipped through a crack in time and space and landed himself in medieval times. A new sheen of sweat burst from his pores, and he felt a whimper in the back of his throat.

Stuck in the Middle Ages, truly, with no doctors or antibiotics, no telephones, and no one whom he knew and loved?

But no, that couldn't be. What of Belch? There was no such thing as dragons.

But was Belch really a dragon? Maybe he was a holdover from the age of dinosaurs, like some claimed the Loch Ness monster to be. Belch looked similar enough to a crocodile that George could believe he was a product of the natural world.

And the hot spring! That would explain why Belch was here. Some warm ocean current had brought him, and he had found a cozy nest for himself, the cave being the only place he could survive in this chilly climate after the warm current had gone away.

It was plausible.

To believe that, he would also have to believe that Athena's antique-mall crystal was possessed of some magical power, as was she; and *that* he couldn't do.

He would follow Occam's Razor: the simplest solution was most likely the correct one. He had been hypnotized, that was all.

Besides, time-travel wasn't possible.

Was it?

He dimly remembered a theory about all time

and all matter existing at once, in the same space—that sequential time as everyone knew it was an illusion.

It would be so easy to believe that this was all real; it certainly felt real enough. Perhaps something about that crystal, its structure, the reflections of light, had opened a window from one point to another—

No! It was lunacy to think that way. He had to act as if this was real, to work through the puzzle of this dream, but it was acting only.

He wondered what his mysterious mistress would say if he told her she was not a real person, but instead the personification of his feminine side.

She would probably drag him down to the cavern and throw him over the rail.

And what would a psychologist say, if he confessed he was having lewd thoughts about the faceless personification of a side of himself? Even George himself had to admit there was something perverse about it.

All manner of kinky thoughts were getting into his head. Thoughts of that hood staying on but everything else coming off. Of lush white breasts and rounded hips. Of the robe thrown back over her shoulders and hanging as a backdrop as the mistress walked toward him, naked and inviting. Of her riding atop him, his hands on her waist as she rose and fell, her soft thighs over his hips, her body wet and hot and tight, squeezing him as she reached her climax, moaning . . .

He felt pressure in his groin as he became engorged, his erection stretching against his briefs and leggings. Thank God for the old shirt he had found in one of those chests in the garrison room. It was cut full enough that he was able to get it on, although it was likely made for a smaller man. It smelled musty and was splotched with stains, but it hung down to mid-thigh, concealing all evidence of his physical attraction to the bad-tempered mistress.

"Here's your supper," his temptress said, dropping his bowl onto the table with a clunk.

"Thank you." It was killing him not to know what she looked like. He went to the hot spring basin and washed his hands.

She sat where she had during his lunch, with nothing in front of her.

"Aren't you going to eat?" he asked.

"I will eat later. I have no wish to be watched while I sup."

He raised a brow at her, but if she recognized the irony of her watching *him* while *he* ate, she gave no sign. He sat, and pulled his bowl toward him.

It looked like the same stew of that afternoon, this time with a hunk of brown bread on the side, getting soggy. Thoughts of multiplying bacteria squirmed in his head. He had been taught to eat whatever was put before him, but he didn't think his mother meant to do so at the risk of his intestinal health. "Er . . . when did you make this stew?"

"Yesterday."

"Ah. Hmm. Where do you store food, between meals?"

"In a pot, of course."

"You have no cool place?"

"We have a cellar for roots and apples, cheeses, things like that."

His eyebrows rose. " 'We'?"

She hesitated for a moment. "Milo and I."

"Milo eats with you?"

"He, ah, stores things here on occasion, and sometimes will eat with me. He prefers his privacy, though. As do *I.*"

He ignored the comment, suspicions aroused. "And no one else?"

"Who else should there be? No one dares come to Devil's Mount."

He stared at her, trying to gain some clue from the shadowed chin and the hands that she held tightly together on the table.

A startling thought hit him. Might she have a boyfriend who even now was somewhere in the castle?

That would explain why she seemed so determined to keep George under lock and key. She might be afraid he would find out and tell the townsfolk. Her days of living in the relative luxury of a castle and romping with her boyfriend would be over.

He wondered who the guy was, and if he might be able to oust him. It wasn't very sporting of him, but dammit! She was *his* personification, his anima, not someone else's!

Oh, Lord. He was losing his mind. He was going to need to see a *real* shrink by the time he came out of this trance. Now he was imagining rivals to his imaginary lust-object. It said plenty about his repressed sex drive.

There had been a time in his wrestling career when picking up an all-too-eager female groupie while on the road had seemed a good way to spend the night, but Athena's single motherhood of Gabrielle had been the beginning of the end of such entertainments. He had started to see things from the girl's point of view, and then all the fun had gone out of it. He had no wish to take advantage of the naïveté of star-blinded young women.

He knew better than to start an affair with one of his female co-workers, and he sure as hell wasn't going to pay for it from some unfortunate, drug-addicted, virus-carrying prostitute.

Which left him with no choice but to abstain. It had been two years since he had had sex with anything but his hand and some pretty pictures. He could hardly be blamed for the wet dream he was having now.

"There should be no one else," he said, belatedly answering her question.

He took a bite of the lukewarm stew. It was seasoned with salt and pepper, and with his own appetite, which made the greatest difference of the three. He was used to eating four or five meals a day, and he had been ravenous for hours.

There had been more than one pale face at the windows, and the giggling and footsteps outside his cell this morning had been female, not male. Neither spoke of a male rival lurking in the castle, but rather of something more supernatural.

Ugh. The ghosts of dead virgins.

He shuddered.

There were too many strange things creeping around in his unconscious. He was getting a headache again. Better to think about something constructive.

He downed several more mouthfuls of the stew, which he now noticed had a slightly bitter taste. He stirred his spoon through it, finding bits of what he assumed to be turnip. He had never had turnips before. Perhaps they accounted for the flavor. He swigged some beer.

"Have you made your plan for killing Belch?" his hostess asked.

He sopped up gravy with his bread and wolfed it down. "I have a few ideas. It would help to know what others have tried, before. The de Burroughs and their soldiers must have tried to kill him."

She shrugged. "Most ran. Whatever stories may say about the bravery of warriors, when faced with such a beast most choose to flee rather than fight. Those that did stay to fight, died."

"And no one has tried since?"

"One or two. Their bones and mail lie at the bottom of Belch's pool."

He scooped up the last of the stew, then set his spoon in the empty bowl. "It's difficult to believe that the townsfolk of Markesew should go on so long, giving up their young women to the dragon without trying again and again to be rid of it."

"Yes, it is difficult to believe, isn't it?" she said, and there was more raw emotion in her voice than he had heard all evening. She was not taunting him now. Her fingertips had gone white where they clenched against the backs of her hands.

"It should be their soldiers going to the lair, not girls," he said, testing what more of a response he could draw from her.

"They claim to be farmers, not soldiers." Her tone was bitter.

"Then they should use their gold to hire men to fight Belch, or they could offer a prize to the one who succeeded. I should think there would be many who would work to win it."

"Ah, but you miss an important point."

"What is that?"

"A poor girl sacrificed once a year is cheaper than a purse of gold."

"I can't believe that an entire town could be so heartless. There must be another reason."

"Must there? If you think so, then you do indeed come from a land far away. One where no one puts the health of their coffers above a human life." She stood up. "More stew?"

"I can get it," he said, moving to stand.

"No, please. Sit." She took his bowl and went to

fill it again, her back to him as she dished from the pot on the edge of the center hearth.

"My land is neither so far nor so distant as that," he said, thinking about the Missouri boys and their injuries, and the money that wrestling brought in. "But what of their sheep, at least? The farmers must have lost enough of them to equal a large prize."

"The sheep they send are the poorest of the flocks. There are times I think the farmers and townsfolk see the dragon as a convenient means of being rid of offal, just as one throws unusable scraps to chickens and pigs."

She brought the bowl back and set it in front of him, and there was such tension in her voice and movements that he thought for a moment she was going to hit him. Instead, she refilled his cup from an earthenware ewer.

He stirred his stew, watching her from the corner of his eye as she again sat across from him. He glanced down into his bowl and noticed some small clumps of white. He mashed them against the edge of the bowl, blending them in. It was probably flour, used to thicken the gravy.

"And what of your own role in this?" he asked, keeping his eyes on his stew, hoping she would answer if she didn't feel accused. "Why not spirit the girls away, instead of feeding them to Belch? Who would ever know the difference?"

She picked at a hangnail, then started polishing a fingernail with the pad of her thumb. Her tone was less defensive than he had expected. "Belch would know. He would attack the village."

"Are you so certain he can tell a girl from a sheep, and of the two wouldn't prefer the sheep to begin with?" He ate some of the stew.

She made a noise suspiciously like a laugh, and almost too quietly for him to hear said, "I once knew someone like that." She went on in her normal voice, "It was only when Belch ate his first young girl that he stopped his ravaging. Everyone knows that dragons prefer virgins."

"And gentlemen prefer blondes. But there are always exceptions."

"Do they?" she asked, sounding surprised.

"Do what?"

"Gentlemen prefer blondes?"

"It's only a saying."

The mistress fidgeted and brought her hand up to her hidden mouth in the unmistakeable gesture of someone chewing on a hangnail. "What hair color do you prefer?" she finally asked, around the obstruction.

"Whatever grows naturally upon a woman's head."

He might have told the truth and said that he had a fondness for redheads—they made him think of autumn and Irish setters, fires and snuggling naked in a soft blanket in a cabin—but then she would turn out to be blonde or brunette, and she would never forgive him for saying he liked a different color best. He might not know much about women, but he knew that much at least.

"Oh," she said.

"What about you?" he asked.

Her hands went down to her lap, and she sat still. "I do not think of such things."

"My ass."

"I do not think about *that,* either!"

He laughed at her misinterpretation and its implications. "You're quick to deny it."

"Because it is untrue!"

"That's not the usual reason protests come so fast. I think you *do* think about my ass," he teased.

She made a grunt of disbelief, then a *puh* sound of ejected air. Another grunt, and a hand waved in dismissal. "You speak nonsense."

"Women look at men's asses," he said. "We all know that. There's nothing to be embarrassed about."

"I do *not* look at your ass!"

"Not even once? Come on. Admit it. I try to look at yours, but you've got it too well covered."

Little choking, gasping sounds came from under her hood. The woman sputtered for a while, then regained the power of speech. "Lecher! To look at a nun's buttocks! You are no saint!"

" 'Ain't no saint.' I've heard it before." He grinned.

"I . . . I . . . I hope Belch *does* eat you!"

"Maybe just a little bite, if you'll kiss it and make it better."

She stood up. "I think you should go to your room now."

"Only if you come with me."

"Go!" she ordered, sticking her arm out to the side and pointing.

He took another bite of stew. "I'm not done."

"That is of no matter. Go!"

"Sit down, mistress, please. I'm not a little boy to be sent to bed without finishing his supper." His intestines made an unhappy gurgle, and what was left of his appetite disappeared. Oh, man, he hoped it hadn't been a mistake to eat that. "And I'll stop teasing you, I promise." At least for now.

Her arm slowly lowered. She remained standing, and he guessed she was considering his size and the impossibility of forcing him to obey her. She was a bossy little thing, and it probably chapped her hide that she couldn't force her way.

"These failed knights, the one or two who have tried to kill Belch . . ." he said, and pushed away his half-empty bowl. "Do you know anything of how they fought him?"

"Neither lasted more than a minute. They went in, they were eaten. As you will be."

"Did you watch?"

"I have no stomach for such spectacles, much as you seem to believe otherwise."

Or maybe she was too young to have been here then. "You were quick enough to drop the sheep down that hatch."

"Would you rather I had not?"

"Point taken." He sipped his beer, hoping the alcohol might kill whatever bacteria were multiplying in his gut. "Did you at least hear about how the battles went?"

She moved slowly back to her place at the bench and sat down. "Each had men with him who watched, although they lacked the courage to join their companion. I do not know how true their tellings may be."

"Tell me what they said. The more I know, the better I can avoid their mistakes."

"One was killed as he descended the stairs. Belch came out of the water at him, as he did at you today."

"Was the man making noise like I was?"

"I do not know."

"Had Belch been fed recently?"

"I do not remember."

This was not proving helpful.

"What of the second knight?"

"He approached Belch as he lay upon his beach. The dragon did not move, so he stepped closer. And closer."

"Yes?"

"And closer. Until he was right beside Belch's head."

"And?" he asked, leaning closer.

"And SNAP!" She clapped her hands together, making him jump. "Belch ate him."

"Christ." He sat back. He was reminded of nature programs, where the crocodile lurks in the muddy water, waiting for the zebra to come close, then lunging up and taking it down in a froth of spraying water.

His bowels gurgled.

The mistress shrugged and dropped her hands back down into her lap. "You are certain you would not rather leave now, with all your parts attached?"

"I can't. I promised Emoni, and I won't break that vow."

"That is admirable of you."

He couldn't tell if she meant it. Damn that hood! He imagined her at this moment with ash-blond hair and large blue eyes, like a disdainful Michelle Pfeiffer.

He sat and thought for a minute. "I won't stand much chance against him if I walk right in. He's too fast." He thought a little longer. "When does he sleep, do you know?"

"A better question might be when does he wake? And the answer to that is, 'At the merest sound.' "

"Could I borrow some sleeping potion?" he asked, half joking.

"Mine?" she screeched.

"You have some?" He sat up straighter, excited. "How strong is it? Would it work on Belch?"

"I . . . You don't . . . You want to drug him?"

"I want to keep my head upon my shoulders, so yes, I want to drug him!"

"Is that not dishonorable?"

"He's a dragon. I don't think he cares about honor."

"But you! How could you kill him while he slept?"

"Much more easily than if he were awake, I'm hoping. The beast has eaten dozens of people—I see no reason to add my name to his list of dining conquests. Hell, yes, I'll kill him while he sleeps."

"There is no pride in that. Is that how men fight in your land?"

He thought of the wrestling ring, and the careful manipulation of the crowd's mood by use of unfair moves and double-crosses. "To be sneaky and underhanded is a virtue, at times. You do have the potion?"

She hesitated. "A powder."

"Great! Tomorrow I'll drug him, and then it will be bye-bye, Belch." His intestines churned, and he suddenly felt a buildup of internal fumes, those of the sort that if let loose would end forever any hope of seducing the woman across the table. "Great! Thank you for supper! I'll go to bed now!" he said. Then he dashed from the table toward the doorway to the dark corridor.

"You do not want a lamp?" she called after him.

Damn! Of course he needed one if he wanted to find the jakes before he fouled himself. "Yes, yes, if you please."

He waited in the arched doorway as she moved slowly—oh, so slowly—to light the wick of a small earthenware lamp. Behind him he felt a faint draft of air, and as he turned to look heard a creak of hinges directly across the corridor, then the soft thud of a door coming up against its jamb.

What the hell? That was the door that led into the great hall, the hall which he had not seen. And which should be empty.

She came over and gave him the lamp, the smoke from it reeking of burning tallow. The light was less than that from a match.

"Thank you," he said, and he would have confronted her about the door to the great hall, only his innards twisted and groaned, and a sweat broke out over his body, accompanied by a roiling sense of nausea.

He made his escape while she might still think him an appealing man.

Chapter Twelve

He wanted to die. The past four or five hours—God only knew how long, there were no clocks here— were the most miserable of his recent memory, even worse than the night he had torn his muscle.

What he wouldn't give for an anonymous, glaringly clean Holiday Inn bathroom, a box of Imodium, and a toothbrush.

Ice water would be good, too. Or anything non-alcoholic, except that he suspected that anything liquid and unboiled would send him back to the garrison-room privies, with their dark holes through which could be heard the distant crashing of the sea.

He lay naked but for an old sheet, on top of two of the beds that earlier in the day he had arranged end-to-end, making a surface long enough for his frame. He had piled them with extra mattresses, trying to make it level. It was a good thing he had done it then; he didn't have the strength now.

Or the wits, he feared.

His head was strangely muzzy, prone to wandering down psychedelic corridors. It was only the twisting of his guts and the waves of nausea that pulled him back again and again to the present unpleasant reality.

Patches of darkness fluttered and rippled above him. He heard the squeak of bats. He closed his eyes and told himself they weren't really there.

He attributed the brain fog to the weird beer. The intestinal disaster had to be the stew. Food poisoning wasn't so fast-acting that he would have felt it at the end of his supper, but he had had the same stew for lunch, and there was plenty of time for *that* to have worked its evil on him.

The small lamp sat on the floor a couple of feet from his bed, its dull orange glow illuminating nothing. He curled onto his side and gazed at it, wishing that he could wake himself from his misery. Athena could hypnotize him again later, and when he restarted this mental game, he would know better than to eat the slop that the mistress served him.

Orange trolls danced into his vision, no taller than his knees. He squinted at them as they joined hands and danced around his flickering lamp.

"Go 'way," he grumbled, and flopped his hand through the air. They disappeared.

A few minutes later came the sensation of something huge standing behind him. Sweat gathered at the nape of his neck and his muscles tensed. He could feel the cold breath of some creature as it breathed on his back, waiting for him to turn over so it could howl into his face.

"Go 'way," he tried again. It came out as a whisper.

There was a soft rustle of movement, and then the sheet covering his body began to move away, off of him, pulled by an unknown force.

The whispers he had heard, the closing door when no one should have been in the hall, the faces at the window in the floor above: he didn't want to know what they all might mean.

The sheet slipped lower. He held it, his fingers weak. With a soft tug it slipped free, then grazed over his hip and was gone, leaving him exposed. Defenseless.

He gathered what little strength he had left, and the even smaller amount of courage, and in one twist turned to face the darkness.

And screamed.

There were a dozen of them! Pale figures in white, gathered together to gape at him with their hollow eyes and wide-open mouths. One held his sheet in its hands, the edge of its face and arm traced in orange lamplight.

It was a *girl's* face.

They were female, every one of the pale horrors! They were the spirits of the dead virgins!

He screamed again.

A spectral wailing rose up from their throats, and then they were whirling, gowns drifting, hands pulling at each other, their screeches rising and falling. He wrapped his arms over his head and curled into a ball, a noise coming from his own throat such as no grown man should make.

Alizon jerked awake. By all the saints in heaven, what was that noise?

She stared into the darkness, ears pricked.

There, again! That wailing!

And then it grew in volume, female voices added to the other.

Christ's curse! The virgins.

She scrambled from bed and grabbed her hooded robe from its peg by the door on her way out, wrapping it around her naked body as she ran on bare feet down the passageway to the virgins' rooms. Her fingertips brushed empty space where closed doors should have been, but the voices were not coming from within.

They were coming from below.

At each end of the passageway were stairs that led to the floor beneath. She had barred the door at the top of the stairs into the soldiers' quarters, in case George should wander in the night.

Apparently, she had barred the wrong doors: It was her own charges who could not be trusted and should have been locked in.

She ran for the stairs, her feet sure even in the

black of night. The wails of women grew louder, then faltered, and then low, quick voices drifted up the stairs, and gasps of laughter.

The deeper groans of George continued, distant and alone.

Alizon waited on the landing until the first pale faces had come around the spiral of the stairs, and then she spoke with the cold edge of fury in her voice. "You swore to obey me."

The gasps gave the leaders away. They were Joye and Ysmay, with Braya right behind. There was much stumbling and bumping as the line of women and girls came to a halt, those still around the bend of the stairwell questioning and complaining.

"You said you had drugged him," Joye said with the defensiveness of the guilty. "He was not supposed to wake."

"You disobeyed me, and now you have ruined everything. *Everything.*"

"We only wanted to look," Ysmay whined. "He did not even know we were there until Pippa pulled the sheet off him."

There was a furious wave of shushing and cursing, and someone shoved Ysmay, almost setting her off balance.

"It is true! If his buttocks had not been chilled, he would have slept on!" Ysmay protested.

"Be *still!*" Joye said.

"It was Braya's idea to go down and look," Ysmay muttered.

Reyne's timid voice came from somewhere behind the leaders. "He will think us nothing more than a bad dream, mistress. Listen. Even now he cries out. It is as if he is tortured by the demons of sleep."

Reyne was right; Alizon did hear George continuing to moan, beyond what a man in an empty room should do. That truth threatened to make her anger ridiculous, which only incensed her the more. "Go to your rooms, and do not come out until I say you may."

Alizon stepped aside and allowed them to file past her, their giggling silenced now and their heads bowed. She snapped after them: "I will deal with you in the morning, *if* we still have a life and a home of our own."

"Yes, mistress," several voices mumbled.

When the last door had closed behind them Alizon wrapped her robe more tightly around herself and descended to the garrison room. George's moans had lowered to whimpers.

The faint lamplight was enough for her dark-adjusted eyes to make out the man as he lay curled on his side, his arms wrapped around his head. No one had replaced his sheet; his skin looked as smooth as polished stone and likely just as cold. Her nose caught the faint odor coming from the privies, which spoke of someone who had been ill.

Guilt washed over her, turning her own stomach. She had not known how much of the powder to use on him; it came yearly with the sacrificial virgin, to sedate her during her final hours, but she had only ever used a sprinkling of it, to sometimes help a new girl sleep. Those who had used it occasionally reported strange dreams upon the morrow, and complained of dizziness, but never had Alizon known that it could do to a person what she saw before her.

She had wanted George to sleep through the night, and had been overgenerous in her dosing of him to ensure it. She had not meant him harm. She had never meant *this*.

She hoped Reyne was right, that he would wake thinking this night had been but a bad dream—and not only so she and the virgins could maintain their secrecy. If he knew she had drugged him and caused this misery, he would hate her. He would think her a fiendish witch. He would like her even less than he did already.

He would never understand that her intentions had been for the best for all concerned. Just as he would never understand that what she had in mind for the days to follow was for the best, as well.

She shouldn't care what he thought of her, but she found it impossible not to. Even though everything depended upon her lying to him about who she was, a part of her wanted him to see the truth. Part of her wanted him to push back her hood, to see her as she truly was.

Deep inside, part of Alizon wanted this man who pretended at being a knight to break down her lonely fortress walls and carry her away from it forever.

She approached his bed, picking up the sheet that was pooled on the floor. George was shivering, the sheen of sweat on his hairless skin telling her his shaking was more from sickness than from cold.

"George," she said softly. "George. It's all right."

When he did not respond she reached out, tentatively, and touched his arm where it was wrapped tightly over his head. "I am here, it is all right," she whispered. They were words she had used to soothe girls woken by their own terrors, or when the bellows of Belch drifted through the windows on the night breeze, causing tears of fright.

His muscles clenched at her touch and then relaxed, his arm coming down and the last of his whimpers stopping. His green eyes were glazed, focused more on internal horrors than on her. "Mistress?"

She shook out the sheet and pulled it over him, glancing despite herself at the dark growth of hair at his groin and his flaccid manhood, which lay there, then just as quickly averted her gaze, ashamed to gawk at his body while he suffered. "I am here."

He grasped her hand, his huge palms damp and hot, engulfing her own. "I saw them. Dozens of them."

"You have taken ill. You saw no one."

"The virgins. The dead virgins."

"Shhh . . . You were dreaming."

His pressure on her hand increased, pulling her toward him. The bed frame hit the side of her knee and forced her to sit, her hip pressed up against his thighs.

"They were here!" he insisted.

With her free hand she brushed his wet hair back from his forehead, unsticking it from his skin. "Hush. Hush, now."

Even lying down and half huddled in on himself he was huge, but for the first time his size did not unnerve her. This man was too helpless to do her harm, but more than that, Alizon realized he had nothing of violence within him. Twice now she had seen him terrified, and neither time had he reacted with anger or by striking out, as other men might have done. She remembered that much, at least, of how the rougher sex behaved.

Why in God's name did this man expect he could kill Belch? A dozen girls set him weeping in terror and Milo could best him in a fight. He stood no chance against a dragon.

The thought should have made her happy, but instead she felt a twinge of concern. George did not seem to be a bad fellow, and she had no wish to watch such an innocent get eaten. She would have to be careful and clever to be sure he did not, and trust that he had at least some ability to look out for himself.

She stroked her fingers through his hair, gently shushing him until the glazed look faded from his eyes and they began to close. He released her other hand, his own relaxing across her thigh, and his breathing smoothed out. He was falling asleep.

His hand slipped lower on her leg, his fingertips accidentally finding their way through the opening of her robe. Alizon caught her breath, feeling the light touch against the inside of her thigh. She was suddenly aware of her nakedness beneath the brown wool, and the short distance from his hand to her sex.

A God-fearing woman would remove his hand.

Yet Alizon had lost her belief in God long ago. She moved her other leg, enough that a space opened between her thighs.

George shifted, sighing, and his hand slid deeper between her legs, grasping briefly at the soft flesh of her thigh and then releasing it.

She sucked in a breath and flicked her gaze to his face. His eyes were closed, the muscles of his mouth relaxed and peaceful. He was unaware of what he did, and he would have nothing to remember of this in the morning.

If he had been awake she would never have allowed this, but he slept, knowing nothing, and Alizon could not make herself pull away from his touch. Warmth was spreading from his motionless hand up her thighs, her sex tingling with arousal. This was so close to what she'd dreamed of! Her body was waking to him, every inch of skin from her neck to her knees aching to be stroked, burning with sensation.

She waited for the next movement, the next dragging of that palm across her skin. When it did not come, she shifted her leg herself.

145

The movement seemed to disturb him, and his hand slid out of its warm harbor between her thighs and pulled the edge of her robe with it, leaving the white of her leg exposed. After a pause, his hand moved again, sliding down the outside of her thigh, pulling the brown wool away from her body.

She felt the rough fabric begin to drag across her nipple as the front of the robe opened, the cool air touching first her belly and then the inside slope of her breast. She raised one hand as if to halt the unveiling, her fingertips hovering inches above the slowly moving material.

Then she let the robe pull away.

Alizon exhaled a deep, uneven breath, her body tense, her eyes closing as she let herself remain exposed in his presence, his hand lying against the outside of her thigh, his fingertips caught between her robe and her skin.

She opened her eyelids halfway and raised her eyes to his face.

He was watching her, his gaze upon her bare breast!

She could not move, horrified he was awake, and at the same moment aware that she wanted him to see her like this. Wanted him to touch her like this.

His expression gave away nothing of his thoughts, his eyes focused but with the internal distance of a fevered mind. He slowly raised his hand toward her breast, with its nipple hardened by the cold, her flesh tight and dimpled. She could feel the heat of his palm through the narrow space of air, soft as a blanket, and then in the moment before he touched her, her courage evaporated.

Pulling her robe back over flesh that ached with desire and fear, Alizon jerked away and fled into the shadows.

Chapter Thirteen

"Joye, what will happen if the people of Markesew know that we are here?" Alizon asked, standing behind the girl who sat at the kitchen table, her bowl of porridge growing cold before her. The other virgins sat lined on either side of the long table, hands in their laps as they stared down at their breakfasts, unwilling to draw Alizon's attention.

"They will come throw us all to Belch."

"Ysmay, how do we know this?"

The dark girl's lips tightened and tears of either distress or rebellion glimmered in her eyes. "Because of what they did to Reyne when she tried to leave."

"How else do we know this?" Alizon asked, coming to stand behind Reyne and laying her hand on

148

the young woman's quivering shoulder.

"Because they fed us to the dragon once before," Reyne answered, her voice hollow. "Because they care nothing for us. Because their sheep matter more to them than our lives."

Alizon remembered the rare sound of Reyne's laughter last night, as they had been climbing the stairs. A stab of regret went through her at having drained the joy once again from the girl.

Then she remembered her own misdeeds, her own succumbing to the temptation that George's presence presented, and her resolve hardened. She must be harsh, for the good of them all.

"Mistress?" little Flur asked.

Alizon looked over at the child, her fair, baby-fine hair making her look even younger than her twelve years. "Yes?"

"Will Saint George kill the dragon?"

Alizon felt all eyes turn to her, bodies shifting in the eager wait for an answer.

"I could go home to Mama if he did," Flur said quietly.

"And where would the rest of us go, Flur?" she said, forcing herself to be heartless. "How many of us have families waiting to take us in?"

Flur's mouth turned down, and she ducked her head.

"We could work as we do now," Joye said. "We need not depend upon families."

"Where would we live? Where would we get our wool?" She looked around at each face. "And what do you think the good landsfolk would do, if they knew we had been living off their livestock all these years?"

"They would demand payment," Braya said, her heavy jaw setting in anger.

"Would any truly be happy to see us, we whom they had thrown away?"

"No," a few muttered.

"We were worthless to them and would only remind them of their guilt and selfishness. Were they glad to send us here the first time, and wouldn't they be glad to send us again?"

"Yes," several more said.

"Did they play music and put flowers in our hair, and tell us to be joyful as we went to our deaths?"

"Yes."

"And is that fair?"

"No!"

"Do they deserve to keep their sheep?"

"No!"

"Do they deserve to live free from the fear of Belch?"

"No!"

She softened her voice. "And is our life better here than it ever would have been in Markesew? Do we have a finer home, finer clothes, finer food, and easier work?"

"Yes!"

"Do we have a strong family among each other? Are we sisters?"

"Yes!"

"Will we let anyone destroy what we have built?"

"No!"

"Will we?"

"NO!"

She let their answer echo up the walls of the kitchen, fading out the windows high above, then she picked up her brown robe and pulled it on, fastening the clasp at its neck. "I will deal with the stranger, who is *not* Saint George," she finished, looking at Flur. "He is an inept fool on a hopeless quest, and within the week he will be gone from Devil's Mount."

"Are you going to let Belch eat him?" Pippa asked, her black starburst of hair making her look the imp that she was.

"We are not Markesew's villagers, Pippa. We do not send innocent people to their deaths. He will leave the mount unharmed in all but pride." She addressed them all. "You had your fun with him last night, and by the grace of good fortune were not discovered for what you are. He thinks you are the ghosts of dead virgins."

A snicker went around the table.

"I do not think we will fool him a second time. Let there not be one."

They nodded, unity apparently restored.

She should have been reassured. She should have felt back in control, confident of their obedience as she sought to keep them safe. If they were anything like her, though, their curiosity was more roused than satisfied about George, and anything might happen if her control faltered.

Nothing was as settled as she wanted.

"There is porridge in the pot," Alizon said as she dumped innards into a sheep stomach. Blood caked under her nails and stuck between her fingers, and threatened the rolled sleeves of her robe. She blew at the wool "hair" hanging against her face, the strands tangling in her eyelashes and catching between her lips.

"Is there? Hmm. Er," George said from somewhere behind her.

She was afraid to look at him, afraid that she might see in his eyes some memory of last night.

She rubbed her face against her shoulder, trying to dislodge a stubborn fuzz of hair. "I would serve you, but my hands are dirty."

He came up beside her, her body sensing his approach in the movement of air. A tingling rush ran down her back.

"That's not dinner, is it?"

Surprise made her turn to look at him, her vision obstructed by the hood. He was asking about the stomach she was stuffing. "No. Whyever would you think so?"

"Oh. Sorry!"

"Do you have a complaint about my cookery?" Annoyance was more comfortable than vulnerability.

"No, no! Not at all!" He paused. "It's, ah . . . just

a bit different from what I am used to. And I feel guilty having you wait on me when you plainly have so many other responsibilities around the castle. Tell you what," he said, then stopped.

She waited. "Yes?"

"If it's all right with you, I'll cook my own meals. And clean up after myself, of course. What do you think?"

She pursed her lips, trying to decide if he suspected her of poisoning him, or of just being a bad cook. Either way, if he did the cooking it would make it more difficult to drug him nightly—using less powder, of course—and he might start poking into places he had no business being. "I would feel a poor hostess if you were to do that."

"You would be making me feel more comfortable if I knew I weren't such a burden. Tell you what," he said again. Then he paused.

It was a peculiar speech mannerism. She waited, allowing her annoyance to grow, but curiosity eventually won out. "Yes?"

"I'll cook for you, too."

A chill went through her. Did he have plans to drug her in return? "No, I could not let you do that."

"Certainly you can. Why not? It won't kill you to give my cooking a try, will it?"

She gripped the bloody stomach in her hands more tightly. A bit of intestine bulged out of the top.

"Say yes," he urged. "It's the least I can do."

"Cook for yourself, but not for me. I am content with my own fare." She stuffed the errant intestine back in, then took a handful of blue-dyed flour from a bowl and dumped it into the stomach.

She felt more than saw him shrug. "Please yourself." Then he added, "What *is* that that you're making?"

"A treat for Belch." She pointed to the harmless dyed flour with one bloody finger. "With enough of that in here, he should be sound asleep when you go down to cut off his head."

"Stab him through the heart, maybe. I don't know that cutting off his head will be necessary."

She used her forearm to shove back her hood just enough that she could see his face. His nose was wrinkled, and his lips curled back in disgust as he stared at the pouch she held.

Looking back down, she pulled open the mouth of the sheep stomach and swirled her finger inside, mixing the blue flour with the blood and fluids there. "This is a bit of lung, right here," she remarked, lifting the sack so he could get a good view. "Plenty of gut, of course, and then, here—" She dug around, organs sliding against each other. "I know there's an eyeball in here somewhere. . . ."

He stumbled back.

"I have sweetbreads left over, if you would like them for your breakfast. You can cook them yourself." She smiled, forgetting he could not see it. "Lung fried in butter, kidneys in gravy, a bit of brain on bread. I know *I'll* be eating well these next few days."

"Thank you, no, I had something else in mind. If you could point me in the direction of your pantry?"

She propped the stomach in a wooden bowl and rinsed her hands. "Tell me what you need and I will fetch it for you." She could not let him see the quantities of supplies they had; he would realize they were not all for her and Milo.

"I'm not sure you'll have everything."

She gestured with her hand for him to go ahead and give her the list.

"Bread?" he asked. "Stale is fine."

She nodded.

"Eggs, butter, sugar, cinnamon?"

Jesu, but the man had expensive taste. "No sugar or cinnamon." Or at least, none that she would give away so freely.

"Honey, then?"

She nodded reluctantly, noticing again how big he was and wondering how much of such dear foods he would put down. She should have insisted he eat the porridge.

Lighting a lamp, she went to the cellar, leaving George to examine the cookware, scraping with his fingernail at spots and frowning as if she and the virgins did not know how to keep a proper kitchen.

Everything about George this morning rubbed her wrong. And it only made it worse, knowing that the reason was her own attraction to him and her shameless display last night. He threatened everything that she was, and she reminded herself she wanted him frightened away so that he could do her no more harm.

Belch would take care of that.

Alizon descended the stairs to the cool cellar hewn from the rock of the mount. Pots of butter, honey, cones of sugar, and other goods lined the shelves, while barrels of rough-milled flour and grains sat about on the floor. There were casks of wine and beer, sacks of nuts, and jars packed with dried fruits. She searched out the items of George's request, pausing to nibble a date.

At the beginning, when she had first come here to Devil's Mount, Belch had been a demon, a creature not of this earth, something thrown up from the bowels of Hell. He had been the incarnation of evil.

Then, slowly, as she took over the role of his keeper, he had become an animal. She had started to see him as a beast with an earthly need for food and warmth and sleep. His evil was simply the evil of a creature without conscience or thought, though unquestionably one with the power to kill whatever crossed its path.

Over the years he had become her ally. It was because of Belch that she could demand an ever-increasing number of sheep from Markesew and have the villagers obey, sacrificing to her that which they valued more than their young women. She knew that even old sheep had their worth, and were not given up without regret, and so she delighted in taking them from the people of her old home. She and the others had earned them.

It was because she alone had the courage to face the dragon that she was the mistress of Devil's Mount. And it was Belch who had, ironically, given her the chance to save eleven girls not only from death, but from lives of poverty and misery, of toiling in fields and from dying young in childbirth.

Yes, Belch had helped make her what she was, and Belch had given her much of what she had. It was that truth that had gradually changed her feelings about the dragon from abhorrent hatred to a sort of protective fondness mixed with fear.

Today George would try to kill Belch, but she would not let it happen.

Alizon popped the rest of the date she nibbled into her mouth, downing it as mindlessly as Belch downed a sheep. She was the mistress of this mount, and she would protect all who inhabited it.

"Come on, try a bite. Don't you want a *bite?*"

Alizon crossed her arms over her chest, lips tight together like a baby refusing food. "No."

"You'll like it, I promise." George waved a chunk of his "French toast" at her, speared on the end of a knife. "It's delicious."

It smelled delicious, certainly. Saliva filled her mouth, but stubbornness and the self-satisfied way George was eating his cooking kept her from succumbing.

"I could teach you how to make it. It's simple."

"It must be."

"You mean, if a bonehead like me could make it? That doesn't mean it isn't good. Here, come on, don't be afraid to try something new." He waved the piece of egg-battered bread, glistening with butter and honey, in front of her hood.

Against her will, Alizon's lips parted. The French toast looked so much better than porridge.

"You know you want it. I won't tell. Come on, try it."

He was tempting her as he had last night. Lust, gluttony, what else would this man encourage in her? He was more of a devil than Belch! To accept anything from him would only weaken her, of that she was sure.

But it looked so good. . . .

"Good morrow, mistress." Milo appeared in the doorway, saving her from the luscious square of golden bread. He nodded to George, gracing him with a grunt of greeting.

"Good morrow," Alizon replied.

"Milo!" George dropped his knife back onto his square wooden plate. "My man!" He got up and jogged over to the corner where he had left his chosen sword propped against the wall. "I need your help. I need to sharpen this thing."

Milo took the sword from him, testing the edge of the blade against his thumb. "I have a wheel in my cottage. I can do it now."

Alizon grimaced. There was a small whetstone

here in the kitchen, if George had thought to ask *her*. Milo looked pleased to have been asked for help, though. Boys and weapons, it had been the same through all time.

"I'll go with you. I've never sharpened a sword before and want to see how it's done."

Milo glanced at George with the same expression she knew she herself wore: one of doubt and puzzlement.

"You've *never* sharpened one?" she asked.

"Er . . . my squire usually did it."

His ignorance, however laughable, provided opportunities for those with knowledge. "Be sure Milo does not put too fine an edge upon it," she said. "It will become brittle."

Milo looked at her with a blank face; then comprehension came to his features—and a hint of disapproval, though he gave the barest hint of a nod to show he would obey: The sword would shine but barely cut through boiled meat when he was done.

"Really?" George said. "I didn't know that."

"It is your strength that will kill Belch, not a narrow edge of steel. Your strength and your wit."

He gave her a doubting look, obviously hearing the touch of sarcasm that she could not keep from her voice. "Don't touch my food while I'm gone," he warned.

She made a noise of disgust and waved her hand at him.

He grinned, then slung an arm around Milo's shoulders. Milo's eyes widened in alarm, his face asking, "What now?" But George just steered him around to the doorway, and off they went.

Leaving her alone with George's plate of "French toast."

She sidled over to the table and looked down at it. There were at least a dozen little cut-up squares, so many that no one would ever notice if one was gone. She bent over the table and sniffed.

Warm, sweet, eggy.

She dabbed a fingertip in the honey and butter, then touched it to her tongue. *So* much better than porridge. Should she try it?

No. It would be giving in. It would be losing. In what way, she did not know, but she felt it with certainty.

She was not going to eat any of that toast.

Chapter Fourteen

"You took a bite, didn't you?" George asked. His sword was sharpened, and he had returned to the kitchen. Here the mistress was finishing sewing up her gory stomach full of dragon treats.

"No. Of course not."

"Yes, you did. I left a piece right there, on the edge, and now it's gone."

She turned to look over her shoulder at the table, where the remains of his breakfast had grown cold and congealed.

"You imagine things."

"I certainly do, but not this. Admit it: You took a bite, and you liked it. You loved it, in fact. You had a hard time not gobbling down the whole plateful."

The mistress muttered something dark in the

depths of her hood and turned back to her work.

George grinned, knowing he had won a small victory. She *had* tried it, and liked it, he was sure of it. He almost laughed, imagining her sneaking the piece off his plate, eyes on the doorway as she slipped it into her mouth. He knew better than to chuckle aloud, though—she had been in a bad mood all morning, and he didn't want to see it get any worse. Maybe it was the stress of what they were about to do that was getting to her.

He should be the one in a bad mood, though, after last night. He had woken this morning with a mouth that tasted like a rat had crawled over his tongue and died in the back of his throat. His head had throbbed, his hands had shaken, and he kept getting glimpses of the weirdly real dreams that had haunted his night.

They *had* been dreams, hadn't they?

His headache was gone now that he'd had something to eat and drink—more of that awful beer— and his muscles had stopped their quivering once he had gotten up and done some basic calisthenics to get his blood moving. The snatches of his dreams from last night, though, would not go away.

Usually, unless he fought to remember them, his dreams slipped away within moments of waking. And even when he did make a conscious effort to keep them in his mind, they were likely to be gone the moment he let his mind drift elsewhere.

All that *had* to have been a dream last night— even though he was dreaming now, while he seemed to be awake. Sleeping dreams inside a waking dream, that's what it had been.

As if that explanation made any sense.

It made more sense, however, than thinking that Mistress Hard-ass had sat on his bedside wearing nothing under her blessed robe, nothing at all, just as he had fantasized. And it certainly made no sense that she would have let him put his hand between her bare, soft, warm thighs, and then uncover her tight young breast, sitting there with her breath audible as he raised his hand to touch its pebbled nipple.

But that might explain her bad mood.

No. It was his frustrated sex drive, that was all, giving him wet dreams. What else should he expect from this journey through his unconscious? Of course there would be breasts and panting women here.

And howling ghosts?

He shuddered, recalling the pale group of wraiths that had surrounded his bed. God help him, he hoped that they had been a dream within a dream and nothing he would have to face again. What could those wraiths mean, anyway?

The Willie Nelson song about all the girls he'd loved before came to mind. Maybe he had treated them worse than he thought, and this was his guilt come to punish him.

The remains of his cold French toast didn't appeal to him, but he had to eat what he could, to keep up his strength. A man couldn't kill a dragon on an empty stomach. He polished off what was left, then cleaned his dishes, including the pan he had used for cooking.

He was aware the whole time of the mistress watching him from beneath her hood while pretending to be absorbed in her gut sack. She seemed more impressed by his way around the kitchen than by anything else he did or said.

He winked at her. "I bet you'd like to see me in nothing but an apron, wouldn't you?"

She straightened. "I think it is more likely that you have spent your life employed as a cook, roasting swine and stirring sauces, than as a slayer of dragons. I can more easily imagine you sweating over a fire in an apron than standing victorious over the corpse of a slain beast."

George made a noise of mock offense, resting his fist with the dishrag on his hip. "You're showing little faith in my manly powers."

She snorted.

"Look at these muscles!" he said, trying to make her laugh. He went through a body-building routine of poses, with accompanying grunts of primitive masculinity. "You've never seen anything like me!"

"Marry! 'Tis true, I have not!" she said, and he heard mirth in her voice, as he had hoped to elicit.

"A man like me comes along only once in a thousand years," he continued.

"For which we shall all be grateful."

"Damn right. Some unfortunates don't get one like me at all!"

He felt her staring at him, speechless in the face of his refusal to be insulted. Eventually she turned back to her gut sack, her attentions going to something more helpless in the face of her abuse.

George found that he was starting to enjoy her uptightness. Whether last night had been real or not, he had an inkling that she was a wild thing under all that control. He wanted to be there when she finally broke free. His imagination wandered down wanton paths on a similar theme.

"Let's go," she said.

"Huh?" He blinked at her. In his mind she had been lying on the kitchen work table, vegetables scattered around her outflung arms, legs in the air as she screamed, "Yes! Yes! Harder!" as he thrust inside her.

Instead, she was standing before him holding a bowl with a bloody sack of sheep parts.

"Belch awaits," she said.

His stomach fluttered. He had been using his lewd imaginings to avoiding thinking about his match with the dragon—in much the way he avoided thinking about a trip to the dentist.

This wasn't like wrestling, where he had someone with whom to choreograph the fight, calculating moves for their most dramatic effect. This was unpredictable. Life or death. He could get his head bitten off. Literally.

Well, it might be just a dream, but he was learning you could still be scared shitless in a dream.

"Right! Off we go! We wouldn't want Belch to get lonely," he said with a bravado he didn't feel.

Fake it 'til you make it, that would have to be his new motto.

So what, that he used to get queasy watching his dad clean a fish. This was a virgin-eating dragon, dammit, and he would skewer it through its cold, miserable, reptilian heart.

And when he did, not only would Emoni's daughter be safe, but his hot-bodied little mistress would finally throw back her hood, and he would see surprise and respect in her Michelle Pfeifferian face. She would be so grateful she could finally leave Devil's Mount, she would fling off her clothes, those perfect pink-nippled breasts of his imaginings offered up, her soft thighs parting as she lay back on her bed and . . .

"Are you coming, George?"

"Just about." He threw the dishrag he held aside and picked up his sword. He had forgone the helmet, or any of the other scraps in the old armory, opting for unobstructed sight and movement over the questionable protection those pieces offered. He had had more than one moment to reflect that it was too bad he hadn't dreamt up some Kevlar and an anti-tank gun for himself.

The mistress was waiting by the closed door that led to the stairwell, a candle in one hand. The bowl was propped on the ledge formed by her slender waist curving into her full, rounded hip. She could visit his dreams any night.

Mentally, he shook himself. Lusting after her was becoming his "happy place." He would do better, though, to plan out the approach he was going to take with Belch.

But that breast, it had been so close to his fingertips. . . .

"George?"

"Yes, yes. I'm here, ready and willing." He held the revolting bowl with the sheep stomach while she unlocked the door, then he gave it back, pulled open the door's heavy, creaking weight, and bowed to usher her inside. "Ladies first."

"Cowardly kitchen boys last," she retorted, passing him.

The stench of Belch was but a whiff on the clammy air, but even that faint trace was enough to bring back in full the terror of seeing that misbegotten son of a crocodile lunging up out of the mist-covered water, jaws gaping, mouth pale pink and lined with ivory pitons of death.

"Fake it 'til you make it," he chanted under his breath.

The mistress paused to light a torch from her candle, then started down the stairs. George let out a shaky breath and followed.

He was always nervous before a match, but that was different, milder. It was a good sort of nervousness, the type that gave an extra boost to stage performers.

This was of a sort that might have him fumbling his sword and getting torn apart like a secondary character in *Jurassic Park*.

"Fake it 'til you make it." He knew how to psych himself up, and that's what he needed to do now.

Ah, crap, who was he kidding? This matchup had an ass-pucker factor of ten, and like a sea slug he wanted to vomit out his innards and creep away. The last thing he wanted to do was step back out on that rickety wooden platform above Belch's lair, much less go down inside and poke that dragon with an oversized cocktail stick.

The mistress's sleeping powder had better be potent, that's all he could say.

In fact, why not give the lizard an overdose and be done with him that way? Not a noble stratagem, perhaps, but wits were more valuable than brawn. Wrestlers knew that, despite perceptions of the public to the contrary. It was intelligence that put a great match together and let one manipulate the crowd—however moronic the results might appear.

He and the mistress passed through the second door, and the wave of stench that rolled across George made his eyes water. Good Christ. It was like summer roadkill, with a dash of septic tank and a smear of sour sweat for piquancy. The vapors from the mineral water below were an added splash of olfactory pleasure.

George and the mistress made their way through the tunnel to find it all quiet at the open archway at the end: no bellows, no splashing, just a faint tinkling trickle of the hot spring draining into the seawater. George's sword tip scraped against the stone wall, making him jump.

The mistress did not notice his show of nerves. Good. She also showed no hesitation at stepping out onto the platform. He followed her as if he weren't on the verge of upchucking his breakfast.

The mist lay thicker and stiller than yesterday, the light from the cave mouth turning it to cotton batting. Rocks protruded from the sea of fog like islands in a Chinese painting, and it was appropriate that there should be a dragon lying in the midst of it, on his raised mound of shore. Belch wasn't half so decorative as a Chinese painting, though.

The last time he'd been down here, he'd seen only jaws and claws. This time, he got a view of the whole beast, and he was guessing Belch measured about sixty feet from snout to tip of tail. The resemblance to an alligator or crocodile was disheartening, as he recalled nature shows where crocs used the power of their tails to launch themselves straight out of a river like missiles from a submarine, plucking monkeys or birds off the branches of overhanging trees.

Ooo oo oo. He was the monkey man.

He was on the verge of voicing his poison-the-dragon idea when the mistress turned and looked at him. Her hood had slid far enough back that he caught his first real glimpse of her face behind the veil of white hair. She had dark eyes—dark, dark eyes—a narrow nose, almost pointy; and lips like Betty Boop's.

She was nothing like Michelle Pfeiffer, with that actress's pastel coloring and soft eyes. Michelle Pfeiffer should be so lucky as to look like the mistress. This woman was fierce; she was determined. And she was young and vulnerable, which he could see from something hurt and expecting of the worst in those dark eyes.

Everything changed. He couldn't back down and poison the beast. She would expect more from him than that, would only want a man who lived up to his title, a man who and proved himself strong and honest and worthy. She needed that. She needed a hero to free her from the dragon.

He sighed. At least it was easier to pretend to be brave with an expectant female audience. He could be grateful for that.

He tore his gaze away, not wanting her to suspect how well he could see her, and looked over the rail at his opponent. "It looks like Belch is already asleep. Why don't I just go down there and kill him now?"

What the hell. He should get it over with. Be a man. Besides, the dragon wasn't looking dangerous at the moment. Sure, Belch had scared the hell out of him yesterday, but the beast hadn't actually *hurt* him. It had been noise and big moves, that was all, just like in wrestling. Or so George tried to tell himself.

"But . . ." she began.

"He *is* asleep, isn't he?" George squinted down at the monster. Damn, but that was a big lizard.

"Wouldn't you rather be certain he will not wake up?"

"That's what *this* is for!" He held up his sword.

"Er. Hmm. Yes, but are you sure he's asleep? He lies like that when he's awake, too."

George propped his sword against the wooden platform wall and took the mistress's dragon treat from its bowl. The stuffed stomach felt like a water balloon, distorting under the pressure of his hands. He felt a lump that might be an eyeball squishing away under his finger. "We'll test him."

He hefted the stomach like a shot-put, holding it in his palm beside his head. He squinted down at Belch, taking aim, then with a heave lobbed it into the air. The mistress pressed up beside him at the rail, watching as the gory bag arced through the steamy air, then went down, down. . . .

It hit Belch on the side of his snout with a *plurp*, then *plurped* once more onto the ground. It began to leak, a trail of purplish red oozing onto the stone.

They waited.

"Maybe he's not hungry," the mistress said.

"A bellyful of sheep shouldn't stop him from such a treat as that. It's not my French toast, granted, but what dragon could pass up a meal made by you? Or does he suspect you of drugging him? Have you done it before?" He grinned at her.

"Just because *you* got sick—"

His grin faltered. "How did you know I was sick?"

"I . . ."

"Did you sneak into my room?" he asked. His grin came back, stretching wide. Was it possible? "You *did,* didn't you?"

"No. Why should I do such a thing? You looked pasty this morning, is all. And a bit sweaty at supper."

"You're a terrible liar."

"I am not lying!" she squeaked.

He leaned close to her. "Hey, I'm glad you came to check on me. I was afraid you didn't care."

"I don't. I wasn't there."

"Oh." He made a disappointed face, as if he believed her. Perhaps he almost did: She wouldn't really have done what he remembered, would she? "Then the beautiful woman I saw must truly have been a dream."

He sighed and cast a sidelong glance at her to see if she was taking the bait. Not that he could tell, given that damn hood, which had slipped back into place. She held a certain stillness, though, a certain angle to her head that told him she was listening.

"What did—" she began.

Below Belch jerked his head, snapped up the dragon treat they'd lobbed down to him between his jaws, tilted his head back, and gulped it down. All three motions were accomplished in a matter of moments.

"Holy moley, did you see that?" George burst

out, leaning out over the rail. "Hell's bells, and to think I almost went down there!" He felt a nervous sweat break out along his skin.

Just noise and flash, he told himself. *Noise and flash, nothing more.* He hoped.

The mistress was silent.

He turned to her. "I owe you one."

She shifted her weight and crossed her arms over her stomach, holding herself. "Owe me one what?"

"One favor. For saving my life."

She didn't answer.

"Is something wrong?"

"No. Of course not. Why?"

He shrugged, still watching her. She uncrossed her arms and started picking at a fingernail, scraping out a bit of dried blood from underneath.

"I think the powder should take at least an hour to work," she finally said. *"If* it works."

"You think it might not?"

She shrugged.

He would say she was acting peculiar, except *everything* she did had an air of secrecy and peculiarity to it. She was one hell of a repressed, mysterious chick.

George paused. They always said the quiet ones were the wildest in bed. He wondered what fantasies traipsed through her mind in the black hours of the night.

"Tell me about this dream woman," she said at last, breaking the silence.

So *that* was it. She had been fighting against her curiosity.

"I shouldn't say. It's not a fit description to give to a nun, being filled as it is with lustful imaginings."

"Lustful imaginings?"

"They're indecent." He waited, trying to keep a straight face.

"I do not think I would be offended . . . if you wish to tell me."

"They would appall you."

"I am of stronger stuff than you think," she insisted.

"Are you sure?"

She nodded.

"If you're sure . . ." He leaned back against the rail and looked up at the cavern ceiling, his voice taking on a wistful tone. "She was like an angel from the darkness, come to comfort me. I could see nothing of her at first—I could only hear her soft voice and feel her gentle touch on my forehead." He lowered his gaze. "But then she bent down and I felt her lips on my own."

The hood jerked toward him. "She kissed you?"

"I told you it wasn't fit for pure ears. I should stop here."

"No, no. Tell me more."

He raised a brow as if in question, playing her as he would play the audience at a CUW event. No one was safe from the Saint! She didn't know what she was up against, the poor sheltered creature.

Or was he the one who didn't know? That fierce look he had seen in her eyes gave him pause.

"Her lips tasted like honey. All my chills and pains faded away. I was grateful for her presence, and then she went even further, taking me to a heaven such as few men have known here on earth."

"Heaven? How so? What did she do?"

"She opened her robe, and she was naked beneath. Such breasts! Round and high, and nipples like . . . like . . . cherry pits."

"Ugh!"

"Not 'ugh'! Hard, delicious cherry pits, pink from the flesh of the fruit."

"As if the flesh had been chewed off? This is a terrible story. I do not wish to hear any more."

"It's not terrible. It's beautiful."

"Cherry stones and"—she choked on the word "and nipples? I do not wish to hear of such things."

"They were perfect nipples! I wanted to suck on them!"

The shoulders beneath the mistress's robe shuddered.

"You would like it if you tried it. Just like my French toast."

"You should keep your foreign ways to yourself."

"I'm trying to broaden your horizons. To get you to try new things."

"I am content as I am. I do not need this sucking, this talk of chewed cherry stones."

He laughed. "Don't you?"

175

She crossed her arms over her chest as if protecting the cherries therein. "No. Nor do you, I should think."

Then she retreated to rocklike silence, quiet coldness answering his feeble attempts at engaging her further.

At last he gave up and found a seat on the ledge of the doorway, his knees up high and his arms resting on them. The mistress remained standing on the platform, her back to the cavern wall, holding herself steel-spine straight as if afraid to relax in his depraved presence. He watched her.

A subsequent half-hour of impatience and a sore, chilled butt prompted him finally to stand and pick up his sword. He looked out over the rail, down at Belch where the beast lolled on its beach. It was hard to tell, but the dragon's eyes looked, if not closed, then at least halfway there—as one might expect a drugged lizard to look.

George tested the edge of his sword against his thumb. It seemed sharp enough.

He sensed the mistress watching him from her frozen silence. "All right," he said. "Let's do it."

"Now?"

"No time like the present. Looks like he's as drugged as he's going to get."

She clasped her hands together before her belly, her knuckles showing white. "You are sure you want to do this? It is not too late to change your mind."

"And let down Emoni and all the virgins to

come?" He shook his head. "I hope I'm a better man than that. So . . ." He stood still, feeling that this was an anticlimactic beginning to his great battle. "Do I get a kiss for good luck?"

She made a rude noise.

He shrugged. "I thought not." He rolled his shoulders and took a few practice swings, making her step back the way one steps back when certain the other person is about to cut off their own foot in clumsiness.

He took one last look at Belch to be sure the dragon hadn't moved—he hadn't—one last look at the mistress—she hadn't moved, either—then gave her a wink and headed down the slippery stone stairs of the cavern to the beach below.

He pretended the stairs were the ramp down through his screaming fans, the wrestling ring what was waiting for him at the end of it, its surface reflective white under the hot lights. His theme music was playing, fireworks were blasting, his muscles were pumped, and he was ready to kick some ass. His opponent was waiting for him, and surely that was a look of worried, deflated cockiness on its reptilian face.

Faking it or making it, the Saint was going to take care of business.

Chapter Fifteen

Alizon watched George go, unable to take her eyes from him. She stepped to the edge of the platform where she would have a better view. She did not want to watch, any more than she ever wanted to watch the sheep being eaten, but something within compelled her to do so. She did not know if it was a sense of guilty responsibility or a simple, sick, morbid fascination.

At the moment, she was not half sure that she *didn't* want George to get thoroughly thrashed by Belch. Not killed, perhaps, but whacked a few good times with his tail.

Cherry stones. How dare he!

Suck on them? She thought not. As if she would ever let him!

A brief imagining of him lowering his head to

her bare breast—taking her nipple into his warm, damp mouth—filled her mind, and her body responded, twisting and tightening deep inside.

Treacherous body! Treacherous thoughts! Bite him, Belch, bite him!

George crept down the slick stone stairs, his steps light and graceful despite his size. He was still wearing the old shirt he had found, with those silver hose and boots, and the black bands around his knees. He had tied back his long dark hair, and a thick shadow of beard covered his jaw. He carried his sword with ease and wore an expression she had not seen on his face before: one of angry determination. He looked as if he had a personal grudge against Belch—as if the dragon had eaten his own sister.

It was a surprising change from his usual demeanor. She felt a quickening of her heartbeat. Maybe this battle was not as pre-determined as she had thought.

Her hands tightened on the rail. Despite the dull sword, despite the false sleeping powder, might George kill the dragon after all?

He reached the bottom of the stairs, jumping onto Belch's beach as if he belonged there and was looking forward to the upcoming fight. If he was afraid, she could see no sign of it.

He tossed his sword from hand to hand and stalked toward Belch. As he neared he got a good grip on the weapon's haft with his right hand, and ten feet from the dragon he stood with feet wide apart, head lowered and a glower on his face.

Belch lay still.

"Candy-ass lizard," Alizon heard him say.

Candy-ass? He could not mean the dragon's arse was sweet, surely.

"Virgin-eater. You think you're a tough guy, chomping little girls?"

Why was he talking to Belch? Alizon wondered. Why didn't he just strike him?

"You've been ruling over this island for too long, lizard-breath. Saint George the Dragonslayer is here to send you back to Hell!" The odd man shook out his shoulders and snapped a sudden glare at his foe. "Well? Got nothing to say?" He strutted back and forth. "I thought not."

Was he going to *talk* the dragon to death?

With a belligerent, wide-legged gait George stomped a circle around Belch's prone body, stopping every few feet and eyeballing the beast as if he had caught it trying to sneak a piece of his French toast.

Strike him! Do something! she wanted to scream. The suspense was chafing her, making her crazy with impatience even as she was fascinated by George's dawdling, wanting to see what odd thing he might do next.

Or wanted to see if Belch might strike first.

George inched closer. Near enough for Belch to whip his head to the side and take his leg off, if he so desired.

"Iguana," George said, with a sneer.

He stepped over Belch's foreleg, as big as George's own thigh, and leaned up close to the beast's half-closed eye.

"You're nothing but an overgrown gecko." He flicked a fingernail against one of Belch's teeth that stuck out along the side of his mouth.

A gurgling sound came from the dragon's gut. George jumped, then made a show of relaxing, shaking out his arms and stalking away from Belch, his back to the serpent as if it was not worth watching.

Belch's eye opened.

Alizon bit down on a screech of warning.

George took a few practice swings at the air, then turned. As he did so, the eye shut again. He circled, coming around to the end of the dragon's tail. Suddenly, with no warning, George ran at Belch: ran up his tail, over his ridged back, his footsteps light and quick, as if crossing thin ice, his balance neatly kept. He stopped only when he reached the dragon's shoulders, standing there with feet apart and sword raised two-handed above his head.

Alizon's breath caught in her throat.

Belch's eyes opened.

George turned the sword around so that its point was facing down, ready to pierce Belch's neck, but then he paused. He stood there, sword raised.

Now! Do something! Alizon screamed in her head, and she did not know if she meant the plea for Belch or his foe.

George's shoulders heaved, his sword rising

slightly for the downward, fatal plunge.

Alizon clenched the rail and whimpered deep in her throat.

The point of the blade came down, and in the same moment Belch shuddered and rolled. The blade skittered off the side of his armored neck, and George lost both aim and leverage. His feet danced on Belch's hide, his body swaying and his arms flailing. He kept his balance and his footing, though, the look on his face one of wide-eyed, hard-jawed concentration.

Alizon felt her own jaw and neck strain against the impulse to shout his name.

Belch rolled onto his back, exposing his soft yellow underbelly. George's feet slid and pranced on that smooth surface, then Belch erupted into a thrashing frenzy, rolling and bending and sweeping his tail.

George lost his footing, bounced off the dragon, and fell to all fours on the ground halfway down the beach. The stirred mist swirled over his hands and knees. Belch snapped his head toward him, jaws opening. George twisted out of the way, the dragon's jaws slamming together where his torso had been a moment before.

Alizon keened in her throat. She did not want to see the first gout of blood. She did not want to see when George lost the first limb, or to see Belch tossing the knight's carcass in the air like a half-eaten sheep, guts spilling out, head missing.

George gained his feet again, and he had kept his

hold on his sword. Belch bellowed, and George echoed the sound, hollering the cry of a warrior and charging his opponent, running up the dragon's foreleg, again finding his perch on the beast's back.

The serpent bucked and thrashed from side to side, trying to dislodge him. George used his sword like a walking stick, digging its point into Belch's hide to keep his balance. Then, when for a moment his footing was secure, he raised the blade again and this time struck deep into Belch's neck.

The monster went wild, tossing and twisting, bellows of pain and rage reverberating off the walls and shaking the hollows of Alizon's chest. The very fog seemed to take the shape of waves, shivering to the sound. George was thrown from the dragon's back, his blade still protruding from Belch's neck.

Alizon lost sight of him for a moment as a thick wave of mist rolled across the cave. Belch reared up onto his hind legs, stubby forelegs clawing toward the wound he could not reach, his cries throbbing through the air.

George rose up out of the fog and danced to the side as Belch came back down, the dragon's body slamming against the ground. He stood gaping for long moments at the thrashing beast, as if unable to believe that he had caused it such pain; then he regained his wits and rushed forward, grabbing the blood-covered hilt of his sword and trying to tug it from the monster's neck.

Belch yanked away as George pulled his blade free, but the sudden loosening caused him to lose both his balance and grip. The blood-slicked sword flew free, disappearing into the mist. Belch's tail flashed round and thwacked against the back of George's legs, buckling them, then the beast lunged for his fallen foe.

Once more, George rolled out of the way with a skin of air to spare. Next, in a move Alizon had never imagined, the knight arched his body and leapt in a single motion from flat on his back to standing crouched on his feet. Belch came at him again, and he sprang into the air, somersaulting over the beast's head to land on the other side.

Alizon's mouth dropped open.

Belch's wound was oozing blood, but the gash was plainly more of an aggravation than a threat to the monster's life. He bellowed in frustration as George continued to dance around him, his foe's eyes flicking from him to the mist-covered ground.

"Mistress!" George shouted. "Where's the sword? Can you see it?"

His calling to her surprised away Alizon's ability to speak.

"Mistress!"

"To your right!" she cried at last, her voice hoarse, then clearing as it gained volume. "But I cannot see exactly where!"

The knight somersaulted and rolled, searching the ground as his foe stomped and snapped above him. He found the sword at last, and rose up with it, swinging at Belch's head as the dragon swung his great jaws toward him.

Man and dragon connected, and George was swept off his feet, flying through the air and landing with a splash in the steaming water.

Belch galloped after him, his belly slapping the water and throwing up spray as he surged into his element. Alizon leaned over the rail, searching for sign of George, knowing the water was deep and Belch was swift within it. Her heart was racing.

Belch sank beneath the mist, and for a moment all was quiet, the white fog smoothing over the dying swirls of his passage.

Suddenly there was a gasp and a splash, and Alizon threw herself to the floor of the platform and stuck her head out around the corner of the low wall where it stopped at the stairs. Thirty feet below, under the platform, George was climbing the rocks out of the water.

He looked up and saw her, and a wild, half-crazed grin lit his face. Water slicked black streaks of hair down the sides of his cheeks, and his thin shirt was a ghost against his skin, warm tones and muscles visible through the fabric.

The mist swirled behind him.

"George!" She stretched out an arm, pointing.

He glanced over his shoulder, and when he looked back up at her the grin had gotten harder. He pulled himself up the rock wall by fingerholds, but not fast enough.

Belch flung himself from the water. George pressed himself into a depression in the wall just as the beast slammed across it. For a moment he was concealed beneath the dragon's body; then Belch fell back, claws dragging at the rocks then slipping off, his body hitting the water with a *boom* followed by a deep, swallowing splash.

George climbed again, this time with fresh, frantic speed, his toes in their silver boots gripping at tiny ledges too small for Alizon to see from her vantage. Five feet from the supporting struts of the feeding platform he stopped, his hands searching for new holds that were not there, his body held slightly away from the wall as he balanced on precarious toeholds.

The mist swirled below, a splash echoing off the walls as Belch swam and circled—preparing to leap again.

George met Alizon's eyes, his own filled with intensity and a hint of desperation.

She could not bear to watch him snatched off the wall like a tidbit of fresh flesh. Instead, she pulled back and yanked the lever that opened the trapdoor. She tore off her concealing robe, there being no time to consider the consequences of being now clad in only her burgundy gown. She twisted her robe diagonally into a bulky, awkward rope, cursing beneath her breath at there being no abandoned sheep tether to use.

She leaned down through the trapdoor and wrapped her doffed garment in a single hitch around the nearest strut, its beam a triangle between wall and platform floor. There was not enough length to tie off the robe, so she held tight to her end and, lying on her side, pulled her knees up against a post of the stall to brace herself as she bent down through the trapdoor. The other end of her improvised rope dangled three feet beneath the strut.

"You won't be able to hold me!" George shouted.

"I'll have to!"

"I can find another way!" He looked over his shoulder, down at the water, and she had a sudden vision of him falling and being snapped out of the air like one of the sacrificial sheep.

"Don't do it!" she screamed.

She could see him changing his posture, loosening his grip to allow himself to fall into the water, and then the mist below swept away for a moment, showing Belch's nose and eyes above the water, plowing toward the wall like a ship before a storm.

"Shit!" George shouted. Then, with a quick look back at the dangling robe, he made his decision. Even as Belch left the water, George released the wall, springing up the two feet between his outstretched arms and the end of the robe.

Belch's jaws clapped shut over empty space, and George's feet kicked at the dragon's snout as his hands found and seized the end of the robe.

As the lizard fell back, George's weight came down on Alizon's robe. Her knees banged once, hard, against the post, and then the world was awhirl as the garment yanked her through the trapdoor, swung her around and dropped her next to

187

George. Her body slammed into his and rose quickly above it, the two of them hanging suspended at either end of her rolled-up robe, which was now wrapped around the beam.

Her slide stopped with a jerk as George found purchase and took some of his weight off the robe. She dangled against him, her lower belly against his face, her arms stretched above her as she held tight. If the man was to let go of his end, she would plummet to the steaming water below. She looked down, trying and failing to see his face past her breasts and the thick braid hanging down over her green gown.

"Hot damn, red hair!" she heard, and felt the words as his warm breath came through the wool over her belly. "I didn't imagine red hair!"

"Devil in your eye! This is no time to speak of hair! We're about to be devoured!"

"I'll show you devouring." He chewed lightly at her belly, through the layers of cloth. "Hot damn!"

She kneed him in the shoulder, then used him as a foothold as she tried to climb up the robe to the supporting beam just beyond her reach. He did not protest, but instead pressed a kiss against her loins as they rose past his mouth. She grabbed the beam, and in a delayed reaction to his touch felt a muscle-weakening wave go through her. She closed her eyes against it, and her grip slipped.

"No you don't," George said, his arm going around her waist. He was suddenly up beside her. "No falling into the soup."

She opened her eyes, and for the first time since the night he had come to the mount, Alizon saw him without the intervening screen of wool and the confines of her hood. Her strength slipped again.

He gave her a shake. "Come on, no going faint with terror now."

She stiffened. "I am not frightened, you lack-wit. My arms are not as strong as yours, is all."

Belch bellowed down below and thrashed his tail in the water like an angry cat.

"Are they strong enough for you to hang on to my back?" He didn't wait for an answer, using his mass to press and hold her against the cavern wall as he turned around, his back against her chest. "Hold tight."

She wrapped her arms about his neck, her legs of their own will going around his waist. Her skirt hiked up her thighs as she did.

"Oh, baby," he muttered.

"What?"

"Ger-on-i-mo!"

"What? What?" she screeched, clinging with all her strength to his strong neck and waist as he leapt upward, catching the edge of the trapdoor and then pulling them both up by brute strength. "Jesu save me!" she cried, hanging from his back, nothing between her and the long drop down.

Again Belch lunged from the water, and this time it was her own flesh that felt the wind of his snapping jaws. George was not fast enough to keep her hanging gown from catching in Belch's teeth. As the dragon fell back, he jerked her with him, she in turn pulling George down. Her legs came free of George's waist, her hands breaking their hold around his neck.

In a flash, George flipped back to catch a beam and the scruff of her gown both. The skirt of the gown gave way, ripping at the tears Belch's teeth had rent, and then all at once Alizon was yanked upward. She found herself lying on George across the floor of the wooden platform, her bum naked to the cavern air.

Before she could move to conceal herself, George was up and had her stowed under one arm, leaping with his light grace into the safety of the tunnel. He set her down and with her hand firmly in his own dragged her at a run all down the tunnel, up the stairs, and into the kitchen.

They burst into the empty room, Alizon struggling both to catch her breath and to pull her torn gown and chemise over her backside. She reached for a hood that was not there, knowing it was too late but trying to hide herself anyway.

"Kee-rist!" George exclaimed, letting her go and digging both hands through his hair. It bunched in a wild, wet mess, most of it still held by the leather band at the back of his neck. "Damn! I don't know whether to laugh or to faint!"

His eyes lit on her, and whatever confusion he felt burned away under an intensity that made her take a step back, her hands gripping her skirt behind her back.

"And you! Hot damn!"

Then he had her face between his hands, and without so much as a by-your-leave, he lowered his mouth to hers.

Chapter Sixteen

Alizon was too stunned to move, her heart still racing from the near escape and the run up the tunnel. Her breath was coming hard, but George seemed not to notice, his lips taking hers despite how they parted to suck in air. She raised one hand to his chest, laying it lightly there as if to push him away, only something strange was happening to her, and she could not do so.

She was dizzy from lack of air. Her senses were being overwhelmed by his closeness: by his damp warmth; by the shadow of his size, which blocked out vision of all else; by the feel of his lips on her own, pressing and tugging, and then the tip of his tongue sliding within to touch briefly against her own.

She should be concerned that he knew she was

not a crone; she should be thinking of explanations to give him; but her breath grew shorter, her mind dizzier still as without thought she pressed her mouth harder against his. George's arms came around her, and one hand slid down to the rent in her gown, reaching in and cupping her buttock.

The touch was shocking, and it startled a muffled "Umph!" out of her against his lips. She started to pull away, but he only held her tighter, his lips parting hers and his tongue stroking gently within, even as his hand squeezed and explored her. Each motion of his fingers pulled against her sex, and she was torn between embarrassment and the tingling, seductive warmth he was building.

She felt his erection hard against her belly.

God's breath, this was what she should have had all those years ago, in the shed with Osbert. It was what she had been longing for, alone in her castle chamber.

She no longer knew if her heart raced from receding fear, the run, or arousal, or all three coming together to weaken her legs and send a warm wash of desire to her loins. This should not be happening, not here, not with him, not now. She had eleven women and girls to protect, wards who needed her clear thinking.

His fingertip brushed over her sex, and she could not care about anything else.

She did not care that his hand was where it should not be, or that he handled her as if expecting her easy acquiescence. Such considerations were of the mind, and it was the body she listened to now. It was the body whose hungers had been roused, and whose decade-long famine was so suddenly near to surcease.

She wrapped her arms around his neck, pushing her fingers into his hair and pressing herself hard up against him. The tip of his finger slid again across the opening to her, and she moaned deep in her throat, the sound new to her, one she had never made. She did not care.

His hurried hunger gave her no chance to pause, his hands and mouth pushing her to go faster and farther than she might have chosen on her own, but she let him set the pace. Each unexpected, demanding touch set off a new flush of excitement, and she wanted to let him do as he would and lead her into this long yearned-for new world.

George lowered her to the floor, trapping her beneath him, the uneven slates cold and hard and strangely arousing against her exposed skin. The stubble on his cheeks burned rough against her as he kissed his way down her neck.

He yanked at the neck of her gown, baring one breast, and took the erect nipple into his hot mouth. Pleasure shot from it to her loins, bolts of sensation making her feel heavy and tensing the muscles of her legs, as if with effort she could steal more and yet more of the feeling he was creating. His tongue went around the pebble of her nipple, then he sucked at her, rubbing the pulled peak with the roughness of his tongue, his chin scraping lightly at her even as his hand went down and found her slickness.

Alizon arched her hips against his hand and the fingertip that rested against her opening. She wanted him inside her, wanted him to stroke her. She wanted everything at once, now, hard and fast and without question.

He moved his attentions to her other breast, leaving the first to tingle in the cold, and she was absurdly aroused by the bite of the air, and by her half-nakedness. His fingers began to stroke her, using her own moisture to slide over her folds and circle upon that hard nub of arousal that she had herself found in her private explorations.

His mouth came back to hers, and she allowed him entrance, sucking his tongue into her mouth, taking him in there as her body wanted to take him in below. He took his hand away from her for a moment, and she felt him yanking down his hose. Suddenly the hard heat of him was against her, the length of his manhood pressing into the soft flesh of her femininity. She arched and stroked herself against it. He guided it with his hand, its tip slick as it circled the heart of her sensation, then he lodged that tip against her entrance.

Alizon remembered how Osbert's fumblings had hurt her, and how he had been unable to gain passage. George's erection began to part her tender flesh, smooth and large and promising to stretch her beyond bearing.

She wanted it. Alizon did not care how it hurt or

how it rent her; she wanted him inside her. She wanted the length of him thrust within her, filling her, stroking her with the power of his muscled hips and buttocks.

He caught her hands within one of his own and raised them above her head, pinning them to the ground, forcing her breasts to arch upward to his waiting mouth. She slid her thigh against the back of his, urging him forward, but he would not be rushed, the tip of him still paused at the entrance to her core.

He raised his mouth from her breast. "Tell me your name."

She stared dumbly at him and pulled at him again with her thigh. He dipped inside her a bare fraction of an inch, then out again, taunting her.

"Your name."

"I—" To reveal it would be too much.

He dipped again, slowly, deliciously stretching her, and her hips followed his retreat.

She should lie. She should use another's name. But she could not think. She knew nothing but that she was being denied the one thing she wanted at this moment more than life itself.

"Alizon."

He smiled, his green eyes looking deeply into her own, then he lowered his head to—

Suddenly he collapsed atop her, his weight knocking the wind from her.

"Mistress, are you all right?" Greta asked. The girl had appeared over George's shoulder, a piece of firewood in her hand. Braya, Ysmay, and Joye were right behind.

Alizon wanted to scream.

"We saw he had you pinned," Greta said. "We did right, didn't we?"

She would flay them with her tongue, scold them from the room, only she could not gasp the air to do so. She took a moment to recoup.

The floor was suddenly no longer arousing beneath her bare flesh, George's inert form an embarrassment lying between her legs. The virgins would never trust her dealings with him if they knew how eager a partner she had so briefly been to his lust.

"Get him off me," she at last managed to gasp, her voice hoarse with frustrated desire, but the sound of it misled the girls into believing the worst, and they pulled him rudely from her.

"He is bleeding, mistress," Joye called as they rolled him to the side. Alizon sat up, pulling her dress over her exposed limbs. The other virgins were drifting in from the great hall, drawn to the commotion.

"From Greta's blow?"

Joye examined his head. "A bit. But it is his body I speak of."

Alizon's eyes widened. George was lying on his side, his sex helplessly exposed to the staring eyes of the virgins, but it was his back she needed to see. She and Joye rolled him onto his stomach, and she pulled up his bloodstained, torn shirt to find on his back a smattering of shallow cuts. She remembered Belch slamming against him as he clung to the wall, and imagined what it must have felt like to have the scales of Belch belly scraping down his back. There were also red weals all over George's body, tokens of the abuse he had taken, that by the morrow would turn black and purple.

"He gave me no notion . . ." she said under her breath. How could he have been so battered and yet so eager to take her?

"Let's leave the barbarian to suffer his wounds," Braya said.

"He fought the dragon as he said he would?" Joye asked.

"He did, and narrowly escaped with his life," she admitted.

"Better he should be eaten," Braya said. "He attacked you. We are none of us safe with him here."

There was an uncomfortable, excited murmur through the virgins gathered around George's prone form.

Alizon's first impulse was to defend him, but she bit down on her lip. She and the virgins would be better served if they feared him and wanted him gone as quickly as possible. They would not be sneaking into his room if they thought him a danger, might keep themselves as well hidden as they should have all along.

And she could not admit to them how eagerly she had parted her thighs and invited his touch!

"We'll wash his wounds and put a clean shirt

Join the Love Spell Romance Book Club
and **GET 2 FREE* BOOKS NOW–
An $11.98 value!**
Mail the Free* Book Certificate
Today!

Yes! I want to subscribe to the
Love Spell Romance Book Club.

Please send me my **2 FREE* BOOKS**. I have
enclosed $2.00 for shipping/handling. Every other
month I'll receive the four newest Love Spell Romance
selections to preview for 10 days. If I decide to keep
them, I will pay the Special Members Only discounted
price of just $4.49 each, a total of $17.96, plus
$2.00 shipping/handling ($23.55 US in Canada).
This is a **SAVINGS OF $6.00** off the bookstore
price. There is no minimum number of books I must
buy and I may cancel the program at any time. In any
case, the **2 FREE* BOOKS** are mine to keep.

*In Canada, add $5.00 shipping and handling per order
for the first shipment. For all future shipments to Canada,
the cost of membership is $23.55 US, which
includes shipping and handling.
(All payments must be made in US dollars.)

NAME: _____	
ADDRESS: _____	
CITY: _____	**STATE:** _____
COUNTRY: _____	**ZIP:** _____
TELEPHONE: _____	
E-MAIL: _____	
SIGNATURE: _____	

If under 18, Parent or Guardian must sign. Terms, prices, and conditions subject to change. Subscription subject
to acceptance. Dorchester Publishing reserves the right to reject any order or cancel any subscription.

The Best in Love Spell Romance!
Get Two Books Totally FREE*!

An
$11.98
Value!
FREE!

**PLEASE RUSH
MY TWO FREE
BOOKS TO ME
RIGHT AWAY!**

Enclose this card with $2.00
in an envelope and send to:

Love Spell Romance Book Club
20 Academy Street
Norwalk, CT 06850-4032

upon him, but that is all the care he deserves. Greta, put on a cloak and fetch Milo. He will help to carry our *guest*"—she sneered the word—"to the garrison room." She looked up at the others gathered white-faced around her and George on the floor. "There will be no doors left unlocked this night if you value the honor and safety of your persons."

"Aye," they mumbled. Their expressions were appropriately uneasy, but in more than one pair of eyes she saw a hint of the light of speculation at that mention of a threat to their honor.

"Flur, Pippa, Malkyn, go find a clean shirt. Reyne, Sisse, Ysmay, water and cloths to wash him. Braya, Lavena, one of my gowns and a chemise."

"Did he tear your dress?" Braya asked in surprise, taking her eyes from George's exposed flesh long enough to notice the state of her mistress's garb. The others turned their eyes from George and truly saw her for the first time as well.

"It was Belch."

A gasp went through them, and those who had begun to leave on their tasks froze and turned. "Belch!" they hissed.

"Tell us what happened, all of it," Greta said.

"I will, but later, when *he* is safely locked away." She and George had saved each other's lives, and she told herself they were even. She owed him nothing.

"But Belch was so close?" little Flur asked.

"Close, but not close enough," she said, trying to

smile through the wave of delayed fright that washed over her. She felt her smile falter, and coughed to cover the need to sniff back threatening tears of emotional strain. She pushed to her feet. "Belch will never get the better of me." She looked down at George with deliberate contempt, pulling her skirt away from where it brushed his leg. "What happens with 'Saint George' is another matter altogether."

It wasn't until much later that she realized those words had more than one meaning.

Chapter Seventeen

George tried another door off the south terrace and found it locked against him—like all the others except the one that had allowed him to leave the garrison room. He stepped back, shading his eyes with his hand as he looked up at the high windows of the great hall.

The great hall whose interior he had never seen. There were too many secrets on this island mount.

He had woken in the middle of the night and spent the small hours of the morning lying in his narrow bed, exploring the deep scratches on his back and failing to unlock a single one of the puzzles that plagued him. Daylight had brought more questions than answers, as the castle remained silent and there was no sign of the mistress.

Of Alizon.

He was 90 percent certain that was her name, her uttering of it the last thing he recalled before waking groggy and dry-mouthed in the garrison room.

Since he had started this adventure he had spent an inordinate amount of time waking up and wondering what had happened. He was beginning to get paranoid that he would go out cold each time things started to get interesting.

Fight with Milo: lights out.

See ghosts and a beautiful naked babe: wake uncertain it had been real.

Be on the verge of sliding home with the most confounding woman he had ever met: good night, sweet prince.

He certainly fared better in the ring than he had been faring here on Devil's Mount.

This morning it had taken him longer than he cared to admit to remember that this was all happening in his mind. It had not felt that way, with Belch huffing dragon breath at him and slamming him against the cavern wall.

He shuddered in remembrance of how close Belch's jaws had come—more than once—to snipping off big chunks of his anatomy. If that was what Belch was like partially drugged, George didn't want to deal with the fiend when he was fully awake.

He returned his thoughts to Alizon. It had not felt like this was all happening in his mind when she had her soft thighs around him, her hips urging him into her slick, wet heat.

Christ, no, it hadn't felt like he was imagining things. He didn't have that good of an imagination. He was an up-front, straightforward sort of guy, never subtle in his playacting. Although Alizon's silly crone costume fit with that, George didn't understand how she could have sprung from his unconscious. He kept getting the feeling that there were convoluted layers beneath her surface, much more convoluted than was native to any aspect of his personality, however buried.

Of course, Alizon's body was 100 percent edible—but he had seen plenty of pretty women, and he'd never been as obsessed with them as he was becoming with her! He never knew what to expect; each encounter with her was a challenge, sending the adrenaline of confrontation pumping through his blood. He didn't know what she wanted: of him, of the dragon, of life, of anything.

He grinned. Except for French toast and his body. He was pretty sure she wanted both of those, although probably in the same order.

Where the hell was she this morning, anyway?

The sea was bright beneath a white haze of sky, wind gentle in its gusts, seagulls holding steady on updrafts. The distant shore was green and peaceful, dots of white sheep moving on the hillsides and pencil sketches of smoke drifting from cookfires in the town. It should have been a beautiful morning, but all he felt was irritated frustration.

His muscles hurt, the cuts on his back stung, he was hungry, his head was throbbing, he had a serious case of blue balls, and no one was giving him any damn answers! What kind of dream was this, anyway?

He needed a cup of coffee. Why couldn't he have imagined himself in a quest to Starbucks? Two-ply toilet paper wouldn't go amiss, either, nor would shampoo, a proper change of clothes, and a razor.

More than any of that, however, he wanted Alizon. He didn't need a psychologist to tell him that she was an important part of his being here, perhaps nearly as much so as the dragon. That, at least, he was able to figure out on his own.

Her name sounded the same as that of Emoni's long-lost friend, the one after whom she had named her daughter. Was it she? And if so, what had she been doing here all this time? Why did her friend think her dead?

He went to the edge of the terrace and leaned against the parapet, looking out over the shimmering ocean dotted with the dark sails of local fishing boats.

He ached with the need to complete what he had started with Alizon on the kitchen floor. Was it a mental ache and not a physical one? Was that what this was about? Maybe he was trying to "connect" with his feminine side.

He grimaced. That made it sound like a creepy, convoluted mental jerk-off—instead of the most exciting physical encounter he'd had since he was sixteen and had a girl go down on him for the first time. He had heard that a near miss with death was an irresistible aphrodisiac, and he could vouch for the truth in that now: after Belch had almost chomped him, he could think of nothing but plunging himself deep inside this Alizon woman.

Hell, it was *still* almost all he could think about, symbolic meanings be damned.

He pushed away from the parapet and stalked around the end of the great hall, around to where he knew the kitchen to be. He found himself on the north terrace, its flagstones as empty of humanity as those on the other side. There was an opening in the parapet, though, that he had not noticed before. He went to it and looked down on a flight of stone steps that descended into the first of several walled kitchen gardens, one beneath the other, like rice paddies on a hillside.

He trotted lightly down the steps, his mind going back to his disastrous fight with Belch. The dragon was supposed to represent the doubts that had been plaguing him about his work. Kill the monster, kill the doubts. Right?

But then why had he hesitated when it was time to plunge the sword into the back of Belch's neck? For hesitate he had. He had been unable to stab that blade into the living flesh of an animal lying quiescent beneath his feet. He'd had to remind himself that Belch was a virgin-chomping dragon before he could force himself to give the blow—a blow that missed, due to his hesitation.

Belch's attempts to turn him into lunch had made the second blow easy to deliver, and George had been surprised when, with a thick, heavy sliding, the blade forced its way through the dragon's hide.

Then there had been all the blood. And the bellows of pain. It had only been Belch's continuing attempts to bite him in half that had kept George from tearing off his shirt and trying to stanch the creature's wound.

Perhaps this fiasco of a battle said something about the way he had handled the assault on his professional life. He had stood there and taken whatever they threw at him, believing himself strong enough to handle it, and believing as well that it would be somehow unfair of him to strike back at mothers who wanted only to protect their children.

Yet none of that answered the question of why his feminine side might be trying to connect with him. It sounded like he had an excess of femininity already, being overly softhearted. Which brought up a troubling thought:

He wasn't . . . gay, was he?

He thought of Alizon's parted thighs and felt a flush of heat through his loins.

No chance.

He stopped, standing still at the edge of a plot of sorry-looking cabbages, and tried to rationally think about this fairy tale he was living, to ignore the nagging conviction that Alizon must be a real person and not a part of his mind.

He had tried to do the nasty with her, had almost succeeded, and then out he'd gone like a light. It had to have been Milo who'd hit him.

Maybe Milo was the important character in this whole scenario. The man's habitual silence and brief answers were like those of a guru, so maybe that's what he was. His short statements were likely fraught with hidden psychological meanings that it was up to George himself to decipher.

Maybe Milo had been forced to knock him out because he knew it was too early for George to fully "connect" with Alizon. George didn't know or understand her well enough yet. He hadn't learned what he needed to from her.

Of course.

A little of the tension left his shoulders, pleased as he was with that bit of nimble brain work. Everything made sense, everything fit, if he just trimmed a few corners, turned it upside down and looked at it the right way.

He should be hanging out his own shingle, to counsel people. Write a self-help book, maybe. Go on "Oprah."

Deep inside a little voice laughed, giggling that he knew less than he thought. A dim memory surfaced, that a man's feminine side could also appear as a femme fatale, a demon of death who would lead him to destruction.

He shrugged off the thought. Not Alizon.

He resumed his walk through the gardens, noting the variety of vegetables and herbs, a frown slowly growing between his brows. He knew a little about the trials of yard work, and he wondered how Milo and Alizon managed to keep a handle on all the beds and espaliered fruit trees against the walls.

The enigma was soon forgotten as he lost himself in musings on the symbolic meanings of gardens, and he was surprised when he came at last to the final walled enclosure, with no outlet except an iron-banded door set in the far stone wall.

He pondered the door as if it had appeared in a glimmer of magic dust, as dubious in purpose as a portal in a fairy tale. Should he pass through? What might await on the other side? The apparently simple decision could be important, and he should ponder the consequences before acting.

Or he could stuff the pondering of consequences and count on his wits and strength to conquer the unknown demons beyond. He pulled back the bar and opened the door.

A sheep stood on the other side. It lifted its head, looked at him without interest, and went back to grazing.

The door divided the fortress gardens from the open slopes of the mount. Maybe not everything had a special meaning. Sometimes a cigar was just a cigar.

He went through and shut the door behind him. Picking a path down the slope, he climbed down rocks, crossed narrow meadows, and passed through pockets of trees and brush. The rhythmic *shoosh-shoosh* of a saw caught his ear, and he followed it down to a small shed near the base of the mount. Milo was there, cutting a rough plank of lumber.

"Milo! Good morrow!"

The man paused in his sawing for a moment, looking up much as had the sheep, then grunted and returned to work.

"What are you making?"

Milo gave him a flicker of eye contact. "Not making. Fixing."

His guru was being stereotypically laconic. George thought he himself should be meditatively reflective in response, but instead felt the impulses of a five-year-old pestering a workman. "Fixing what?"

"Platform."

"You're going to go down the tunnel and repair it?" he asked, startled by the answer.

"No. You will."

George grimaced. Was he going to have to go back down there so soon? Entering Belch's lair was not, he felt, going to get any easier with practice. He understood now why Milo never did, and he could only wonder at what inner resolve kept Alizon descending time after time.

"Fair enough, I suppose," he said, trying to sound casual and not as if the thought made him ill. "It was my fault Belch smashed the end of the thing."

He found a seat on a chunk of wood, watching Milo saw.

"I understand why you did it," he said after a few minutes had gone by.

Milo glanced up at him, a question in his expression.

George lightly touched the bump on the back of his head in explanation. "It took me a while, but it makes sense. I almost feel I should thank you—but jeez, man, a tap on the shoulder would have stopped me just as well. It's not like I would have continued with an audience. Take it easy on the brain case next time—I promise, I'll get the message."

The puzzled look on Milo's face took on a shading of alarm. He wore the expression of someone who was slowly realizing that the normal-looking person he is sitting next to on the bus is actually in need of heavy doses of psychotropic medication.

That, too, only made sense. George was breaking role, and if he wanted to kill the dragon and get it on with the girl, he had to play his part by the rules. Tempting as it was, there could be no knowing asides to his guru.

He changed the topic. "So, I have a new idea for killing Belch, but I'm going to need your help in gathering supplies."

Milo grunted. Warily.

"I need a few logs, of different lengths and widths, preferably of dry wood. Do you think we can get them?"

"I must ask the mistress."

"Alizon, yes. She *is* the one to go to, isn't she? But damned if I can find her."

Milo gaped at him.

"What?"

"She told you . . . ?"

It took him a moment. "Her name? You didn't hear her tell me?"

Milo shook his head.

"That's all I did get out of her, and it's my own fault, for rushing things. You know how it is, sometimes a guy thinks with the wrong head."

Milo seemed not to have heard him. "She must trust you," he said in wonder.

"You think so?" The thought was both cheering and sobering. Trust imposed the obligation that it not be abused. He must be more honorable in his treatment of her, for her own sake as well as for his, if he was going to learn what she had to teach him.

No more sex on the kitchen floor. At least, not until he knew her better.

Dammit.

Personal growth through creative visualization was proving to be a lot more work than he'd expected.

Chapter Eighteen

"Alizon! Yoo-hoo! Alizon! Where are you?"
George called from outside the great hall, his voice
floating in through the high windows.

Alizon hunched her shoulders and leaned closer
to the tapestry she was working on to hide the burning of her cheeks. The tapestry on its frame was
mounted vertically before her, a sketch of the picture it would represent drawn onto the wall directly
behind. She worked from the reverse side of the
tapestry, sitting on a tall stool, just as several of the
other virgins around the hall were on stools before
other tapestries.

"Yoo-hoo! Alizon! Come on, I'm starving out
here! Don't make me eat those scraggly cabbages I
saw!"

"Are you going to let him in?" Greta asked.

Alizon felt the eyes of the others all turned to her. "He will settle down if I ignore him."

"Alll-i-zohhhn . . ."

Glances of doubt were exchanged, and Joye made a noise of disbelief from in front of her tapestry. Hers depicted six young women in a garden—young women whose faces were those of six of the virgins. They often used themselves as models for their work, and the resulting hangings sold well.

Every six months a closemouthed trader from France arrived in their harbor to take the tapestries they had produced and to bring such luxuries as silk and velvet, silver mirrors, illustrated books that they gazed upon but could not read, ivory combs, spices, sugar, and sweetmeats. Milo handled the transactions in the dark of night, with Alizon standing hooded and silent in the shadows nearby.

There were virgins in Alizon's tapestry as well, albeit in the background. From the walls of a castle they watched the scene playing out in the foreground: a knight in black armor mounted on a rearing white horse, his surcoat displaying the red cross of St. George, his spear piercing the throat of a dark dragon. The dying beast, teeth bared, writhed on the ground amid the bones of sheep and humans. Lizards crept from a chasm in the ground nearby. Between the saint and the castle, a red-haired princess in pink robes and ermine watched in serene confidence.

"Allie-allie-allie-zohn!"

She ran her fingers over the face of the knight,

completed many weeks before. Was there something of George in his features? She had not been striving to create any particular face when she wove that visage, but that nose, the line of the jaw . . .

A flutter of uneasiness went through her. Surely not. She had none of Emoni's predictive powers.

Marry! There were only so many ways to weave a knight's face. A dozen other men would fit the features just as well.

This was not the first tapestry she had woven of the legendary St. George. None of those other weavings had drawn a knight to her castle, so it stood to reason that this one had not done so now. By the rood, she had had no wish to summon a dragon slayer!

But that jaw did look the same. And there were those imaginings that kept her awake through the nights, betraying her wish for something more than she had. Mayhap those imaginings had been caught within the spell Emoni wrought when she summoned the man.

"Alizon! I know you're in there!" George banged on the heavy doors to the north terrace, making them all jump.

"He does not sound as if he is settling down," Joye said.

"You should have locked him in the guard room, like on the first night," Braya said. She was sitting tailor-fashion, sewing a border onto a finished tapestry. "I do not know why you let him outside. We

are all trapped in here, as if he were a hound trying
to find his way into a sheep pen."

"If he is made to feel a prisoner he will fight me,
and lose his faith in my goodwill," she explained.

"Alll-i-zohhhn . . ."

"Verily, he howls like a hound," Joye gibed.

The younger girls snickered as they spun wool
on their spindles. Joye took the encouragement and
started a soft yowling, adding Alizon's name into
it. The young girls joined in, until they sounded like
a pack of wolves baying at the moon.

"Hush! He'll hear you," Alizon scolded.

They cut off their canine cries and were met with
silence from without. Gazes met gazes, anxious
that they had given themselves away. Long moments passed.

"Alizon?" George called, sounding worried.
"Was that you?"

A giggle of relief went around the room, followed
as quickly by an exaggerated hushing of each other.

"He probably thinks we're the ghosts again,"
Pippa said, her wild black hair quivering with the
shaking of her laughter.

"Scared in the daylight!" Braya sneered. "Such a
man is he! And one who would attack our mistress
as soon as he sees she is no crone."

"Alizon! Dammit! If you don't come out, how
am I going to apologize for yesterday? I shouldn't
have done that, and I regret it. Deeply."

Wide eyes turned to her. Greta spoke the thought
they all shared: "He is sorry?"

Maybe he was. The thought soured her mood further. It was bad enough to have shamelessly given in to her lustings, and to have told him her name in her desperation that he take her, but it was worse by far to have him now say he regretted touching her. His apology embarrassed her far more than her own enthusiasm had.

George shouted again. "There is no excuse for what I did. It was unforgivable. Unpardonable. Disgraceful. I ought to be whipped."

Yes, he ought to be.

"He doesn't *sound* very sorry," Joye said.

True, he did not. Perhaps there was hope.

"Alizon! Please forgive me. I beg of you. It won't happen again!"

She *wanted* him to try it again. It was better if the virgins thought him a beast, but *she* wanted to complete what the beast had started—on her own terms, of course, and somewhere more private than the kitchen floor.

She could not lose her wits like that again, but as she lay in bed last night she had concluded that she could take what he had offered without losing control of the situation. If she could outwit a village, survive a dragon, and provide for eleven women and girls, then she should be able to maneuver one naïve foreigner into her bed and have him obey her instructions.

She would not let down her guard. She might not have her disguise to protect her any longer, but strength was not to be found in a brown woolen robe. It was inside her, and she would use it to take what she wanted and to reveal nothing of herself. He would see only red hair and "cherry stones," and be happy with what was offered. Her secrets would remain safe within the fortress of her heart.

She would reveal nothing of the presence of the virgins. She would reveal as little as possible of her own past. He would see nothing of the yearnings that plagued her in the night, that if discovered and exploited could tear apart the world she had built upon Devil's Mount.

When he had lain between her thighs, she had cared about nothing but her own pleasure. She had cared nothing for dignity, secrets, revenge, the lives of others. Nothing.

She had enjoyed feeling that she was of flesh and blood, and was no longer the effigy lying in cold perpetuity above a crypt.

She had, sickening as it was to admit, enjoyed letting someone else take the lead for a change.

She would not allow herself such weakness again.

George would not be allowed to take her. *She* would take *him*.

"Alll-i-zohhh-ohh-ohhhn!"

"All right, all right!" she groused under her breath, sliding off her stool.

"You are going out there?" Greta asked.

"The hound must be fed, must he not?" Fed and subdued, and put in service to her own desires.

* * *

"Anything you want, you got it!" George sang, standing with his back to her as he sliced cheese on one of the work boards. He was swinging his butt back and forth, in time to the strange song he sang.

Alizon sat at the kitchen table, hands clasped before her, wishing for the hooded robe that was now at the bottom of Belch's pool. She felt exposed and awkward, especially with what had last happened between them in the kitchen fresh in her mind.

George had said nothing to her about her lost disguise, and the accompanying subterfuge. After a brief apology for yesterday, he had discussed nothing at all except for food and the possibility of a bath and doing some laundry afterward. He had not even mentioned the battle with Belch.

She did not know what to think, and it was making her tense. He must have questions that he was waiting to spring on her. She found herself on the verge of volunteering answers, if only to end the anticipation.

"Anything at ALLLL, you got it, BAAAAAY . . . BEEEE!" He spun around to face her, a pair of wooden spoons in his hands, beating them on invisible drums while making "doo doo doo doo" noises.

She frowned at him.

"Doo doo doo doo."

"Is this what music is like in your land?"

"Only the best," he said, grinning. "Roy Orbison is my god. He's the one who sang that song."

"Perhaps you will become a minstrel like him, when you tire of dragon-slaying."

"An interesting idea, but I doubt anyone would want to listen."

"As I am being forced to do," she grumbled.

He laughed. "You would like my sister. She shares the same opinion of my musical talents."

Her lips parted. "Sister? You have a sister?" For some reason, it surprised her.

"Athena. She manages my house for me while I'm away. She has a daughter, Gabrielle, my niece." He smiled, his gaze focusing on some internal thought.

"You sound fond of them." For the first time, she realized that whoever George truly was, he had a life waiting for him somewhere beyond Devil's Mount. Nothing else he had said about his homeland had struck her as being real as did his simple mention of sister and niece, and the gentle smile that accompanied it.

"I am. Athena talks sense into me when I'm being mule-headed, and Gabby . . . Gabby reminds me that my worries aren't as important as I think." A faint expression of surprise drifted over his face as he said it, as if it were a truth he had not recognized until now.

"How old is Gabby?"

"Five."

"And your sister's husband, what of him?"

A look of disgust twisted his features. "Gabrielle's father was a musician in a small troupe.

219

His only words to her when she said she was pregnant were—excuse the language here—'What the fuck you telling me for?' "

"God's blood! There is a snake of a man! I hope you served him what he deserved!"

"I wasn't there, or I would have been tempted. By the time I heard of this, he had already left town. The good part of it all was that Athena, having been unwisely seduced by this loser's musicality, was now wisely disillusioned as to his character. She didn't mourn his leaving."

"But she must have been frightened! To bear a bastard—the shame of it! And what if her family threw her out, how would she survive?"

"Ah, well, I think she knew I would never let either her or her child go wanting. Athena is one of those people who goes through life assuming that everything will work out in the end, and somehow for her it always does."

She pursed her lips, finding such a trait annoying. "You are remarkably accepting of your sister bearing a child out of wedlock."

"It wasn't the most intelligent thing she's ever done, and I could have wished for her own sake that she had waited until she was older and married to a good man. Punishing her wasn't going to stop the baby from being born, though."

Verily, she could barely wrap her mind around his calm acceptance of his sister's bastard child. There had always been plenty of children conceived out of wedlock in Markesew, but they were born securely within the bonds of matrimony. It must indeed be a different world that George came from, that he could speak so openly of his sister's shame. "Athena is fortunate to have you to provide for her."

He shrugged, as if it were not worthy even of consideration. He brought the food he was working with over to the table and sat down across from her. "What of your own family? Do you have brothers or sisters?"

"None."

"Parents?" he asked, as he took a round of bread and began to slice it.

"Dead."

"I'm sorry."

"I do not remember them, so there is nothing to grieve."

He gave her a sympathetic look from under his brows, then went back to his slicing.

"There was the widow Bartlett," she offered, not wanting him to feel sorry for her. "One might say she was like a mother."

"Who was she?"

"A tapestry weaver. She took me on as apprentice when I was yet a child. She and her sister fed and lodged me, and taught me skills to earn my keep."

"Very . . . motherly," he said.

"I was fortunate to have her," she responded, hearing the defensiveness in her own tone. Something in George's voice made her feel that he pitied her. "She took me in when no one else would have, and gave me hope for a better life. It is not common for a girl to be made an apprentice, as well you must know. My life was better with her than it would have been elsewhere."

"Mmm. And when did you meet Emoni?"

"When I was eight. We—" She stopped, suddenly realizing what she had given away.

He raised his clear green eyes to hers. There was no accusation in them, only a frank desire to understand. "And she has no idea that you're alive. What happened, Alizon? Why are you living here alone, while your dearest friend believes you died in the jaws of the dragon more than twelve years past?"

Her breath was frozen in her lungs. She had not meant to tell him that; had meant if asked to say that her name and that of Emoni's lost friend were a coincidence. "You tricked me." She started to push away from the table.

He reached across and grabbed her hands. His palms were warm around her cold fists, gentle even as they held her in place. He pulled her hands toward him and bent down to kiss the backs of her knuckles.

"No trickery," he said, his gaze capturing hers as his soft lips left her skin. "I want to know."

Her heart beat quick as a rabbit's in her chest. She had no defense against this gentle manner of assault. She was torn between retreat and striking out, and balanced too evenly between the two to act on either.

His gaze did not waver, and she found that she was the one who looked down and away. She did not want to tell him anything, this intruder, this disruption to everything she had known for more than a decade. She did not want him examining her life and passing judgment, or interfering in the course she had set.

And at the same time, she wanted to tell him all. She wanted to share her burdens, and see what he from his outsider's standpoint had to say in response.

His thumb brushed over the back of her hand, gently, the simple movement more powerful than he could know. How long had it been since anyone had touched her in such a way? As mistress of the mount she was sometimes sought to give soothing comfort, but never was that same soothing directed back at her. The virgins saw her as invulnerable.

Damnable man! His sympathy was killing her. She felt tears start in her eyes. She did not want to feel this way, to feel the stones coming loose in her fortress. He was not assaulting her walls, he was coaxing her to push them down from within.

She tried to tug her hands free.

He would not let her. "Alizon. You have been alone for too long. Talk to me. Tell me what happened."

"Peace! You know not of what you speak!" she said, betraying tears in her voice.

He released her hands and she pulled them to her stomach, holding them there and looking down at them. She heard him rise and glanced up to see him coming around the table. He straddled the bench beside her, and she scooted away.

"Come here, you nut," he said, and wrapped her in his arms, pulling her sideways, awkwardly, against his chest. Her head came to just beneath his chin. She felt him kiss her crown and lay his cheek lightly atop her head.

She sat stiff against him, her eyes wide. His hand began to stroke slowly up and down her back. There was nothing erotic in his touch: just warmth, and a promise of caring.

She did not know what to do.

Except from Emoni long ago, she had had no one offer her such comforting. She did not know if she could trust its veracity from George, or survive without harm the weakening she felt. She felt a welling of pain rising up inside her, seeking to pour over the walls, and feared that it might wash them away entirely.

He paused in his stroking to massage her lower back, then moved up to gently knead the tightness of her shoulders and neck. Her eyes closed halfway, and she allowed herself to relax a bit against him, turning so that her breasts were pressed against his chest and her cheek rested on his collarbone.

"Tell me what happened," he said again, softly, and stroked down to her hip, massaging it and her upper thigh.

He already knew who she was. She would lose little by telling him how she came to be mistress.

Perhaps the waters of her anguish could be allowed to trickle a small stream over the walls, to ease their pressures.

"I was fourteen when I was chosen in the lottery," she said softly.

He went motionless for a moment, startled, perhaps, that she had chosen to speak. Then his hand came up to her hair, fingertips combing lightly through it against her scalp, following the course of it back toward the loose braid at her neck.

"Emoni said she had a vision of me in the lair of the dragon, so I was not surprised when my name was drawn."

"She's a woman of strange talents," George said.

"Yes." For the first time, she wondered if perhaps Emoni truly *had* called George, not just from a far country, but from some unearthly realm beyond this solid one. It was not to be believed, yet if anyone could have done it, it would have been Emoni.

"What happened after they drew your name?"

"They gave me a white gown to wear, and undid my hair and put a crown of flowers upon it. I looked like one of the sheep, penned and likewise bedecked. It was a wonder they did not salt me, for better flavor to please the beast."

He chuckled, the sound a rumble she could feel in her own chest. She wrapped her arms lightly around his waist, sinking a little more deeply against him.

"The tide was out, the causeway uncovered. Milo was waiting at the start of it, a shepherd's crook in his hand. He barely looked at me, and I was terrified of him—so big, and no expression on his face.

"I was led to the causeway, and then the townsfolk began to sing. It's the same short, horrid song they've sung every year."

She began to sing, in little more than a whisper:

"Go gently, good child
Thine innocence to save us.
Go gently, good virgin,
Thou art bravest."

"Bastards," George hissed. "Sending a fourteen-year-old girl to a dragon. Asking *her* to be brave, when they themselves are cowards."

She tightened her hold on his waist, pressing her face against his chest. It was the first time an outsider had spoken the thoughts that had screamed their injustice at her year after year. It felt as if he had transfered her anger to his own shoulders, and now there was nothing under which to hide the pain of that long-ago day.

Again, she was standing on the shore, looking one last time at the faces that had filled her young life. Faces that expressed bliss and relief more than sorrow, and whose mouths were singing her to her death.

Only Emoni and the widow Bartlett showed any sign of regret. Emoni wept openly, but Alizon's mistress maintained her stiff and upright posture, her eyes averted. Alizon's mistress did not sing with the others, though, and the stony stillness of her countenance had been marred by the trembling of her tight-pressed lips.

Alizon sniffed back tears and took a breath to settle herself. She shrugged within George's hold as if to say, "That's the way of the world."

She went on with her story. "I stepped out onto the causeway. The sheep were herded after me, with Milo following. I did not want to go forward, but I refused to look back. They had thrown me away, and I would not humiliate myself by begging them to keep me. They weren't worth it."

"Bastards," George said again, under his breath.

"I crossed the causeway, the sheep bleating behind me and before me the distant figure of the crone in a brown robe, hunched and leaning on a cane." She shuddered. "She had long white hair, unkempt, wisps of it blowing about in the wind. Even from so far away she looked like a standing corpse. Walking toward her was like walking into the arms of Death."

"Why didn't she come to the town with Milo?"

"She never did. She wasn't wanted there. She was too much of the mount, too much of the world of the dragon. Milo, like the causeway, is the bridge between the worlds."

"What fun for Milo."

"It suits him well enough."

He made a noncommittal noise. "What happened when you reached the crone?"

"She was older even than I had expected. Frailer.

227

Unwashed, as if she hadn't the strength even to wipe the food from her chin. I was scared half past thinking, but it occured to me that I was stronger than she was. If it was not for Milo, I could have overpowered her.

"Milo penned the sheep, and then they brought me up to the castle. Into the kitchen, right here. Milo gave her a small packet—they must have given it to him in Markesew—and the crone mixed the powder it held into a mug of beer.

" 'Drink this,' she told me, setting it on the table. They were the first words she had spoken. She barely looked at me.

" 'What is it?' I asked her.

" 'It will put you to sleep, girl. Drink it.' "

George twined his fingers into the hair at the base of Alizon's neck. "You didn't, did you?"

"Didn't I? With Milo standing there, ready to force it down me? I drank it, at first as slowly as I could in hopes of finding a way to dump it, but then I realized that whatever was in it would have me half-senseless by the time I finished. I downed the better part of it in one long draught.

"I could see the crone relax. The difficult part was over for her. I had obeyed. All would go as she wished, with no trouble.

"Milo went to stand by the door to the hall. The crone sat. They were waiting for the drug to take effect.

"I waited as long as I dared, then squirmed a bit and with half-closed eyes asked to use the jakes. 'I haven't had a chance all day,' I said. 'I don't want to foul myself when I die.'

"I had been so cooperative, and they thought the drug was already taking effect. Milo took me to the jakes, and as quietly as I could I forced the brew to come up."

She felt the chuckle in George's chest. "How does anyone manage to do that quietly?"

"Aye, well . . . the sound of retching is not one to be mistaken. You hear someone in the jakes cough, and then a splash, and you know what is going on."

"Did Milo know?"

"He looked at me when I came out. Stared. He knew what had happened, but not whether it had been on purpose. He said nothing, though, not then and not when we returned to the kitchen.

"I could feel the drug working on me a little, and exaggerated the effect, acting more tired than I was. After ten minutes or so, the crone had Milo open the door to the passageway. She lit a torch and beckoned me to follow.

"I hadn't gotten rid of all the drug in my gut and was dizzy. It took all my concentration to keep to my feet as we went down the stairs. I thought of shoving the crone but was afraid that I would break my own neck tumbling after her.

"It wasn't until we reached the second door, which she had to open herself, that I realized Milo had not followed us. I could have attacked her there, as she strained to pull it open, only I couldn't think how to do it. I might have only one chance, and knocking her to the ground was not going to be enough."

"You intended to kill her?" George asked, his fingers tightening in her hair.

She leaned back against his enfolding arms, meeting his gaze, expecting to see condemnation there and beginning to raise her angry shields against it. There was nothing of horror in his eyes, though—it was with a sort of fascination that he gazed back.

"I intended to save myself. I was thinking of nothing more," she said, relaxing somewhat. She kept the small distance between their bodies, missing the warmth of his chest against hers but unable to lean forward and reclaim it. Her pride would not let her show she wanted the comfort.

A misgiving snaked through her, that she should not be sharing so much of herself with him. The desire to continue her tale dried up inside her, the words dying in her throat. She suddenly wanted away from him.

He seemed to sense her withdrawal, and before she could move had drawn her back against his chest, his big hands again stroking her spine and massaging the resistance out of her muscles. He did not talk, and soon she found the words returning to her, spilling out into the waiting quiet.

"You know what it smells like when that second door is opened. I knew I would do anything to save myself from being thrown to whatever made that stench. And yet, at the same time, I felt I had to *see* it. To know what this dragon was that had been ruling our lives for so long.

"She prodded me ahead of her, and a minute later we came out onto the platform. As when you first went down to the cavern, there was nothing to see but fog. The crone rapped her cane against the floor, three or four times, then pointed to the stall and told me to lie down in there and go to sleep.

"Part of me wanted to. I had taken enough of the drug that I *did* want to lie down and rest. It wouldn't be such a bad way to go, after all, in my sleep, and then I could be done with the worry of it all."

"You were too stubborn to give up," he said.

"Too angry," she corrected. "I refused to do as the crone bid.

"She ordered me again to lie down. Again, I refused. She tried to poke me with her cane, tried to prod me into place. I grabbed the end of it and tried to jerk it away from her.

"She had more life in her than I expected. We had both been fooling each other on that, I think. She did not let go, and we tussled over it, both of us stumbling to the rail."

Alizon felt his arms tighten around her. "Somehow the cane got between us, across her chest. I pushed at it. At her. I was heavier than she was— I had at least that advantage—and I bent her back over the rail, her shoulders and head hanging out over empty space.

"There was a splash, far below, and I saw her eyes widen. I was slower to think than she was, and was still holding the cane against her chest, forcing her to lean out over the rail, when Belch's jaws snapped shut on her, snagging her by the head and shoulders. A moment later she was gone, torn out of my grip. I could feel wetness on my knuckles, from where his snout had grazed my hands."

George leaned back, loosening his hold on her so he could see her face. "Good God. No wonder you were so frantic that first day you brought me down there."

The stubble over his jaw was taking on the rough looks of a new beard. She wanted to run her short nails through it, and feel it scrubbing against her fingertips. "I had no wish to see it happen again. Once was enough."

"I can't think you were too sorry to see the crone go, though."

"It was neither sorrow nor relief I felt. Stunned terror might fit my feelings better. I had caught only a glimpse of Belch's head, but that was enough. I forced my legs to hold me and stumbled back up the tunnel."

"Milo must have gotten quite a shock when you came out that door."

She smiled crookedly, feeling more at ease with George in that moment than she had ever expected. Desire for him was slowly heating her blood as she sat between his thighs and within the circle of his arms, but she felt no need to rush it. The growing lust was a pleasure in itself.

"I was halfway up the stairs before I remembered Milo. The thought of him waiting for his mistress stopped me where I was, and I sat on a step in the dark and tried to figure out what I was going to do.

"In the end, there seemed to be only one thing I *could* do. I got up, walked bold as you please into the kitchen, and told Milo, 'I am your mistress now.' "

George laughed. "What did he do?"

"Stared at me for a long moment, then nodded. Once. And that was it."

"So what happens to the virgins now, when they come every year? I know you don't let Belch have them."

"How do you know that?" she asked, flattered and alarmed both.

"I know at least that much about you. Your sense of justice would not permit it."

"You do not think my wish to save myself might be stronger?"

"Not with the innocent."

"You do not know me as well as you believe," she corrected quietly, thinking of the night she had drugged him, of her sabotaging of his battle with Belch, and of her intention to continue undermining his efforts to kill the dragon.

"You are fierce, my sweet, but fierce only to protect a tender heart."

She snorted with laughter. "A remark that shows you know me not at all!"

He only smiled and traced the curve of her cheek with his fingertip. "Do you toss the girls to the dragon?" he asked.

She tried to keep the smirk on her face, not wanting him to see how important it was to her that he had gotten this, at least, correct. "It was only as I got to know Milo later that I learned how much he hated his own role in the sacrifices. He was more than happy to help me buy passage up the coast for the yearly virgin," she lied, and felt her ease with him die as the false words left her lips. She forced herself to go on. "It is my hope that they make new lives for themselves, but I have no way of knowing if they succeed."

It was something she *had* thought of doing, only to discard the idea as she had when having her own thoughts of running away from Markesew before the lottery. The virgins were safe here, and well provided for. The world was too cruel and dangerous a place for a girl alone, without family or friends on whom to rely.

She could not tell *him* that, though. If he knew that the virgins were in the castle he would want to see them, and then his sense of honor would have him taking them all away from the mount. She knew it, to the center of her bones.

She should have been remembering that, instead of sitting here basking in his attentions. Marry! It was a miracle she had not told the truth, such was the power of his hands upon her back, and the feel of his heart beating beneath her cheek.

He frowned, cocking his head to the side. "But why do you stay here at all? And why send the girls away? You have proven that Belch does not need to eat a virgin every year to be controlled. Why continue pretending as if he does?"

"Because *they* will not believe anything else," she said bitterly, nodding her head in the direction of Markesew. "Several weeks after she was supposed to have been sacrificed, one of the virgins tried to return to the town. They stoned her nearly to death. Milo carried her back to the mount, bloody and broken, scarred for life."

"I would think they could be made to see reason—"

"You are welcome to try it! Do you think they want to admit that all those sacrifices already made were unnecessary? Do you think they want to take the risk that Belch might emerge from his lair? They are satisfied with how they have arranged things. It is convenient."

"They won't be able to argue with a dead dragon," he said. He suddenly reached up and held her face between his hands, gazing intently into her eyes. "I will kill Belch, and free you from this island."

She could only stare back, frightened. She did not want to be free. There was nothing else for her in this world but Devil's Mount.

"Better that you keep your wits on staying alive,"

she said. "When your three tries are finished, I want you to take Emoni and her daughter away from Markesew."

He chuckled, and leaned forward and kissed her on the forehead before releasing her. "You have so little faith in me. Belch will be dead after my third try, if not my second."

She placed her hands on his thighs, which straddled the bench. They were hard with muscle, long and sleek under her palms. "George, listen to me. Fighters better trained than you have died in that cavern. This is no game. Do not risk your life to kill a dragon that is no longer a threat to anyone."

It was her own sabotaging efforts of which she was perversely trying to warn him. George could surely not beat Belch as long as she was secretly aiding the dragon. All his risks and efforts were for naught.

"But he *is* a threat. All those girls, torn from their families, their lives uprooted. And you, Alizon, trapped here alone to watch over a dragon." His expression held deep respect. "For twelve years you have borne the responsibility, putting the lives of others above your own. You have given enough. It's time you had your own life."

His praise made her feel sick. She had saved the virgins, aye, but as for the rest, it was revenge against the heartless scum of Markesew that motivated her. She was no self-sacrificing martyr, forgiving those who had harmed her or laying down her life in order that they might live free of the threat of the dragon.

"Do not do this for *me*," she said harshly, feeling the chasm between whom he thought she was and whom she knew herself to be. "I can take care of myself."

"That is more than obvious," he said, laughing again and reaching for her.

She scooted back and swung her legs over the bench, standing. "Are you going to finish making this 'sandwich' you told me about?" she asked, gesturing to the abandoned food. She did not want to talk any longer about who she was or what her future should be. He was being too kind and gentle with her, and it made her feel monstrous and evil in contrast. She wanted to kick and scratch and push him away.

Only, she knew it would get her nowhere. He would just hold her until she calmed herself, and then she would start weeping out more of her secrets to him, becoming weak and soft and helpless. She could not stand it.

She was mistress of the mount, and he was making her forget that. Worse, yet, he was stirring those nighttime doubts that mistress was what she wanted to be.

He gave her a long assessing look, as if trying to figure out what was going on in her head. He stood, and for a moment she thought—hoped—he would take her in his arms despite her protests, but then he shrugged and went back around the table, directing his attentions again to the food.

She felt bereft and betrayed, and angry at herself for feeling so. The simplest actions of one man should not have such a powerful effect upon her. It was like a sickness within her. She should cure herself of it as soon as possible.

If she only knew how.

"I was wondering if, after we eat," he asked, as he started to lay slices of cheese atop a piece of buttered bread, "you could show me around the rest of the castle?"

"Why?" she asked, crossing her arms over her chest.

"Curiosity."

"That is hardly reason enough for me to give up my privacy."

"I do not need to see your private chamber, not unless you wish me to." He gave her a hopeful look that almost made her smile. "But surely the rest of the castle is free of the underclothes, diaries, what-have-you, that would keep me from your bed-room."

"I thought you wanted to bathe and wash your clothes."

"I can do so after."

"Better to do it sooner. You smell." He did, a bit, but nothing strong. The dunking in the mineral pool had rinsed him well.

He plucked his shirt away from his underarm and sniffed at it. "I've smelled worse, and I'm still sweeter than Milo. At least show me the great hall."

"No."

"Why not?" he asked, abandoning his cooking and putting his hands on his hips.

"You have no need to see it."

"I want to enough that it is nearly a need. Just as I want other things."

His hungry gaze sent a flush through her, and she suddenly felt exposed, standing there across the table from him. Again she felt the desire that he should ignore her resistance and take her. She felt ignorant and stupid in the face of the forces at work in her own body, and having him take charge would end the chaos.

Jesu mercy, but he tempted her.

He was the devil on the mount, more than Belch ever was.

"No," she said. "You have seen all of the castle that you need to. Be content."

"I shall never be content, as long as there is a door left locked against me." His voice was soft, but his gaze was intense.

She felt a flutter of frightened uncertainty, no longer knowing if it was only the fortress of which he spoke. He sounded as if he meant to find his way inside her, body and soul, leaving no corridor unexplored however carefully she barred his entrance.

"Then you shall live a discontented, miserable life!" she snapped.

With that, she ran from the room in ignoble retreat. It wasn't just George she wished to escape, but her own confused and fragile heart.

Chapter Nineteen

Sweat streamed down his forehead, through his eyebrows, and into his eyes, stinging them with salt. He blinked away the pain, and maneuvered the last thin log into place, jamming it in amid the others in the mouth of the hot spring.

He was squatting inside the low, narrow opening where the mineral water poured into Belch's lair. There was just enough room for him to crouch, safe from attacks from Belch, and he had paid the price of security with his cramped muscles.

The hot water that had once run freely was now down to a trickle. Two dozen logs and poles were crammed lengthwise into the small tunnel, damming it. He hoped that as the dry wood soaked up water, it would expand and set itself even more tightly into the passage.

He had thought of using mortar and stones to do the job, but he couldn't figure out how to manage it with the water constantly running and keeping the mortar from setting. As it was, he hoped the pressure of the water behind the logs never grew so great as to spit them out like so many toothpicks. There were other outlets for the water, though—the kitchen was one—so he kept his fingers crossed that such a pressure buildup wouldn't happen.

He also kept his fingers crossed that there weren't spring openings hidden in the bottom of the pool. With the main source of heat gone, the steaming pool of water should cool to the temperature of the sea that sloshed in from outside the cavern. Belch, as a cold-blooded reptile, would have no way to warm himself. He would either leave the region, in search of more temperate climes, or he would die of hypothermia.

He gave the logs a last testing shove with the flat of his hand, then swung out the entrance onto the rope ladder system he had rigged, leading up to the trapdoor of the platform. Alizon was peering down at him through it, her braid hanging and the neckline of her lavender gown offering a view she probably hadn't intended.

"Are you done, then?" she asked.

"Done as I'll ever be. There's nothing to do now but wait."

"I have never heard of such a way of killing a dragon," she said doubtfully.

George hung on the ladder for a moment, looking across the pool at Belch. The monster had been fed a sheep this morning, and lay quiescent on his beach, seemingly uninterested in the goings-on at the spring. Alizon had stood watch for any movement while George worked.

"You were the one who said that strength *and* wits would kill him. This is a far more intelligent approach than fighting him man-to-dragon."

"More likely it is foolishness, and either way it counts as your second attempt."

"Ye of little faith." He tugged playfully on her braid and released it, and she drew back to give him space to climb up through the trapdoor.

He sat on the floor of the platform, legs dangling through the opening, glad even of this small distance from the heat of the spring. He wore only his soggy, mangled boots, a pair of braies that Milo had found for him (he had washed them, not knowing on whom they had been), and his knee and elbow pads. The braies were like baggy shorts, at first held to his hips by a cord, but now plastered to his body by sweat and steam. He felt like one of those loin-clothed laborers building the pyramids in an old Hollywood movie.

"Are you going to bathe yet again?" she asked.

"Of course. And then I have a surprise for you."

The look she gave him was more wary than thrilled. "What would that be?"

"You'll have to wait and see. It is my gift to you, for helping me this past week."

"Gift?" She said the word as if it was a foreign concept.

"Don't ask me what it is. I'm not telling." He wasn't sure she would have known what it was, even if he *had* told her. And truth be told, it was as much a gift for himself as for her, although he intended they should use it together.

"I need no gift." She sounded as if she might not need it but certainly wanted it. The gleam in her eye spoke of tightly reined curiosity and greed. He was delighted.

"Sure you do. Every woman does. And you arranged for the logs and the ropes, and watched my back while I was down there. I couldn't have dammed the spring without your help."

He was getting wise to the ways of Alizon. If she needed a reason to be given a gift, a reason he would give her.

After spilling her heart about the day she had been given to the dragon, she had closed herself off and avoided talking with him. She reminded him of a wild animal, and instinct told him that the way to tame her was to let her tame herself: He would sit still and let her come back to him. Pushing would only scare her farther away. She kept up her porcupine quills because she was, at heart, frightened of him.

It was a truth of human nature he had learned coming up through the ranks of the CUW. Those who were sure of their place and of themselves had no need of posturing and back-stabbing. It was only those who felt their own vulnerability who behaved like sewer rats. A pissy attitude was a sure sign that someone was feeling scared and helpless.

Alizon was scared of him in the same way that men and women had been scared of each other for millennia, wanting one another and yet afraid of letting down the shields on fragile hearts.

So, he had gone about his business while talking about his family and his friends. He told anecdotes from his life, tailoring them to fit this medieval world. He asked nothing from her, not even that she listen.

She had gradually thawed, and started hanging around him, offering her own tales about the time she had lived in Markesew. She liked especially to speak of Emoni, and asked him over and over the same questions about her long-lost friend, as if through repetition she could gain some new crumb of information. She had started behaving like a friend.

He stood up and helped Alizon to her own feet. He couldn't get enough of looking at her, now that the hood was gone. In the hood's place he had the certainty that she would flee if stared at to keep his glances furtive. He liked it best when she was engaged in some task in the kitchen and he could watch her for minutes at a time without her knowing.

Sometimes she did catch him looking; then she would get either flustered or angry.

George & the Virgin

And sometimes he caught her looking. He would pretend not to notice.

"I may have arranged for the materials, but I still do not think they will do any good," she said. "You have likely wasted your efforts here."

"We'll see."

She gestured to the trapdoor. "Are you going to leave the ladder?"

"I'll want to check the dam tomorrow. I doubt Belch will do anything to it if we leave it overnight."

She shrugged and started up the tunnel. He followed, watching the sway of her hips and resisting the urge to squeeze her buttocks. Keeping his hands off her while he won her confidence was taking the patience of a saint.

And he wasn't one.

While waiting for the logs and ropes this past week, he had spent most of his time working on the gift, chopping and hauling wood, weeding the gardens, cooking, and attending to personal hygiene. The personal hygiene and cooking took unholy amounts of time, but he couldn't allow himself to stink with Alizon nearby, and even if he had trusted her cooking, he wouldn't have been comfortable making her wait on him.

Besides, like tempting a wild bird into the hand with sunflower seeds, the simple meals he made lured Alizon to the kitchen table. She had started eating whatever he put together, and however basic the sandwich or omelette seemed to him, its novelty appealed to her.

245

He liked watching her eat. He liked the feeling that something he had done gave her pleasure, and liked the way she pulled bits out of her sandwich, tasted them, and put them back. He liked the darkness of her eyes, and the way they flashed at him over the top of her sandwich when she took a bite, like a hyena wary of a nearby vulture.

He liked the challenge of their encounters.

He liked *her*.

Alizon would never let anyone use her as a doormat. She would never cling, or look for others to solve her problems. She was a survivor, independent and proud, but best of all was the heart that beat beneath her dragon-scaled exterior. Again and again he found himself in awe of how she had saved so many young girls, and how despite the risk to herself she descended weekly to Belch's lair to feed him.

Again and again, he found himself wanting to take the burden of the dragon from her, to set her free to live the life she deserved.

And again and again, as he lay in bed at night, his imaginings wandered to what it would be like to have her in his real life, living in his house, traveling with him from city to city, waking next to him in his bed every morning, her unshielded heart in her eyes. What might it be like, to be loved by a woman such as Alizon, and to love her in return?

What might it be like?

They came out into the kitchen, and he grabbed

his usual buckets and scooped them full of hot mineral water.

"I do wish you would use the tub," Alizon said. "It is indecent, your standing naked on the terrace to bathe."

He grinned at her. "You're the only one who might peek, and I wouldn't mind if you did." There was a big, heavy tub he could have used for his bath, but he found it more efficient to take the buckets out onto the terrace and give himself a scrub in the open, dumping water over his head to rinse. It was fast, though chilly.

"Marry! Please yourself, but I shall not be peeking!"

"Don't go anywhere, and for heaven's sake, don't lock the door. I'll be back in fifteen minutes with your gift." She had a fondness for locking doors behind him and leaving him to knock and shout her name when he returned.

She was either paranoid about intruders, or she took some sort of sadistic pleasure in making him beg entrance again and again. What might it be like to have her in his real life, indeed!

She crossed her arms over her chest, apparently trying to look petulant and uninterested in the promised gift. She was a poor actress. "I won't sit here waiting all day. I have things to do, you know!"

"Porridge to boil, hearths to scrub, yes, I will try not to keep you long from such joys." He might have to dawdle at his bath, for her own good. Half the fun of a gift, after all, was the anticipation.

She followed him as he retreated into the corridor. "I do more than that with my time."

"I should like to know what."

"My tapestries. I weave."

"Ah, yes, these tapestries you say you were trained to create. I have yet to see one," he goaded.

"Mayhap one such as you would not appreciate it."

"Mayhap you have none to show." He suspected she wanted to be prodded into bringing one out. She was probably too proud to show him if it looked like her own idea, as if she was seeking approval or praise. "Are you coming with me, to scrub my back?" he asked as they reached the door to the terrace.

"Fie on you! Your thoughts follow but one course."

"It is the curse of being a man. We know that women never dirty their minds with such thoughts."

"By Saint Nicholas, we do not!"

"That is what I said. Now will you let me bathe, so that I may bring you your gift?"

"I am not keeping you."

"No, of course you're not. My apologies." With a whisper of a laugh, he pulled open the door to the daylight and went out to take his bath. She was definitely starting to like him.

*   *   *

Alizon watched the door close behind George and felt an odd impatience that he should be out of her company, even for the space of a quarter hour. These past few days she had had the strange sense that George was backing away from her, and that she was the one who was pursuing. She knew she was doing no such thing, and was keeping tight control over her impulses, and yet . . .

The closed door was a frustration, and she had half a mind to open it and continue their conversation.

She made a rude noise and threw up her hands.

She no longer knew if she was coming or going. There was the damming of the spring to worry over, and whether it might not do as George said and chill Belch to death. She did not know what to make of his promise of a gift, or of her own impulse to show him one of her tapestries. She had barely controlled the wild desire she had had, staring at his bare chest, to strip off her gown and slide her naked body down his slick and sweaty skin.

She was upside down and inside out. Mayhap she should go out there and bathe him, as he had dared, and see if it cleared up any of the confusion.

The noise of the bar being slid back on the door to the great hall saved her from acting on any such thoughts. She knew that someone had been listening, and knew as well what was coming next.

"Hurry, hurry, he is much too fast," Joye said, opening the door a crack and then disappearing, running after the rest of virgins toward the door at

Lisa Cach

the other end of the room, leaving Alizon to enter the hall on her own.

She tightened her lips into a hard line and barred the door behind her, watching the flying skirts and bouncing braids of racing girls. She wanted to forbid this spying upon George at his bath, but if she tried, no one would obey. Her authority would be irreparably undermined, for there was no force on earth that would keep the virgins from their daily dose of naked male flesh.

At least George had no idea of what happened each time he stripped off his clothes and reached for the soap. That was a minor mercy.

A dark little voice inside taunted her: *It's not his modesty you care about. You want to keep him all to yourself.*

And what if she did? Surely it was a less sinful desire than one to share him would be.

She jogged after the virgins, toward the other wing of the castle. She had to be there, to keep them under control: It wasn't that she wanted to spy on George herself, like a lecherous old spinster. By the rood, she had not sunk so low as that!

By the rood, she had not. Those long flanks and the dark hair at his groin need not be gazed upon, nor did the thick maleness that nestled upon it. The sculpted buttocks, the broad back with the healing slashes of Belch's scales, the wide shoulders: She had no wish to stare and slobber over such a forbidden view. She had no interest in watching water sluice through his rich, heavy hair and down his

250

body, caressing his skin like eager hands.

Up ahead, Braya lost her footing rushing around a corner. The virgins left their fallen friend and dashed onward, some leaping over her sprawled form. Alizon helped her up and was rewarded with a view of Braya's back as she galloped on ahead.

By the time Alizon reached the long upstairs room that offered the best view of the terrace, the virgins had swathed their heads and faces in black cloths and were crouched as near as they dared to the windows. They had worked together to come up with the veil idea, having recognized that white faces were too easily seen at a window.

It was a good thing they hadn't visited George in the night in such garb: He would have lost what wits he had left. Even in the dim light of this room they looked like headless corpses, with pale slits of eyes floating above.

She took a piece of black cloth and swathed her own face.

The bath began. The virgins watched in intense silence, with a concentration that was unnerving, and that made Alizon worry for George's safety on the mount amid them. It was a wonder he could not feel their gazes upon his skin.

She *had* tried to get George to use the tub in the kitchen, where there would be privacy. She had done all that anyone could expect. If she herself took a small bit of pleasure from watching his bare skin gleam in the light of the setting sun, it should

Lisa Cach

be considered her reward for keeping her hands and mouth off him these past days.

She still intended to use him to lose her virginity but hadn't yet figured out exactly the right approach. It wasn't that she was *afraid* of him, or of what would happen. She was just cautious.

It was too bad that watching him only made her nighttime fantasies all the wilder, and the lust in her blood the stronger. She might do something rash.

Like lick those droplets off his body, running her tongue up his thigh, across his belly, over the planes of that delicious chest . . . She swallowed, her mouth watering. Then she would start over, on that bit of maleness that she unaccountably wished to feel in her mouth, somehow certain that it would feel silky and taste wonderful. Her naked breasts would brush his legs, and she would grip his buttocks in her hands . . .

Down on the terrace George toweled off and donned the shirt he had left to dry on the parapet earlier in the day. A sigh went through the room as he covered up, Alizon's included. She tried to shake off the fantasies that belonged more to the night than to the day.

She watched him a moment longer, amused by his fastidiousness. He was always cleaning himself, his clothes, his dishes, or even his food. He behaved toward dirt the same way others behaved toward a leper's sore: as if disease would come from touching it.

Alizon backed away from the window and removed her veil. She had to get back to the kitchen before he returned. She gestured for Greta to come with her, to bar the door.

"What do you think he is going to give you?" Greta asked as they hurried back through the castle.

"Some trinket, most likely."

"I don't know where he would have gotten one," Greta said.

"Nor do I. Like as not he has found some bit of nothing in that pile of armor and polished it up."

"Why would he do such a thing?"

Alizon shrugged.

Greta lay her hand on Alizon's arm, stopping her. "Why would he do such a thing?"

Alizon frowned at her. "I do not know. Who can say why he does anything?"

Greta kept looking at her, a strange tension in her features.

"What?"

"I know he was not truly attacking you on the floor of the kitchen."

Alizon's lips parted, but she was too surprised to speak.

"I didn't think you'd want us all to see what was about to happen, so I hit him on the head."

Alizon's throat was dry. "Do . . . do the others know?"

"Some suspect you've been visiting his bed. Some are jealous and think you are being selfish by not sharing." Greta smiled awkwardly, her harelip twisting aside. "Some think you would not let him so much as touch the hem of your gown."

"And what do you think?"

"I think . . . it is curious that he wishes to give you a gift. And I think you have had a lighter step and more color in your cheeks than I have seen for many years."

Alizon crossed her arms over her chest. "Which means nothing."

"So you say. But what if he asks you to leave with him?"

"I would not go. My place is here."

Greta's eyes narrowed. "Even at the cost of losing him?"

Alizon matched Greta's intensity with her own, staring her down. "What wouldn't I do to keep us all together? What *haven't* I done?"

Greta was stiff a moment longer, then suddenly her harsh expression collapsed. Her eyes filled with tears and she embraced Alizon, hugging her against her own quivering body. "I knew you wouldn't leave us. I *knew* it."

Alizon stood startled within Greta's arms, and awkwardly patted her back. "Never, Greta. I would never leave you on your own." She had forgotten, for a brief time, how much the virgins needed her. Her mind had been too caught up in George.

"I know, I know."

She patted Greta once more, then stepped away, feeling the weight of responsibility settling again onto her shoulders, cold and heavy where once it had been a warm mantle. Whatever lightness there had been to her step would be gone now.

She forced a false cheeriness into her voice. "Quick, now, I have to get back to the kitchen before he returns. We don't want him suspecting anything, do we?"

Greta sniffed and shook her head.

Alizon exited to the corridor, and listened for the sound of the other woman barring the door to the great hall behind her. The archway to the kitchen was across from her, doors to cellars on either side, the door to the terrace a dozen steps to the right.

She stood alone in the dark for several moments, aware of the doors all around her. To the virgins. To George. To the kitchen and Belch. Those doors awaited her choice, but with a heavy heart Alizon realized that whichever she reached for, the end would be the same: She could never leave the mount.

Her fortress had become her prison.

Chapter Twenty

The legs of the sofa made a hideous screeching as he dragged it across the terrace. It seemed to be protesting being born, and he could hardly blame it. It had to be the butt-ugliest sofa ever to grace the sight of man, uglier even than the furnishings to be found in a bachelor pad or a college student's apartment.

It was so ugly, so misshapen and queerly fashioned, it could almost qualify as a piece of art. "Modern Primitive Sofa," it might be called, and placed in the center of a white gallery floor.

Looks, however, were not the point. Comfort was. He had had enough of sitting on those hard, backless benches in the kitchen. He had cobbled this beauty together from cots, lumber from Milo, several lumpy mattresses, and rope to keep the mattresses in place and provide the illusion of cushions.

He dragged it through the doorway, bumping and scraping at the frame, and a moment later Alizon appeared in the archway to the kitchen, her mouth agape.

"Jesu mercy, what in the name of heaven is *that?*"

"A sofa, my darling. You'll love it."

"But what *is* it?"

She backed away as he dragged it through the arch, and then over to the central hearth. He dropped the end, then shoved the sofa into a better position, close enough to the hearth to be warm, and placed so that a sitter looked across the fire to the worktable.

He came and took her hand and pulled her over to his handiwork. "A sofa is a fine piece of furniture, meant for dozing upon when one should be working. It's a good place to read, or to sit and talk with friends. And," he said, sitting down and pulling her down beside him, then stretching his arm over the back and dangling his fingers down to her shoulder, "it's a favorite spot for young men and women. They spend hours and hours on sofas."

"Doing what?" she squeaked, leaning forward away from his hand, and still looking at the sofa as if it were a three-headed cow he had dragged into her kitchen.

"It never requires explanation. Sit back," he said,

gently pulling her shoulder, "and understanding will come to you."

She did as he bid, an inch of space between them as they sat side by side. Her hands were clasped in her lap, her knees together. Seconds trickled by, and he had the feeling she was waiting for something to happen, as if the sofa should give them a bouncing pony ride around the kitchen.

She leaned forward suddenly, and with a hand flipped her braid out from behind her, then as suddenly sat back again. She squirmed. She sat still. She glanced at him, and then forward again. She twitched her pointy nose, as if she had an itch.

Then, slowly, she let her head rest against the high sofa back, her hair lightly touching his arm. Her knees lost their magnetic grip on each other, and her hands fell open.

The sofa was working its magic.

Alizon felt her muscles relaxing, and as they did she seemed to sink more deeply into the bedraggled mattresses tied to George's *sofa*. The thing was an abomination to the eyes, but she had to admit that it felt wonderful beneath her. It was almost like being in bed.

The outside light was dying, the last hints of orange sunset turning gray upon the walls opposite the high western windows. George threw a few more logs on the fire, sending the flames flaring, their flickering the only light to be seen against the dark shadows of the kitchen.

He would probably get up soon to start fixing their supper, but she hoped he would wait for a bit yet. She liked the nearness of his giant's body, on this piece of furniture he had made for her. For *her*.

A wave of possessiveness washed through her, for George. She did want him for herself. She wanted his kindness and good humor, and his way of looking at her as if he never wanted to stop, and as if given the least sign he would drag her down to the floor and have his way with her.

She wanted his peculiar chivalry, that besides for having him promise women he did not know that he would slay a dragon, had him serving her food and finding chores to do to help her.

She wanted the way he talked to her, as if she was neither an underling nor a superior, but rather a friend he would trust, and whose thoughts he wished to know.

She had never known a man like this George, and she loved the feeling, however brief it would be, that there was nothing and no one on this earth but the fire, the sofa, herself, and him.

Would that it could last forever.

He was barefoot, wearing only his well-scrubbed hose and loose shirt, his damp hair free. He smelled of soap and fresh air, and she imagined she could sense warmth coming off his body—or perhaps she truly could. The hairs on the backs of her forearms were standing up, as if trying to feel his presence.

Would that she *could* leave with him, as she had

sworn to Greta she would not. Resentment against that promise stirred itself into her pleasure, the vow made all the more vexing for being of her own choice.

If she was going to deny herself any thought of a life beyond Devil's Mount with this man, then she would not deny herself anything with him while he was here.

She used her toes to slide off her own leather shoes and pulled her feet up beneath her, rearranging her skirts. Her knees pressed against his thigh, but he made no comment, gracing her with a glance and a wisp of a smile before closing his eyes and leaning his head against the sofa back.

His throat lay exposed, showing the ragged line past which his beard did not grow. The short beard had filled in during the week, and she was sure if she touched it that it would be more soft than coarse.

If she touched it.

She wanted to know what it would feel like, to touch her lips against his smooth ones, set amid such growth.

She rose up on her knees and leaned over him, her body hovering over his. When she looked down she could see the pulse in the hollow of his throat, and the rise and fall of her own breasts, so close to touching him. She brought her mouth close to his, near enough that she could feel the breath from his nose against her skin.

"Thank you for the sofa," she said softly. And she lowered her mouth to his.

He was motionless beneath her touch. She moved her lips over his, feeling their smooth texture and the prickling of his beard around the edges. She rested her hand on his chest for balance, and with the tip of her tongue traced the line where his lips met. They parted under the gentle pressure, and she rested her own parted lips against his, sharing his breath with her own.

She did not know what to do next. She began to pull back, feeling suddenly lost without his guidance, but he reached up and cupped the back of her skull with his hand, pressing her mouth again to his. His lips moved on hers, strong and sure, and she felt a jolt of excitement run through her.

His other arm came around her waist, pulling her down onto his lap where he could wrap her in his arms, caught, unable to escape. She let him, her own hands going up into the hair at the back of his head, gripping it as she held him to her.

Yes.

Yes, this was what she wanted. *Yes,* she would take everything she could from him. She would not be stopped this time.

She opened her mouth to the thrust of his tongue, feeling a power in being able to stir such a quick and strong reaction in him. She wanted him to lose all control; she wanted to arouse him to the point where he would be helpless beneath her hands and unstoppable in his quest to have her.

She let instinct and a lifetime of lonely fantasies guide her. She slid her lips away from his and down the grain of his beard, working her way to just beneath his ear with nips and kisses. She pressed her open mouth against his skin, in the place that was sensitive on her own body, and sucked, rubbing her tongue against the skin. He was salty and sweet, and she scraped her teeth down his neck, unable to get enough.

He groaned, and she took it as encouragement. She pulled up the hem of his shirt and kept tugging until he raised his arms and let her take it off. She threw it behind the sofa and stroked her palms over the smooth contours of his chest.

And got her palms tickled.

She pulled back, startled, and looked.

George touched his chest, himself. "Stubble."

"Marry!"

"Certain . . . ah, *fighters* like myself shave their chests, in my country."

She touched his chest again with her fingertips. The hairs were short enough to be bristly, but sparse enough not to scratch. She played her fingers across the skin there, lightly dragging them, then dawdling over his small flat nipples, so different and yet similar to her own.

She glanced at his face, not certain how he would take this casual examination. His green eyes met hers with the reflections of firelight upon them, and his look was as intense as flame.

Again, she felt that surge of power. His desire in

turn ignited her own, and she felt a heaviness full of tingling sensation in her groin. She bent down her head and ran her tongue over his nipple, then caught the tiny nub between her lips and played with it as he had done to her, on the kitchen floor.

She ran her hands down his sides, then back up the front of his chest, feeling his muscles contract and relax as she touched him. She left his nipple and traced a trail up to the base of his neck. She straddled his lap to give herself better balance, hiking her skirts so that her naked sex rested against the rigid bulge of his arousal.

His hands slid along the outside of her thighs, up under her skirt, and cupped her buttocks in his hands. He held half the span of her hips in his big hands, and when he pulled her against him in a slow grind she could do nothing but follow where he led.

She loved the feel of him moving her where he wished and wanted more. She wanted that ferocious passion of the day on the floor, when he had asked nothing and taken what he wanted.

She put her hands on his shoulders and rode him, looking down from under her lids to meet his gaze. She felt the ridge of him parting her, and she tilted her hips on the downstroke so that the most sensitive part of her ran his length.

He took his hands out of her skirts and reached behind her to tug at her laces. She cupped his face between her palms and kissed him, maintaining it as she felt his fingers work the cord at her back.

The wool parted, and he pulled the neckline of her gown down over her shoulders. She reached up to untie the fine cord at the neck of her chemise, so that it, too, could slide off her skin.

The fire was warm at her back, but it was nothing compared to the seductive heat when her breasts were bared and he broke their kiss to lower his mouth to them.

He pulled the leather thong from the end of her braid and worked his fingers through her hair, spreading it over her bare back in heavy waves. He pushed the gown down to her hips, then bent and rolled until she was lying under him on the sofa. He rose up and yanked the garment down off over her legs, tossing them to join his shirt somewhere on the floor.

He kissed his way down her belly, sliding off the sofa to kneel on the floor as he worked his way down. He took her knees in his hands and jerked her toward him, parting her legs.

For once she was not the one making a decision. There was a freedom to it she had never expected: It made her feel that her only duty was to enjoy what he gave her.

He bent down, slipping her legs over his shoulders. Her pleasure was shaken by a queer embarrassment, the intimate folds of her sex, that even she had never seen, so closely exposed to his view.

He gave her chance to neither ponder nor protest, giving her a slow, strong stroke with his tongue.

She arched off the sofa. "Holy Mother Mary!"

She thought she heard him chuckle, but couldn't be sure as he laved her again, and she ceased to care about anything but that he did not stop.

She felt the tip of his tongue dip into her core, pushing against those tight confines. She pushed her hips down, trying to increase that fluttering pressure, but he swirled away and traced the twin ridges of her valley, and she forgot whatever she had been yearning for before.

He suckled at the hooded junction of her folds, tongue working delicately at the hard pebble of pleasure within.

She felt his fingertip then, at the entrance to her. He gave it hardly any pressure—just enough for her to know it was there.

Just enough to drive her insane.

She wanted him inside her. His finger, his tongue, his penis—she would take what she could get. His tongue continued its work, but each intoxicating touch only drove her further into her desperation.

She could not stand it.

She curled away from him, taking her legs off his shoulders. He reached for her, but she rolled away on her knees on the floor beside him. She grabbed the waistband of his hose and pulled them down.

He froze for a moment, then helped her to disrobe him. His erection sprang free, long and thick, a nest of black hair at its base. She shoved his shoulders toward the sofa, and he took the hint, climbing up and under her continued pressure, lying back.

"Are you sure you know what you're doing?" he asked.

She ignored him, the very sight of his ready manhood sending a shudder of desire through her. She grasped it lightly in her hand and moved her palm up over the silken skin, then back down. Her fingertips barely touched each other around the base of it. Some inborn knowledge warned that he would stretch her beyond her ability to take, but the thought did nothing to dissuade her.

She wanted this. Twenty-six years, God's breath, it was time! And that erection was an invitation.

She mounted his body like a horse, his manhood pressed flat to his belly beneath her.

George propped himself up on his elbow. "Alizon, what—"

Her knees were on the sofa on either side of his hips, the width of his body forcing her to open wide and lay her wet folds against him. She bent forward and brushed her breasts against his chest. She licked him across the lips, then changed it to a kiss, pushing her tongue inside his mouth.

She did not know if what she was doing was right or was pleasurable to him; she only knew that she was doing what her body and its instincts demanded. His hands stroked her buttocks, the tips of his long fingers gliding over her sex.

It was more than she could bear. She pushed upright and reached beneath her until she held him again in her hand. She moved her hips and his erection until the head met her waiting dampness.

"Christ, Alizon," George gasped, lying back again and grasping her by the hips, holding her in place above him, as if he would keep her from sliding down on him. "You can't be ready yet."

"I've been waiting my entire life. I'm past ready." She wasn't going to let anything stop her this time. No more waiting!

"This isn't the best way—" His words were cut off by a groan as she eased the tip of him into her.

The head stretched her, pressing with blunt force, her tender flesh crushing beneath the pressure. The pleasure of his presence at her entrance turned quickly to pain, but she would not allow herself to stop. She set her jaw and eased herself down.

And went nowhere. She pushed harder, but only felt his manhood begin to angle off to the side.

She squirmed atop his unsunken shaft. His thick tip hurt her, but it frustrated her more with its partial entrance. This was becoming more a matter of stubborn determination than of pleasure.

"Alizon, wait," George said.

"No! I *will* do this!"

She reached beneath her and held his penis steady, trying again to impale herself upon it. She gained a finger-width's advance, and paid with scraping, pinching pain. A whimper escaped her throat as she again forced herself down.

"Stop it! Alizon, stop it!" George said, and his

hands gripped her waist, lifting her off him.

"No!" she cried, and fought him with her weight and the grip of her thighs on his hips. "I'm going to do this!"

"Get off me! I'm not going to let you hurt yourself like this. Christ, Alizon, you're not meant to be torn open with a battering ram!"

"I don't care."

"I do."

She gave a sob of frustration as his strength won out over hers, and he lifted her off, then pulled her down next to him, so that she was caught on her side, between him and the back of the sofa. He lay his leg over hers, forcing them together, and cupped her cheek in his hand as he kissed her tenderly on the forehead.

"Hush. You can't hurry this."

She turned her face into his chest, humiliated by the reminder of that long-ago day in the shed with Osbert. She could do nothing right with this deflowering. No one had ever wanted her, and now George, too, had shaken her off as if she were an oversexed cur having sex with his leg.

"We have all the time in the world," George said into her hair, his hand stroking down her shoulder and arm. "Let me take care of you."

"Why wouldn't it go in?" she sobbed, too embarrassed even to look at him.

"It's not just a maidenhead a virgin has to worry about. You're tight, your muscles down there need to be stretched. Gently. Some women are like that, more so than others."

"How do you know this?"

"Never mind how." She felt him kiss the top of her head. "You need to relax. You'll only tighten yourself up more if you try to take charge, and it won't be good for either of us. I don't want you forcing yourself down on me."

She felt the softening of his erection against her, and knew he didn't want her, just as Osbert had not, and just as no one in Markesew had. It was more humiliation than she could take, and she had to be away from him, and from the burning embarrassment.

In a burst of energy she beat the heels of her palms against his chest, punching him back. "Let me go!"

He leaned away, looking at her. "Alizon, what is it?"

"Devil take you, let me go!"

His hand gently gripped her shoulder. "What's wrong?"

She couldn't stand the confinement of being wedged between him and the sofa back, his leg still over hers. She thrashed and shoved, wanting only to escape from this humiliation where she was naked and unwanted.

He tried to hold her, tried to wrap her in his arms.

The threat of his physically subduing her with his strength put her into a frenzy; being under his control, a state that had been appealing just ten minutes past, was now unbearable.

She bit the nearest piece of flesh: his chest.

"Ow! Dammit!" he said, releasing her. "Alizon, what the hell?"

She scrambled up and climbed over the back of the sofa, grabbed her clothes off the floor, and without looking back dashed from the room.

She pulled at the log, sweat dripping down her forehead and her feet burning in the trickle of hot water at the bottom of the tunnel. Her chemise was tied up around her thighs, her gown left on the platform above. A torch wedged into the rocks gave her light, though her shadow obscured most of the dam George had built.

Belch seemed to be sleeping. Even if he had been awake, she would not have cared. She almost would have welcomed his killing her.

The log was not moving. She gripped a smaller piece of wood and wedged her feet against the opposite wall. She used all her strength and weight, waggling it back and forth, then crouched directly in front of the dam and pulled.

With a soggy scrape it came free, and she plopped onto her butt on the rock floor, the long stick in her hand. Hot water poured from the opening. She got back on her feet and yanked at the nearest logs.

A medium-sized one came free, and as she dragged it out of the dam and out the opening of the fissure, the other logs shifted, the ones nearest the hole she'd made beginning to slide forward on their own.

She dragged the wood the rest of the way out and let it fall to the pool below. Behind her, another log came halfway out, its end hitting the rock floor with a soft thud, water pouring over it. She went back and pulled it away, and then others, one after the next, until they covered the floor and there was nowhere for her boiled feet to stand.

The water flowed freely now, and the logs inched their way toward the opening. She scrambled on all fours on top of them, and crawled out the mouth, swinging to the side to the rope ladder. She plucked the torch from the rocks and hung there, watching, as first one and then two more logs came out, teetered on the brink, and then plunged over the edge.

She was mistress of the mount. She might be nothing else to anyone, wanted by no one, but she was, and always would be, that.

Chapter Twenty-one

George looked down at the water pouring from the spring and felt his mood drop another notch. Mist covered the pool, testament to the cozy temperature of the water. Belch lay on his beach, his inexpressive reptilian face still somehow managing to convey smug self-satisfaction.

Or perhaps that was just George's imagination.

Disappointing as it was to see that the dam had come apart in the night, he wasn't surprised. Nothing was going right, nothing at all.

He didn't know how he had messed things up last night. He had tried to find Alizon after she'd run off, but as always the castle doors were locked against him, and there was no answer when he shouted her name again and again. He had retreated to the garrison room, where he found to his horror the blood of her virginity on himself.

She had accomplished that much, at least, to her own agony and to his guilt—not guilt for having taken it, but for not having made the experience better for her.

Sleep wasn't to be his, and he had lain awake in helpless frustration, needing to hold and talk to her.

In his past experience, it was always the woman who wanted to stay and talk things out, and the man who ran away. He was getting an unwelcome taste of life on the other side. It was no wonder women got so pissed off at men, if this was what it left them feeling like.

He would give Alizon whatever it was she desired—if she would only tell him. *What* did she want? Things had seemed to be going so well between them.

She surely could not have wanted to deflower herself in such an abrupt and painful manner. And if she truly *had*, he should never have let her climb atop him. He should have paid attention to the part of his brain that said she couldn't be ready to take him yet, instead of the part that had felt her hot wetness easing down and had urged him to do whatever she wanted.

Damned if he did, damned if he didn't. To let her continue would have guaranteed even greater pain for her, but it was when he had thwarted her that she had gone nutso.

He couldn't win.

He pulled the rope ladder up through the trapdoor, looping it into a heavy coil. He'd like to tie Alizon up and make her sit and tell him what was going through that impenetrable head of hers. He wasn't a friggin' mind-reader, for God's sake.

He looked at the coil of rope over his arm, then over the rail again at Belch.

Old sheep-breath down there wouldn't be able to bite his head off if he had this ladder wrapped around his snout. Visions of "Crocodile Hunter" flashed through his mind, of that crazy Australian subduing giant crocodiles with a bit of rope, wits, and brawn.

He'd need more rope than this, but it might work. He had one try left, no better ideas, and with the Alizon affair presently in shambles, he had nothing else to do with his time than prepare for attempt number three.

What a lousy morning. The only good thing had been that Alizon had neglected to lock the kitchen against him, and forgotten as well to lock the doors down to the lair. She must be seriously upset to have left them all open.

He hefted the coil over his shoulder and headed back up the tunnel to the kitchen, still stewing uselessly over what he could have done differently the night before, and what might be going through Alizon's head.

Halfway up the stairs his steps slowed, then stopped. He had left the kitchen door the slightest bit ajar, and now through the crack he heard giggling and female voices.

Voices.

The hairs rose on the back of his neck, the white faces at the windows and that night with the wraiths coming back in bowel-loosening clarity. His heart thumped, a clammy sweat breaking out over his skin. For a long moment he stood frozen, too horror-stricken to move or think.

In the movies it was always a mistake to go check out the scary noise. The audience said, "No, no, no! Don't go!" while the brainless character crept up the stairs to the door, a baseball bat or other useless-against-the-dead weapon in his hand.

He understood now why the character *had* to go. To not go was worse.

He set down the coil of rope and lodged his torch in a wall bracket. Step by careful step he quietly made his way to the door.

The voices were still going, and the giggling, and he could hear now the creaking of wood and soft thumps. He heard dishes and utensils move, the sound sending a fresh wash of supernatural dread down his spine.

He pressed his eye to the crack but could see nothing.

This was one mystery that he would solve. Whether they were the ghosts of long-dead virgins or the spirits of all the romantic partners he might have unknowingly mistreated, he would face them.

Heart thundering, sweat glands in overdrive, he put his palms on the door and shoved it open, some impulse he did not understand making him shout "Boo!" as he did so.

Five young women screamed and scattered. A sixth was caught mid-jump on the sofa and missed her landing, falling with a thump onto her stomach on the cushion. She gaped at him as her comrades fled out the kitchen archway.

He gaped at her right back. She couldn't have been more than twelve or thirteen, and had black hair cut in a very modern, hip, ragged explosion of tresses. Her garb, though, was thoroughly medieval.

And she was thoroughly human.

She regained her wits before he did, and rolled off the sofa onto her feet. She dipped into a deep curtsy. "Saint George, I am pleased to meet you. I am Pippa."

He made a noise in the back of his throat.

She peered at him, delight in her eyes, a mischievous smile on her lips. "Did you make this thing?" she asked, gesturing to the sofa. "It is wonderful fun."

"Who . . . ?" he managed.

"Pippa. Pih-pah." She tilted her head toward the archway. "Those were Joye, Kit, Malkyn, Braya, and Ysmay. We didn't know you were down there. Mistress will be very upset that you have seen us, but *I'm* glad. We were so tired of only watching and never getting to talk to you!"

"How many . . . ?"

"Of us? Including mistress, twelve."

"Where . . . ?"

She skipped across the floor to him and grabbed his hand. "Come, come!"

He let her pull him out through the archway and across the corridor. She gave a series of raps to the double doors, and he heard a bar being drawn back.

"Is he gone—" someone started to say, and then there was a yelp, and the door started to close.

"No, no, it's all right!" Pippa cried, and shoved the door back open.

He followed her into a great hall that was nothing as he had imagined.

There were the women, for one thing. With Pippa there were eleven of them, staring at him with big eyes, their ages ranging from Pippa's to the mid-twenties. They were wearing gowns in rich colors, their hair—except Pippa's—in thick braids down their backs or looped beside their ears, ribbons woven through.

One of the women had a harelip, and one looked like she had been badly beaten long ago, and the damage never repaired.

"Who are you?" he asked them.

The answer came to him before anyone had a chance to explain. With Alizon, there were twelve. It had been twelve years since she had gone to the dragon.

She had never sent the virgins to start new lives in a town up the coast. They had been here, locked away in this castle, like lost princesses in a fairy tale.

Then he noticed the tapestries on their frames, a half-dozen of them in various stages of completion, silver mirrors on the walls behind them. Did the women weave all day, seeing shadows of the world in their mirrors, like a dozen ladies of Shalott?

"This is Joye," Pippa said, dragging him to the first young woman. She was a pretty girl, with big breasts and a dimple in her cheek when she smiled a flirtatious greeting.

He barely noticed.

"This is Braya, and Ysmay. She is Sisse, that's Reyne, then there's Greta over there, Lavena, Kit, Malkyn, and this little one here is Flur."

The "little one" looked eleven or twelve, with a fairy's petite build and fine, flyaway blond hair. She gazed up at him with big blue eyes. "Are you going to kill the dragon? I miss my mama and want to go home."

"Flur!" one of the women scolded. She was a broad-boned woman with a rough voice.

Flur's little jaw set in a stubborn line, and she turned on the woman. "I don't care what any of you say, I want to go home. I. Want. To. Go. Home!"

"You can't, and you know it, so hush!" the woman said.

George did not want to believe that anyone could have sent that little girl to die in Belch's jaws. He imagined Gabby being torn away from Athena and sent to a similar fate, and it became harder still to fathom it.

His eyes went to the woman with the battered face. He remembered Alizon's story, about the girl who had tried to go home. This must be she.

The woman turned slightly, so that the less-damaged side of her face was toward him.

There was no question that Alizon had saved eleven lives, and provided well for them, but at what cost? Eleven women, locked away weaving, never to leave this tiny island. Never to marry or raise children. Never again to see their families or friends.

"Why?" he asked through his confusion. "Why are you all here?"

They looked at one another. The buxom one named Joye answered with a shrug. "We have no-where else. They tried to kill us once in Markesew and would do so again."

"Why have you not gone to some farther town, where no one knows you?"

She shuddered, and there was a whisper of distress through the room. "Go where, and do what?"

"Work. Marry. Anything."

"We work here," the rough-voiced woman said. "Come, look!"

"Yes, look!" Pippa said, and grabbing his hand again pulled him over to the nearest tapestry frame.

The two women who had been working on it, blushing, explained to him how the picture of women in a garden would look when finished. They were timid in their description, but there was also a certain pride in their voices.

And there was reason for it.

He had seen machine-woven tapestries once or twice, hanging in hotel lobbies or on the walls of a friend's house, but he had never seen anything like this. He leaned closer and closer to the finished portion of the hanging, astonished by the detail and the fine gradations of color.

Pippa tugged his hand. "You are looking at it from the wrong side. We work from this side, which is why we need the mirrors."

He looked questioningly at the women, and one of them pulled the frame away from the wall at one end. He peered around at the other side, and his breath stopped. What had been lovely on the back side was heartbreakingly beautiful on the front, the vibrantly colored threads blending into a smooth surface that from a short distance away would have looked like an oil painting. He had never known that it was possible to do work like this with strands of wool.

"Mistress taught us," one of the women said modestly, seeing his amazement. "Like any girl, I knew how to spin when I came here, but that was all."

"Surely you could ply your trade elsewhere in England, now that you have learned it?"

"I could not leave my sisters," she said.

He turned to the group. "You could all go. Together. Find a town far from the dragon and set up shop."

Furtive glances were exchanged, and weight shifted from foot to foot. No one spoke.

"Come, look at the other tapestries," Pippa said, and dragged him onward.

He knew she was trying to distract him, but from exactly what he did not know. Why didn't they want to leave?

Or was it that they couldn't for some reason he didn't yet understand? It was like the unknown curse upon the Lady of Shalott, keeping her caught within her tower.

The other tapestries were as remarkable as the first, but it was the last one Pippa brought him to that sent a quiver of eerie recognition through him. Déjà vu made the hairs stand up on the back of his neck, yet he had the paradoxical certainty that he had never seen this exact image before.

It was of St. George, killing the dragon with a spear. And in it, *he* was unmistakably the saint. Alizon stood some distance behind, gowned in pink and ermine, her curling red hair flowing over her shoulders. The virgins were crowded together, looking eagerly over the parapets of a castle in the background.

"This is Mistress's," Pippa said.

"When did she start it?" he asked, barely finding his voice. He stared at his face done in wool. The features weren't exact replicas of his own, and yet something in the cast of the countenance captured the essence of who he was.

"Many months past."

Long before he himself had arrived on Devil's Mount. Long before Alizon had ever seen him. It was an impossibility easily enough explained if he still wanted to tell himself that this was all happening in his head.

But he couldn't.

He looked again at the figure of Alizon, her dark eyes intently focused upon the battle waged beneath her. Mysterious, brave Alizon, who was so fiercely protective of her hidden virgins and of her own fragile heart.

A dragon, he could have dreamed up. A castle. Bad food and old armor. Even Milo, he could have dreamed up. But not eleven virgins and a hall full of tapestries.

Not Alizon, with her contradictions and complexities.

And not the aching feeling for her that was spreading through his chest, of mingled respect and pity, admiration and frustrated adoration. What he felt was real.

Alizon was real. She *had* to be.

He thought he should be shocked at such a realization, but he wasn't. It was as if he and Alizon had a bond that transcended time, and he had been waiting all his life to come here and find her. Part of him had started believing in the reality of this world as soon as he'd crossed the causeway to Devil's Mount, but he hadn't had the nerve to face it.

He touched his fingertips to the woven dragon, the black and green scales undulating with evil. This dragon had devoured helpless innocents and had kept the virgins locked away from normal life. It had to be destroyed, and it was his job to do it and to do it right. There could be no more goofing around, taking the task only as seriously as a video game.

If there was any chance a man had to prove himself worthy of a woman's love, this was it.

Pippa saw his intense interest in the tapestry and leaned closer, examining it. "Marry! It is *you!*" She turned to the others who hovered nearby. "Look! Look! It is the saint! Mistress knew he was coming. It is a miracle! He truly *is* Saint George!"

George stepped back as they crowded around, exclamations of "Marry!" and "Jesu mercy!" whispered between them. The glances they gave him were even more shy than before—almost shamefaced. Cheeks turned pink with embarrassment. It was like being surrounded by teen fans.

Pippa met his eyes for a moment, then glanced away.

Joye, her face a deep scarlet, curtseyed before him. "We are sorry for spying on you. We should never have done such a thing to a saint."

"I am not truly a saint," he said. "And there was no harm done." What had they seen, anyway? Just him walking around, or talking to Alizon.

Then he remembered his baths out on the terrace, and Alizon's frequent suggestions that he wash in the kitchen, instead. He felt heat suffuse his own cheeks.

"Mistress told us you were merely a man, and we believed her," Joye said. "But such cannot be true."

George almost contradicted her again, but then thought of the baths yet to be taken, and remembered the dream of lying naked while spirits wailed around him. Spirits? Virgins, gawking while he lay ill and helpless!

Better that they think him a saint, if it would preserve his privacy. He was suddenly feeling uncomfortable around these "innocent" young women.

He was, as well, beginning to feel a stirring of anger that Alizon had been willing to sleep with him, but had not shared such an enormous secret with him as the presence of these virgins. What was he, just a piece of meat to be used and enjoyed?

Alizon was going to have to give up the secrets of her heart to him before she had any more of his body, and that was a promise from the Saint.

"Where *is* your mistress, anyway?" he asked.

Alizon stirred, coming half awake. A feeling that there were things she did not want to remember nudged her back toward sleep, the same as it had several times already this morning.

A noise beside her bed dragged her fully awake. She forced open her eyes a slit, then widened them completely.

George was sitting on a stool, watching her.

She gripped her sheet and pulled it tight against her neck in maidenly surprise. "What are you doing here? How did you get in?"

"Pippa led the way, but Joye and Braya seemed equally eager to show me where to find you. Greta, I'm not so sure about, nor the others, except Flur. She's a darling girl, is your Flur. It's a pity she will spend her youth locked away in this castle, weaving tapestries."

"Jesu mercy . . ." she whispered, and felt her world crumbling down around her.

"Yes, pray for mercy, but you'd be better to ask it from me rather than Jesus." He looked away for a moment, breathing deeply as if to control his anger, then met her eyes. "Why the hell couldn't you be honest with me?"

Which lies did he want explained? There were so many, and the most important yet to be discovered. "Will you hand me my chemise?" She tried to sound unruffled, and as condescending as a true mistress of the mount. "I would rather be dressed if you are going to question me like a naughty child."

"And let you run away and hide again? I don't think so. I like you right where I can see you, with no door you can lock between us."

"It hardly seems fair for you to scold me while I cannot so much as sit up," she stalled. She was aware of her naked body beneath the sheet and blankets, stretched out and vulnerable.

"*Fair* is not a concept that seems to concern you overmuch."

Had he guessed about the false sleeping powder for Belch? Had he seen the broken dam? She had yet to see him lose his temper, but if he did, she would have no defense against someone of his size.

Her fear, instead of making her cower, pricked her ire. "What would you know of fairness? You know nothing of what we have all been through, and what we have had to do to survive."

She sat up, holding the covers over her chest, freeing one arm to gesticulate. "You cannot come tramping onto my mount and tell me what is best for myself or my virgins. You know nothing of what the world out there is like for women. You, with your strange clothes and ways, who can walk into a country without even a sword and know yourself safe because you are a man and are physically strong."

"If I know nothing, then tell me. Tell me, Alizon, why you had to lie to me about the virgins living here, and not on the mainland. What were you afraid I might do?"

She stared at him.

"What? What did you think? That I might throw them to the dragon?"

"No."

"That I might try to take them to my bed?"

"No! And not that I would care if you did."

"Liar."

She tightened her lips. She could not very well

deny the accusation, not when he had caught her in so many other lies.

"Tell me. Why?"

She wrapped her arms over her chest, staring at him, lips still tight together.

He stared back.

"I was . . ." she started, then stopped herself. She did not have to tell him anything! Interloper! Foreigner! He would be gone soon enough.

"Tell me," he said softly.

She felt the corners of her mouth draw down, and she clenched her jaw against the emotion. He was still staring at her, green eyes withholding judgment. When she told him, though, then what might she see in those eyes? How could he ever understand?

It came home to her then how much she wanted his approval. His respect, even. She wanted him to keep looking at her with interest and affection. She did not know if she could bear it if he turned away from her after having drawn so close.

Or would all people forever turn away from her when they got close enough to see her fully? All but the virgins, who could not leave, who needed her.

Let him show his true colors. "I was afraid that if you knew they were here, you would try to take them back to Markesew."

"Damn right I would!"

She reached for him, grabbing his arm, not caring that her shoulders and half her breasts were exposed. "You cannot!"

287

"The villagers can hardly throw them back to Belch when it's so clear that he doesn't need virgin flesh to be controlled. There is no reason for them to remain here locked away from a normal life."

"You do not know them as I do! They do not listen to reason. Look what they did to Reyne, and that several weeks after she was to have gone to Belch."

"She was just one virgin. Twelve of you, coming back, would be proof enough for anyone."

She shook her head. "Not for them. I will not take that chance."

"Is it your decision to make?"

"It is not yours!"

He clasped her hand in his. "It is neither of ours. You've done a great thing here, Alizon, saving those girls from horrible deaths, but you've taken it too far. They're old enough to decide for themselves whether they should stay or go."

"They will not leave. They know what would await them."

"You've been locked up together here for too long, with nothing but your fears to guide you. Of course no one would venture out if every time someone brought up the idea, Reyne was held up as an example of what would happen to her."

She tugged her hand out of his. "We would not wish to go back, even if we could."

"I don't believe that. Maybe some of you are happy here, but little Flur isn't. She misses her mother. How can you keep her here, knowing that?"

"It is for her own safety."

He shook his head. "Alizon, don't you see? None of this secrecy is necessary. Whether Belch lives or dies, the virgins can leave. And if they're afraid to go to Markesew, they can at least go together to a different town. You've taught them a trade that they can use to support themselves."

"They may be able to support themselves, but how will they protect themselves?"

"I can do that, until they settle. The least I can do is give those women a chance at a normal life, by acting as their guardian as long as they need me."

So he would leave, and take everyone she cared about with him.

"You could come, as well," he said. "You don't need to stay here."

"Who else would feed Belch? Who else would wait here for the yearly sacrifice? If the dragon yet lives, I cannot leave."

"He won't live. I'm going to kill him."

"And if you don't? You'll take everyone away?" It came out more plaintive than she had wanted.

He looked at her for a long, hard moment, and then he spoke in soft amazement. "You don't want them to go. You want to keep them here, whether or not there's any danger. You would have them grow old, virgins still, weaving their tapestries and never seeing the outside world again. My God, Alizon, don't you see what you're doing to them?"

"I only see that you are bent on destroying the one safe home we have had!"

"It's a prison, and you are the jailer."

"I saved them."

"You did, but for what? To be your pets? To be slaves in your tapestry workshop? You have to set them free, and let them live their own lives."

"They need me."

"They needed you. Give them the chance to find their own way and they'll grow strong. You weaken them by keeping them within these walls. You steal their lives from them as surely as if they had gone to the dragon."

His words pierced her heart. She did not want to listen to him, did not want to believe what he said, but there was an answering tremor in her heart that said he had struck the chord of truth.

"Take them, then," she said, as if she did not care.

But she did, and the pain of it lodged in her throat. She struggled to keep it hidden there, her jaw tight, her eyes stinging.

St. George had come to the mount and destroyed her world. She wanted to hate him, but her sense of justice would not let her do even that. He was right about the virgins.

Ah, Jesu mercy, she had lost everything. Everything. And she could not even fight against it.

He bent down and started untying his boots.

"What are you doing?"

He pulled off the left one.

"Do not think you are getting into this bed!" She scooted back a couple of feet, to the middle of the enormous mattress. She might not hate him, but neither was she feeling amorous. The disaster of the night before drifted unhappily back into her mind, and a flush of embarrassment heated her cheeks. Her stomach fluttered as she remembered both pleasure and pain, and felt their echoes in her body.

He pulled off his right boot, and lifted the covers and slid into her bed. Before she could say one thing or another, he reached over with his long arms and dragged her down beside him, her naked body pressing up against his clothed one.

"Alizon, Alizon," he said, pressing his lips to the top of her head, his hand stroking down her back in that way he had that she could not resist. "I don't know that I've ever met anyone as stubborn and as brave as you."

Brave? She did not know what was brave about letting him take everything away from her.

"You face so much that others never could."

She did not know what he meant. It seemed to her now that she had spent years avoiding facing the people of Markesew, as well as the truth deep in her heart that the virgins should be given their own choice of where to live. She wouldn't think about such uncomfortable thoughts now, though. It hurt too much.

She stretched her arm over his chest, her breasts flattening against him. The warmth of his big body and the solid presence of it beside her was strangely soothing. His hands on her moved with tenderness, but she could detect no sexual intent.

She reminded herself that he did not want her that way anymore, after she had botched their coupling last night. Tears of self-pity started in her eyes.

He massaged the small of her back, and she fought between a sudden impulse to push him away, and wanting to accept the undemanding comfort he offered. His hand on her back won out, and she sniffed back her tears and let herself relax against him.

He was assaulting her with kindness, and once again she had nothing against which to fight. She was helpless in the face of it, as she never was against an attacking foe.

She knew she would be sorry for her capitulation when he left the mount; that her heart would ache the more for these moments together. She decided not to think about that, either.

"I should have been sleeping here all along," he said, and she felt a rush of warmth and hugged him. Yes, he should have, with his arms wrapped around her, their two bodies safe together from the world beyond the walls of the fortress. "This mattress is much more my size."

She could have bitten him.

Chapter Twenty-two

"So what I'll do is catch the end of his jaw in this loop, and then with a bit of luck Belch will start to thrash and roll, and he'll wind the rope around his own jaw, tying it shut."

"Then you'll take the spear and run him through the heart!" Pippa enthused, and feinted with the weapon.

"Right. And it will be good-bye, dragon."

"Awesome!" Pippa said, using the new word George had taught her.

Alizon stood with her arms over her chest, feeling uncomfortably like an outsider in her own kitchen. Six virgins were packed together on the sofa watching the antics of George and Pippa, while Joye was sitting at the table fluttering her eyelashes and offering food or drink. The others, including Braya, shyly drifted around the edges of the group, and yet had small, excited smiles on their lips.

It was appalling, the difference in behavior that the presence of a man could bring. Hair was tossed and touched with unseemly frequency, voices became higher and temperaments decidedly sweeter. It was nauseating.

The day since George had discovered the virgins had been filled with near-constant giggles and talk, the only moments of quiet uncertainty coming when Alizon herself had announced George's offer to take away anyone who wanted to leave the mount, and act as their guardian until they settled in a town and set up shop. No one had immediately asked to go, but neither had anyone insisted they would not.

It left her feeling both hurt and ashamed to see in their faces the indecision. She could tell from the glances they sent her that they worried how she would react if they chose to return to the mainland. How much *had* she been imposing her will, listening only to her own desires at the expense of theirs?

George's presence lit them like candles. They shone where most days would have found them dully going about their business. It was hard to admit, but most of them probably would be happier if given the chance to marry and live in the outside world.

Such could never be her fate, though. She had been at the mount too long, her life too intertwined with it. And there were yet girls to be saved, if

George failed again in his quest to kill Belch.

Greta came and stood beside her, and slipped her hand into Alizon's. "I do not want to go back," she said.

Alizon squeezed her hand. "You will not be made to. I will stay here, as I always have."

Always, safe and alone within her fortress.

"You're sure that lock will hold?" George asked.

"She is just a girl."

"Mmm. Is that supposed to reassure me?"

Pippa had begged to be allowed to watch his final fight with Belch, but both he and Alizon had, in one firm voice, refused. He didn't want there to be even a chance that the wild-haired girl would see him chewed up. No one needed a sight like that in their memory.

And, too, he was afraid she might come down into the lair proper and try to help him in his battle. From what Alizon had told him, the girl seemed a right little hellion, a medieval Huck Finn.

George shifted the coils of rope over his shoulder. He carried several long lassos and plain lengths of rope, and was counting on his memories of the techniques used on the show "Crocodile Hunter" to help him subdue Belch. He wore his white surcoat for good luck.

They tramped down the now-familiar tunnel to the platform, and he wished he had his entrance music playing. He needed something to hype him up. Now that he knew the dragon was real, all the fun had gone out of fighting it. This was no longer a game, where he could reset and start over. It was no longer something he was doing to feel better about himself or his career. It was, now, something that must be done for others, and something that had real consequences.

Belch *had* to be killed—for the sake of Emoni, for the virgins, and most of all, for the sake of Alizon. She would never let herself leave this island if Belch still lived.

From where he stood now, George's depression over the negative publicity in his "real" life looked silly and self-absorbed. There were more important things to worry about than if someone called him names: important things like taking care of the people who needed him. Important things like taking care of the one he loved.

He loved her. They walked out onto the platform, and he met Alizon's dark eyes, the realization taking him by surprise. Honest to God, heart and soul, he loved her. How the hell had that happened?

She was ornery and stubborn, and defensive past reason. She was secretive and controlling. He had to be crazy to be in love with her.

Crazy, or a saint.

Or maybe she wasn't those things, and instead was strong-willed and determined, with a tender heart in need of protection. She knew how to keep a secret when others depended on her, and was a natural leader. He would be crazy *not* to love her.

He supposed the reasons why didn't matter, only that love her he did. He would free her from this castle, and then . . .

And then what? Live the rest of his life in the middle ages? Try, somehow, to take her back with him to the future?

He'd have to wait to figure that out. First things first: kill the dragon.

And get a kiss for good luck.

He leaned his spear against the wall, took her face between his hands, and before she could say *aye* or *nay* kissed her long and hard. She swayed when he released her, her eyes half-closed.

"I'll be expecting more of that when I'm done," he said.

"Will you?" She sounded both amazed and hopeful.

"Damn right. We have some serious unfinished business between us, Mistress Alizon."

A soft smile touched her lips. "Such pleasures will give me something to remember you by when you are gone."

Was that a joke? He chuckled uncertainly, then picked up his spear. First things first.

She touched his arm. "Take care."

He put his hand behind her neck and pulled her close once more, kissing her first on the forehead and then again on the mouth. "I will."

He took a deep breath, squared his shoulders, then started down the stairs.

This sucked. This really sucked. He'd liked fighting the dragon much better when it was imaginary.

He tensed his jaw against the fear, shoving it away into a corner of his brain, and called up every ounce of grit and determination he had. *Third time's a charm*, he told himself. *Fake it 'til you make it.*

It was time to make it.

Belch was lying in his usual place on the beach, yellow eyes open and watching as George descended. "Yeah, you'd better watch me, wormgut," he muttered, getting into the fighting mood. "Sorry-ass piece of lizard poop. Breathing blob of genetic misengineering. Yeah, how do you like that one, reptile-brain?"

Belch made a gurgling growl, like a giant garbage disposal full of water. The deep sound flipped switches of mammalian alarm in George's body.

"You can scare me, but you can't eat me." He was on the bottom step, and he jumped onto the beach.

Belch swung his head and snapped. The side of his jaw hit George and batted him into the water, making him drop his spear, the ropes uncoiling off his shoulder as a loop caught on one of Belch's teeth.

He surfaced thrashing and sputtering, trying to clear his eyes in time to see the beast bearing down on him. Alizon was screaming, the sound disorienting. He swiped water from his eyes and saw instead that Belch was lying with his head down and that smug, fixed grin on his green leather snout.

One of the ropes trailed out of his mouth like a piece of brown dental floss.

Alizon's screams cut off as George sat up in the shallows, and Belch showed no sign of doing anything more than reclining and gurgling, as if in amusement.

Something bumped against George, and he flinched, then looked down to see, of all things, his long-lost pitchfork floating beside him.

No wonder Belch was laughing.

He picked it up, found his footing, and slowly moved out of the water.

Belch opened his mouth as he approached, and hissed at him on a breath of cold, foul air. George saw that one of his lassos was caught firmly around a lower tooth. The stupid dragon had no idea.

He carefully bent down and picked up the end of that rope. What he needed to do now was to get Belch to roll, and twist this line around the beast's jaws like spaghetti on a fork.

In his first battle, it had been standing on the dragon's back and poking him with the sword that had set off the bout of rolling. George could see the gash where his sword had cut the huge lizard—it was an area of white and pink that looked already to be healing over.

Thinking, he took aim, then threw the pitchfork javelin-style at the raw patch on Belch's neck. It hit and stuck for a moment, then fell away, leaving twin puncture wounds.

Belch lunged.

George danced aside, taking his rope with him, and with a quick flip of his wrist pulled its length under Belch's jaw. As the dragon swung his head at him again, he dashed back in the other direction, this time bringing the rope over the teeth of the beast's lower jaw.

Belch shook his head, and George clung to the end of his line, feeling like he had hold of a bucking bull.

Roll, dammit, roll! he silently urged.

The rope snapped, halfway between George and the dragon.

"Shit!"

He dashed behind Belch, leaping over the lashing tail to the other side where his other ropes had dropped. Belch swung his head back and forth, looking for him.

George grabbed his second lasso and turned to face Belch head-on.

The dragon's lowered snout made a ramp up to the top of his head.

What the hell.

Before he could think better of it, George charged the dragon, putting foot to snout and then running up the lumpy slope until he was right between Belch's eyes.

He turned around and dropped onto his butt, straddling the dragon's head as if it were indeed a bull he was riding. Belch slowly opened his mouth, and George's seat began to rise.

He sent a prayer heavenward, swung the lasso

around his head, then tossed it the short distance to the end of Belch's snout.

The loop fell perfectly over the end. Almost not believing his good luck, George yanked on the rope, tightening it.

Belch decided it was time to fight, and tossed his head. George clung for several bucks, then his thighs lost their grip on the beast's snout, and he was thrown off.

He still had the rope in his hands, though, and he was jerked up and down, back and forth, like a rubber ball against a paddle board. With a quick snap of his head, Belch flung him off.

He hit the beach, hard, and took it on his back the way he had learned in the ring, distributing the force of his fall to avoid injury. Belch threw himself forward and George rolled, but not fast enough. Belch's claw landed atop his ankle, pinning George in place, the pressure of that one dragon toe over his bones nearly enough to snap them.

His pitchfork was out of reach. He had nothing but his bare hands with which to defend himself. He heard Alizon shouting, calling Belch's name, trying to distract the dragon. Belch paid her no mind, his cold eye focused on George, watching him with the same detachment as a child with a pinned insect.

Belch lowered his snout, sniffing at him. George kicked at the beast's nose, his foot bouncing off with no effect. He reached wildly around him, hoping against hope for a loose rock, a stick, anything.

And then there was the flash of a green gown to the side, and all of a sudden Belch was bellowing, the tip of a spear jammed into his nostril. His claw came off George's foot, and George jumped to his feet even as Alizon dashed back to the semi-safety of the stone stairs.

There was no time to thank her. He jumped for the dangling rope, caught it, then swung forward and kicked the spear.

Belch rolled, the spear coming free of his nostril with a gush of blood.

George hit the ground, then swung around into a sitting position, bracing his feet against a bump of stone as he played out the rope, keeping it taut as the dragon rolled again and again, each turn wrapping the line another time around his jaws, tying them shut.

Just as all the slack was used up and George started to be dragged toward the thrashing beast, Belch stopped his rolling and lay still.

George tentatively stood and approached.

The lizard's yellow eye was baleful, but Belch did not move.

Cautious, George came near enough to touch. Belch thrashed, the tip of his tail coming around and knocking him down. George rolled away and jerked his surcoat off over his head. Before Belch could strike again, he found his feet and in three bounds was vaulting onto the dragon's snout. He threw the white silk over Belch's eyes, and held it there until the dragon's thrashing halted and its head lowered to the ground.

He stayed there for a long moment, not trusting Belch, then carefully dismounted and tied off the end of the dragon's rope muzzle. On the nature shows, blindfolding a crocodile always took the fight out of it.

The dragon lay still, his sides heaving.

Holy cow. Had he done it?

George grabbed more rope, and in the interest of safety over sorrow quickly tied Belch's legs, jerking the beast's elbows back behind it as if it were a criminal.

He still couldn't believe he had succeeded.

He fetched his fallen spear, then came back for the killing blow that must be dealt. Right through the heart, as Pippa had said.

He got a good grip on the spear and trained his eyes on the patch of scaly hide that was his target. And again, he felt a hesitation at killing the beast.

To let it live, though, would be to keep Alizon imprisoned in this fortress. Belch had killed and eaten dozens of people, and, given the chance, would do so again. Grisly and unpleasant as the task was, the dragon must be destroyed.

And then, from halfway up the stairs, came Alizon's voice. "George, no. . . ." The sound of the quiet plea carried across the cavern.

He paused, spear raised and ready. He looked up at her, for the first time since the battle had begun. "No?" He could not have understood.

"Don't kill him."

He frowned up at her, glanced at the lizard lying trussed before him, then frowned more deeply as he looked back to her. "Why the hell not?"

"I . . . will have nothing left."

He set the butt of his spear on the ground. "What are you talking about? It's the damn dragon that has taken everything away."

"No," she said, her voice still soft. "You're the one who is going to do that."

"What?"

"You're going to take the virgins away with you. There will be nothing left for me but Belch."

What the hell was she talking about? She couldn't mean that. "But he is the source of all your misery," he said, incredulous.

Her answer came in a voice whose softness had been replaced with a cold edge. "He is the instrument of my revenge."

What? "Against whom? Surely not against whatever poor girl they plan to send here in a week."

"Against the people of Markesew. They do not deserve to live free of fear. They do not deserve to keep their flocks of sheep. They must be made to pay for their crimes, and Belch exacts that justice."

George looked again at the immobilized dragon, trying and failing to understand her warped viewpoint. "Have you *never* wanted him dead?"

She didn't answer for a long moment, and then, quietly, "No."

He looked at the broken rope that hung off of

Belch's lower jaw. A gut-sinking suspicion formed. "The ropes. You weakened them." He looked up at her, anguish in his heart. After they had been growing so close, to have her do such a thing—

"I did nothing this time! I could not bear to. I could not risk your getting hurt! Didn't I save you, when Belch had you pinned?"

"*This* time?" He suddenly thought of his dam, which he had left so secure in the mouth of the spring, and the doors he had found unlocked the next morning. And then there had been the "sleeping powder" that had done little to sedate Belch. "That blue powder . . ."

"Dyed flour," she admitted softly.

His heart twisted with pain. "Alizon . . . why?"

She held her hands apart, her palms open and empty. She was a cold and distant angel, looking down upon him from the stairs, but her voice cracked when she spoke. "This mount is all I have."

He let go of his spear, and it fell to rest against the side of Belch's head. He plopped down on the beach, elbows resting on his knees, and dug his hands into his hair, staring at nothing.

She had never wanted the dragon killed. She had never been the helpless virgin, awaiting rescue. She wanted the damned dragon alive, to wreak vengeance on the town that had thrown her away.

What was he doing here? What the hell was the point of being St. George, and killing the dragon, if the damned virgin wanted it alive?

He dropped his hands from his head and looked

up at her. She looked frightened now, although of his reaction or from the threat to her lizard, he couldn't say.

All he did know was something that contradicted every reason for which he had originally thought he was sent here. Something he said now: "He isn't my dragon to kill." He stood up, and without a glance at Belch went to the stairs and started to climb out of the cavern.

"What are you doing?"

"He's not my dragon to kill," he repeated, still climbing.

"You're not going to slay him? I thought that was what you came here for!"

"I thought so, too."

"But—"

"Doing so won't make me a hero, at least not in your eyes." He laughed, dry and short. "That's what I wanted: to be a hero. Kill the dragon! Rescue the virgins! Be the biggest name, the best fighter! Be a hero, and everyone will love you." He paused beneath her on the stairs and shook his head at his own folly. "I had it all wrong. I thought heroism was something I could seek out and then grant to myself, but that's not what it's about. It's about putting other people first, about using your life to better theirs. I'll help the virgins leave the mount and settle elsewhere, but if you don't want the dragon killed, I'm not going to kill it."

"You can't just leave him tied up like that!"

"He's your dragon. You do with him what you want."

"He'll kill me if I go down there and untie him."

"It's your choice, Alizon. It's always been your choice. The dragon has always been under your control. Do what you will. Stay here with Belch or exchange Devil's Mount for a new life. Kill the dragon, or let him live. It is all your choice."

"It is not so simple!"

"It is. You created this world on the mount, for yourself and for the others. You can create a different one. You just have to want to."

"I've always wanted that."

"No, you've wanted revenge, and to hide. You would rather lock yourself away, alone here with a dragon, than take a chance on living in the world, with all its risks to the heart. You've been a coward in everything that matters."

"What is it that matters, if not keeping eleven young women alive?"

"Love matters. Above all, love." He closed the distance between them, and stood on the stair beneath hers. "Love, Alizon. As I love you."

She was silent, her face a pale mask of shock, her lips parted.

"I can't make you love me. I can't make you choose me over that damn dragon. I saw the longing in that tapestry you were weaving. Now I understand it. Everything you ever wanted is waiting, if you just have the courage to take it. If you have the courage to give up your hatred of those villagers—villagers you haven't seen in a dozen years, for God's sake—and the courage to build a new world for yourself, with me."

"I don't know how," she whispered.

"You do know; it just takes more guts than dumping a sheep to Belch ever did. I'm not going to force you to come out from behind your walls. Come of your own free will or don't come at all."

She stared at him, mute once more, and gave no answer.

He shook his head and stepped past her, continuing up the stairs and feigning an indifference that was a hundred miles and a thousand years from the pain that was crushing his heart.

Chapter Twenty-three

Alizon sat on the middle cold stone stairs of the staircase and stared down at Belch. It wasn't the dragon she was seeing in her mind, though, but George, telling her he loved her. Telling her that she could have a life with him, if only she were brave enough.

Was she?

She had been too shocked to respond when he confessed his feelings. She had never suspected them, had never thought that what she had felt growing in her own heart might be returned by his. She had not believed it was possible, knowing inside how unlovable she was. How like the dragon.

George was different, and she could not understand him. How could it be that he could love her?

Even after hearing that she had sabotaged his efforts to kill Belch, he had said he loved her. He had not abandoned her after she had put his life at risk and secretly fought against everything he tried to accomplish. She had betrayed his trust, and still he could love her.

He loved her, despite being put through more than anyone should be asked to endure.

He loved her.

And she loved him. That gave her all the courage she needed.

She stood and descended the stairs into the lair. Belch was making his gurgling sound, the noise ominous in the quiet of the cavern. The mist drifted off the water and up the bank of the beach, then was blown back again in swirls by the breath of his nostrils.

Alizon trailed one hand along the stone wall to keep her balance on the slick stones. They were steeper than they had looked from the platform, and she wondered at George's easy agility on them.

She wondered at George, who might or might not truly be a saint. Against her every expectation he had managed to subdue Belch, showing a physical skill and bravery that one would never expect to be paired with such a kind, gentle, forgiving man.

What had she been thinking to ever put him in danger? Where had her heart been?

She shuddered at the thought of what she had become, during all these years on Devil's Mount.

Thank God for George, who had come to save her from herself.

She reached the bottom step and jumped down onto the beach. Belch's rumbling vibrated in her chest, shaking her like a reed. She felt another spurt of respect for George, that alone he should be able to bring down such a monster.

God save her, she had been housing a hero without even knowing it.

Keeping a safe distance, she circled around Belch's snout. The spear was where George had left it, leaning against the side of the beast's head. Alizon dashed forward and grabbed it, then danced back, heart thumping, staring at the blindfolded monster.

This was her dragon to kill. Her choice to make. George had been right about that.

Would it live, or would it die?

Its death would be her total freedom. Its death meant she could be with George. And its death meant that no other young girl would ever have to worry that her future lay in its jaws.

She made her decision.

In the course of daily living Alizon had slaughtered her share of chickens and sheep, and she was no stranger to the death of animals. She knew that the kindest end was the swift and unexpected one, accomplished before the creature suffered fear or pain. Lowering the spear, she took aim and ran full-tilt at Belch. The spear's head pierced the beast's hide, Alizon's weight and momentum pushing its shaft in a full foot. Belch bellowed through his tied jaws, and he started to thrash his tail and head, his body arching.

Alizon felt tears start in her eyes, Belch's agony her own. She did not want him to suffer, no matter what suffering the monster had caused in the past. She gritted her teeth and took better hold of the moving spear, and she shoved on it with all her might.

"Damn you! Die!" she cried, and pushed again, tears spilling down her cheeks. The spear went in another inch, then stuck. "Die! Please God, die." Blood poured out of the wound and down the shaft of the spear, coating Alizon's hands and soaking into her dress.

And then there was another pair of hands added to her own, shoving with greater strength than she could muster. George was beside her. Together, they sent the spear homeward, deep into Belch's heart.

The dragon gave one last bellow of pain, his head thrown back, and then his head crashed to the ground. He lay still.

Alizon released her hold on the spear and stepped back, shaking. She met George's eyes. "Is he truly . . . ?" she asked.

George looked at the dragon a long moment, then back at her. He nodded his head.

She closed her eyes and tears spilled anew down her cheeks. George's arms closed around her, and she let herself sink into the warmth of his embrace.

Chapter Twenty-four

Her tears for Belch did not last long. Tucked within the safety of George's arms, Alizon began to feel the weight of the past lifting from her. With the monster's death came the end of all that had been . . . and the birth of all that could be.

Giddiness bubbled up inside her, an almost hysterical sense of relief and burgeoning joy. She reached behind George and squeezed his buttocks. He jerked back in surprise, then looked down at her in question. She grinned. "You said we had some unfinished business," she began.

"You don't want me to take care of it *here*, do you?" He seemed a bit shocked.

She licked his salty chest in reply.

He laughed in amazement, then swept her up into his arms and carried her to the pool. There he plunged with her into the steaming water. Alizon clung to him as the water billowed her gown and soaked through her sleeves and bodice.

"I cannot swim!" she cried.

"It is only waist deep here." George set her down, and he yanked loose the laces of her bloody gown. Soon the soggy garment was tossed over his shoulder, her chemise following, and then his clothes as well. Slowly he helped wash every trace of dragon's blood from her skin, then she returned the favor, at last running her hands down his body as she had wished to do all those times she had spied upon him at his bath. At last she felt comfortable doing so.

As she was finishing, George caught her again, and she wrapped her arms around his neck, her naked, wet body flush against his. He lifted her up into his arms and carried her from the water, up onto the beach. There he lowered her to a smooth patch of stone, the mist swirling over their bodies. Alizon dug her fingers into his hair and coaxed his head down to hers for a kiss.

His hand stroked down her side, then up again to her breast, massaging it, his fingers playing with her nipple. "Will you be all right here?" he asked, and she knew he meant making love in the lair.

"This is where it has to be," she said, not fully understanding why, but knowing it to be true.

He started to lower his mouth back to hers, but she stopped him, her hands still in his hair. She looked up into his green eyes, alight with caring and with passion; they held nothing back from her of what was in his heart.

And she was truly no longer afraid to show him what was in her own. "I love you," she said, and then she said it again, liking how the words felt, and liking the way his gaze deepened as she said it, as if his soul were opening even wider to her. "I love you. I love you. I love you."

"My little dragonslayer," he replied, and she thought she saw a glimmer of tears in his eyes. Then he was suddenly lowering his mouth back to hers, and she was feeling his chest against her bare breasts, his legs entwined with her own, and his hand—oh, his hand!—moving up between her thighs, to stroke there her most sensitive place.

She parted her legs and tilted back her head as his lips moved down her throat. She opened herself to him, trusting him with her body and soul. He had seen into every dark corner of her heart, and he loved her still.

No, there was nothing to fear. He had taught her how to free herself, and now she gave herself over to his touch, trusting him to lead her into this new world.

His fingers played against her, moving slickly over flesh grown full and sensitive with desire. Alizon arched her hips up against him, wanting more, that emptiness growing in her that ached to be filled.

George positioned himself against the entrance to her body, the head of his member as large and blunt as she remembered. He held himself up on his forearms, his face close to hers. "I love you," he said.

Alizon felt her body relax, open. George pierced her and slid deep, and this time, instead of being rent, she was filled. She wrapped her arms around his back and let him guide her hips into a rhythm, rejoicing in the feel of his muscles moving beneath her arms, and in the sweat that dampened their skin as they moved together.

She wanted it to go on forever, this thrusting fullness inside her, these deep waves of pleasure, the sound of his breathing beside her ear broken only by his whispers of her name. Then he pulled slightly away from her and reached down between them. He touched her as he thrust once more, and then she was lost within her climax, feeling the contractions of her sex around the thickness of his shaft.

He held her tight in his arms, his hips barely moving against her own, and he was saying her name over and over and over again as she felt the pulse of his release.

The cold stone virgin was gone forever.

The cold stone virgin might be gone, but a cold naked woman had taken her place. Alizon roused from her doze against the side of George's chest, feeling the chill of the beach beneath her body. She shivered and snuggled closer.

"Cold?" George asked and rolled her up on top of him.

"A little." She kissed his chest as he held her in place with his arms.

"I would suggest we get dressed, only I don't know where our clothes are."

"That *is* a problem," she agreed dreamily. "Perhaps we'll have to stay here forever."

"I might almost be tempted."

She was quiet a moment, thinking. "Where will we go, George, when we leave the mount? I know the virgins will return to Markesew, but where will *we* go?"

"Where do you want to go?"

She thought. Only one answer seemed right: "Wherever it is that you are."

He ran his hands down her back, cupped her buttocks, and kissed her deep and hard in reply.

When the kiss ended and she got her breath back, Alizon went on: "I think I should like to see this homeland you have spoken of, and to meet your sister. If I could."

"You would not miss Markesew?"

"I have no one there but Emoni. It is perhaps weak of me, but I should rather go to some town and country that are new to me, and me to them. I can truly begin anew that way."

He was quiet, his hands idly playing in the small of her back.

"What is it?" she asked, a little thump of anxiety in her chest.

He squeezed her and smiled, albeit not entirely reassuringly. "I did not lie to you when I said that

Emoni had summoned me with her magic. The only way I know to reach my home again is through that same magic. I do not know that it will work, and do not know that it will allow another to accompany me."

A cold flush went through her body, and Alizon began to shake. "You are going to leave me?"

"No! No, never! *You* are what I came here for, not the dragon."

"I thought you said you came to be a hero."

"That's what I thought, but I was an idiot. That tapestry you have been weaving, Alizon. Doesn't that tell you something? You wove my face into it, before you ever met me. We were meant to be together, no matter the distance in time or space."

He might be right. She set her mind on that and refused to think about any other possibility. "If we were meant to be together, then Emoni's magic should work on us both."

"But it might not. I do not want to take the risk."

"I do not want to stay in England," she said softly.

"It might not be so bad; we could find a different town . . ."

"Please take me away."

He met her gaze, a frown of worry upon his brow. "Even if the spell does work, you may not be so happy with the result. My world is different from yours, in ways you would think me mad if I tried to explain."

"I don't care. If there is French toast and sand-

318

wiches, I will be able to eat. If there is a sofa, I will have someplace to sit. And there will be you."

"That is enough?"

"It's more than I could ever have dreamt."

He kissed her and smiled. "There is one other good thing about returning to my world."

"What's that?"

"I'm filthy rich. You'll be able to buy anything your heart desires."

She traced his lips with the tips of her fingers. "Then may I buy another kiss from you?"

He growled, and nuzzled her neck. "A penny will get you that . . . and plenty more."

"I'm going to like your world."

Then he showed her again just how very much she had to look forward to.

"*You* should be wearing the surcoat, not me," George said several hours later, standing on the dark stairs in the passageway to the kitchen.

"They're all women. I don't care if they see me nude, but you can be certain I care if they see *you*."

"They've already seen me plenty of times," he grumbled. A draft wafted up under the hem of the surcoat, brushing his butt with coolness and pressing its chill touch to him in uncomfortable places. He felt absurdly naked without his pants or briefs, bits of his body hanging much looser than comfort demanded.

Their clothing, so happily discarded in their passion, had unhappily sunk out of sight in Belch's pool. The only garment remaining was George's surcoat, which had been thrown across Belch's eyes as a blindfold—and Alizon had insisted that he be the one to wear it.

"What are they going to think when we open that door?" Alizon fussed. "I still haven't been able to come up with an excuse for losing my gown."

He laughed. "Did you really think you could?"

"Greta is going to be so disappointed in me."

"She doesn't like me much, does she?" he asked. There was always one relative or girlfriend who didn't like a guy, no matter how nice he tried to be.

"She's scared she'll be abandoned. I promised her that that would never happen, though. It won't, will it?"

"Does she have family in Markesew?"

"Yes, but I don't know if they will take her back," Alizon said. "If worst came to worst . . ."

"Yes?"

"If worst came to worst, could we take her with us?"

"I'd be willing to *try*, but . . ."

She turned to him, and he could only barely make out her features in the dark of the passageway. "Would you be willing to try with all your heart, the same way you will try to take me with you?"

"I don't know if—"

"But you'll *try*?"

"Because you love her, I will try with all my heart," he said.

She threw herself into his arms, nearly knocking him off his feet. She planted kisses all over his face as he found his balance, leaning up against the damp wall. He might get used to doing as Alizon wished, if this was the reaction he always got.

He let his hands roam freely over her naked body, then lifted her up so that she was straddling his hips. He was so caught up in what they were doing, he barely heard the sounds of scraping metal and soft female curses of frustration from behind the kitchen door.

He noticed when the light flooded down upon them.

"Got it! I told you I could pick the lock," Pippa cried in triumph at the top of the stairs. Then she gasped.

He and Alizon both looked up to see the silhouettes of half a dozen heads limned in the doorway.

"A little privacy, if you don't mind?" he called up to them.

There was a collective gasp, a quick mad shuffle complete with Pippa being dragged forcibly away, and then the door slammed shut.

"You needn't worry about an excuse for your missing gown, now," he said to Alizon, as she hid her face in his neck.

"Jesu mercy," she whispered.

"Another good thing about my home: good locks on all the doors."

Chapter Twenty-five

"Are we ready, then?" George asked.

The question was met by a dozen pale and frightened faces. Alizon and her eleven charges were standing on the north terrace, dressed in their finest gowns, hair loose and woven with wildflowers from the banks of the mount. The breeze caught at tresses and skirts, swirling them around these figures who stood still as stone.

It was the day of the summer solstice, and the virgins of the mount were returning to Markesew.

He and Alizon had decided that waiting the few days until the solstice would make for the biggest impact on the villagers. They would all be waiting there on the seawall, a perfect audience for their procession.

He did know a thing or two about making an entrance, after all.

The wait also had given the virgins time to adjust to the idea that they were leaving, and time to pack up those things they wished to take with them. Their makeshift bags, filled with gowns and small treasures, were piled on a cart that Milo would pull behind them, like a medieval skycap.

"You're going home! This is good!" George said. "No one can hurt you any longer. Belch is dead." There was no response, as if they were unconvinced. "No one can throw you to a dragon that's dead. And even if they don't believe our words, they'll believe *this.*" He held up the foot-long tooth he had pulled from Belch's jaw as a souvenir.

He had wanted to bring the dragon's entire head with them, but Milo had refused to go down in the cavern to help him, and it was too heavy to carry or drag on his own.

Not that anything could have stopped him from trying, after he had pulled the tooth. He had tied a rope to Belch's head and had dragged it halfway up the cavern stairs before it slid off over the side and splashed into the pool, sinking out of sight.

He had spent a good fifteen minutes cursing Belch for that. Now all that the villagers would see when they came to the lair—if they had the nerve to come to it—would be a headless, rotting body. The dragon did not look half so intimidating as it should, without its head.

On the bright side, maybe when the decomposition was a little further along, Belch's head would float to the surface and scare someone silly.

"Don't you want to see your friends and families?" he asked them.

It was Flur, standing beside Alizon and clinging to her hand, who finally answered in a small voice. "What if they don't want us back?"

"But . . . your mother," he said in confusion.

"What if they don't recognize us?" someone else said.

"Or remember us?"

"What if they won't take us in?"

"What will we do?"

"Can we come back to the mount if we want?"

"Peace!" Alizon said, breaking in. "If they don't want you, then you'll come with me and George, as we discussed. No one is going to be left alone, to fend for herself. No one." She locked her gaze with George's, her black eyes widening in a prompt for him to speak.

"There is room for everyone in my house," he said, and for the hundredth time prayed to God that Emoni's magic would be powerful enough to accomplish the miracle. It had been Alizon's idea to offer such an option to all the virgins, and her determination was strong enough that he almost thought they could be transported on it alone. "It is far away, and in a land different from this one you know, but it is a good life you'll have there." Assuming they got there.

What was he doing, telling them he could bring them back with him? He didn't even know if he could take Alizon—an uncertainty that still had him considering staying here forever.

Alizon, though, had utter faith in the powers of Emoni and in the prophecy of her own tapestry, and had refused to listen to any further suggestions that they stay in her world.

When Alizon was adamant, the forces of heaven and hell could not move her.

George's other concern was the creepy certainty he had that his "real" body, or a version of his real body, was still sitting in that wingback chair in the great room of his house back home, his sister sitting across from him. This was real, here with Alizon, but it was somehow also real there.

The dragon had been killed, the virgins were leaving the mount, he had found his Alizon: he had accomplished all he needed to, in this world. He feared that Athena would soon be waking the other him, and he might disappear from this world whether he wished it or not. If he must go, then he wanted to go on his own terms, with Alizon.

Somehow.

God help him.

"So. Now that that's settled, are we going? It's nearly noon." He heard the reluctance to leave in his own voice, not wanting to bring them any closer to the moment when he might be separated from Alizon forever.

"Think of that girl they are about to choose in

the lottery," Alizon said to the virgins. "She, at least, will be happy to see us coming."

That won a smile from the group.

"All right, then," George said, and motioned Alizon to come stand beside him. He was wearing his washed and mended surcoat, with the red cross of St. George. Alizon might know he was no saint, but the villagers would react better if they thought he truly was the legend come to life.

Alizon took her place, and then the virgins lined up behind them in order of when they had come to the mount. Flur was last, with Milo behind her.

The shepherd, quiet as always, was nonetheless grinning like a lunatic, and kept making sniffing noises suspiciously like those of a man hiding tears.

Pippa dashed out of line and back to the cart, rummaging amid the bags until she found her own. A moment later she pulled out a wooden flute. She played a few notes, her eyes meeting George's in question.

He nodded. Entrance music. Of course!

Pippa stepped back into line, playing her merry tune.

George took Alizon's hand and raised its back to his lips. "Are you ready?" he asked softly.

"With you, I'm ready for anything."

Together they took the first steps.

Alizon's heart beat with sickening thumps in her chest, her muscles trembling as she walked beside George across the causeway. They were half-way there, and she could see that the gathered villagers had begun to notice that something strange was going on. More and more people were crowding up to the seawall, their murmuring, excited voices carrying over the empty bay.

"They're about to get the surprise of their life," George said, giving her hand a jiggle of encouragement.

"I hope they fall dead from the sight."

He leaned over and kissed the top of her head. "Don't be frightened."

Curse the man. It was galling that he seemed to know whenever she was scared. The tougher she tried to be, the more he soothed and coddled. And the kinder he was, the more she wanted to crawl into his arms and stay there, with her face pressed to his chest.

"I'm not frightened," she lied.

"You shouldn't be. Remember," he said, and deepened his voice, "You have Saint George to protect you!"

She laughed, and he squeezed her hand again. She moved closer to him, so that they bumped together with each step, the contact a reassurance that there was one who loved her, one who would stand by her, come dragons both real or of her heart.

The only other person who might love her enough to forgive her her crimes would be waiting on the seawall: Emoni. It was seeing her friend again, and admitting that for twelve years she had given no sign that she yet lived, that had her scared more than facing the villagers.

The villagers could rot in Hell for all she cared. She doubted she would ever fully forgive them, and certainly would never forget what they had done, but with George and a new life she thought she could at least leave them in the past. She could start over, in a place that held no memories of hurt, and with a man who would give her anything, even the freedom to choose her own fate.

The years on the mount had been worth it, if George was her reward.

The murmurs of the crowd grew louder, and then began to quiet as they drew near. Pippa's music floated out from behind her, and the sun broke through the clouds, sparkling on the seabed all around them. Alizon felt a smile tickling at the corners of her mouth. Verily, they must make quite the spectacle! She wished she could hear the thoughts of the gape-jawed men and women who were staring dumbfounded.

She was too nervous to focus on the faces long enough for recognition, her eyes skipping from one to another, her thoughts slowing down and clogging up.

George, however, was in his element.

"Greetings!" he shouted, and the mob jumped. Pippa's music tweetered out.

Alizon felt a nervous giggle in her chest. God's body, she wished she could stop shaking. She wished she could focus on a face.

"I am Saint George," her love called from beside her, "and your dragon has been slain!" He released her hand and used both of his own to raise Belch's giant tooth up above his head. "Behold, the fang of the beast!"

The crowd murmured, and glances were exchanged. No one seemed to know what to make of this.

"Behold!" George shouted again, and gave the tooth a punch in the air. "The dragon is dead."

"The dragon is dead?" a male voice from the crowd asked.

"Yes! Dead! Behold the fang of the beast!"

"Someone killed it?"

"Yes. I am Saint George," he repeated, sounding to Alizon's ears as if he were getting a little annoyed by the slowness of the villagers.

She felt another giggle coming on. She had tried to warn him.

"Saint George the dragonslayer?" another man asked.

"Yes."

"What are you doing here, in Markesew?"

Alizon heard him sigh. "I was summoned to *kill the dragon*. Which I did, with the help of this fair maiden you once knew as Alizon." He put the tooth under his arm and with his free hand pulled her forward.

She heard the mumbling of the crowd, her name repeated in question, "Alizon? Alizon?"

They did not remember her. She felt the pain of

it even deeper than their rejection could have cut. All those years she had seethed over their acts, and they had forgotten her the moment she was gone from their sight.

"Yes, Alizon!" a woman's voice said. "Damn you sorry lot, do you not recognize the girl you sent to her death twelve years past?"

Alizon searched the crowd, saw movement as a woman pushed her way to the front. She caught her breath on a sob. "Emoni?"

"Alizon! By the rood, but you're beautiful for being dead!"

Alizon stumbled the few steps left between them, and they fell into each other's arms. "I would never have let your daughter go to the dragon," Alizon croaked past her suddenly rough throat, not knowing why it was the first thing she chose to say after all these years.

"Marry, of course you would not have!" Emoni squeezed her tight, as if not quite believing she was real. They held each other for long moments, and then Emoni said, "God's breath, is that Greta?"

Alizon pulled back, and realized Emoni had seen over her shoulder. "Greta, and more."

George took the cue and stepped up onto the seawall. "Behold, the virgins you cast unto the beast! Greta! Lavena! Reyne! Sisse!"

One by one he named them, and as he did they came forward, up onto the seawall, their steps and faces uncertain, their eyes skimming over the crowd for some sign of greeting or recognition. The crowd backed away, forming a half-circle, leaving the virgins to stand like freaks, surrounded by a space that no one wanted to cross.

"Braya! Joye! Ysmay!" George called. "Kit! Malkyn! Pippa! And last, but certainly not least, Flur!"

There was a gasp from a woman, who fell to her knees at the edge of the circle. "Flur?"

"Mama!" Flur cried, and ran to her mother's open arms.

"Joye?" an old man asked. "Joye? Is it you?"

"Papa?" Then Joye was gone from the small group.

One by one names were called, and girls reunited with what members of their families remained. Alizon looked at George, and caught him wiping at his eye with a knuckle. Milo, behind them, was openly weeping, the tears dripping off his cheeks.

And then no more names were being called. Greta, Braya, Reyne, and Pippa still stood in their small group. Alizon saw Greta's brother in the crowd, and saw him turn away from the searching gaze of his sister.

Pippa had been an orphan, and both Braya and Reyne's parents had died during the time they had been on the mount: each year's new virgin had brought news of births and deaths from the village. If the remaining virgins had siblings here, none were coming forward to claim their lost sisters.

"How?" Joye's father asked. "How come they to be alive? Did you find them in the dragon's belly?"

"We never went to the dragon," Alizon said, finding her voice. Her anger over the hurt she saw in the faces of those virgins who remained unclaimed gave her the strength to speak out. "He was satisfied with the flesh of sheep. We have all been living in the fortress these many years, afraid to return. It was never necessary to send a virgin to her death. All those lost lives were for nothing."

Voices rose in protest.

"Aye, that is right! No one need ever have died!" she shouted.

"They were in the belly of the beast," a different man called. "That is the truth of it. When the saint cut him open, out they fell!"

"No!" Alizon shouted. "We were in the fortress!"

But no one wanted to hear her. "In the belly!" people were repeating. "Fell out like a nest of tangled snakes!"

"You never had to kill us . . ."

"Let them be," George said, laying his hands on her shoulders, "They won't listen."

"But they must! It was unjust, what they did."

"They can't allow themselves to believe you. Let them be."

"It's not right."

"No, it's not. But it's for you to choose if this battle is worth fighting. Look instead at those who have been reunited. And look at those who haven't. You know what matters most."

She looked to the four who remained, and to Milo. George was right: They were all that need concern her. She could do nothing about whether the villagers accepted what they had done, or changed their way of thinking; and she had already had her years of vengeance upon them, for what little joy it had brought her. Time now to live with love, and to leave hatred behind.

"Are you ready to come with me and George?" she asked the others.

Milo sniffed back the rest of his tears. "Mistress, if you do not mind, I would stay in my cottage."

"Milo, are you certain?"

"It suits."

George turned to the man. "I could have a cottage built for you, near my home."

Milo shook his head.

George slapped him on the back. "Good luck to you, then, my friend. And take a word of advice from a man who knows the value of a spectacle: Put up a gate and charge admission to the castle and cavern. You'll be rich."

"No one comes to Devil's Mount."

"They will. Believe me, my man, they will."

Alizon spoke to Pippa and the other virgins. "Will you come with us? It will be a long journey, to a faraway place, but at least we will be together."

Pippa wrinkled her nose at the villagers and spoke for them all. "The farther, the better."

Alizon, George, and the remaining virgins spent the rest of the day with Emoni and her family, the words flowing fast between them as they tried to share years in the space of a few hours. Alizon wished they could have a month together, but George and Emoni both felt something that told them that their time was short.

So it was that she now found herself in Emoni's barn, standing with the others in a circle around a curious crystal in a gold base. Candles surrounded the crystal, their flames reflecting deep within the faceted stone.

She hadn't given much thought to the method of travel when she had insisted that she and George return to his world, and insisted as well that the virgins accompany them. She felt a stab of superstitious anxiety now that she was face-to-face with it, though.

What in God's name had she been thinking, to ask to be sent through a crystal to another world? How could such a thing possibly work, and how could she and the others possibly survive it?

"Hey. Are you all right?" George asked.

"Huh?" she grunted, coming out of her panicked reverie.

"I did this once before, you know. We'll be fine."

"Yes, I suppose."

" 'Suppose' nothing." He tugged her hand until she looked at him. "I love you."

She smiled. "I love you, too."

"We'll come through. All of us."

She found herself believing him. She turned her gaze to each of the girls, seeing their fright and trying to reassure them without words.

Then she met Emoni's hazel eyes. There were no

words that could encompass what she felt for her friend, and at leaving her once again. "I will never forget you," she finally said, feeling it inadequate, but the closest she could come to what was in her heart.

"Nor I you, not in a thousand years."

Emoni came to her, and Alizon embraced her friend one last time. Sniffing back tears, she whispered, "Good-bye."

Chapter Twenty-six

George held Alizon's hand on one side, Pippa's on the other. They were all six standing with clasped hands in a circle around the quartz crystal on its small table, candles glowing around it. He had Belch's tooth hanging from a rope around his neck, and the others wore their improvised satchels of belongings crosswise over their chests. Alizon had her rolled-up tapestry between her feet.

He squeezed her hand, and Alizon looked up at him, nervous uncertainty in her eyes. He felt it himself. Would this work? Could it possibly? Would he awake to find himself surrounded by virgins in his own living room, or would he wake with nothing more than memories and a broken heart?

But no. Love was real. Even if all else in this world was but whispers of the imagination, there was no questioning what he felt for Alizon, and what he saw shining back from her. This was real.

He would believe nothing else.

The spell would work because it had to, because Alizon was now too finely woven into the very fiber of his soul for them to ever be separated.

Emoni began her chant. He looked at Alizon one more time, tracing with his gaze the line of her profile and the smooth arch of her brow. He *would* carry her back with him, if he had to trade his soul to do it.

There was no force more powerful than love. There was no truth greater. There was no corner of the universe, in time or space, where it couldn't reach.

There was nothing else that mattered but love.

He turned his gaze to the crystal and sent the plea of his heart to the flame that glowed deep within it.

Alizon centered her vision on the crystal, the dark barn around her fading away. Emoni's chanting voice grew faint, and then she could not hear it at all. She was aware only of the crystal, and of holding George's hand on one side and Greta's on the other. She felt a fluttering of fear in her chest.

Would they make it? And what would they find on the other side?

She held to her faith in Emoni, and to her own love for the circle of people who stood with her around the crystal. Whatever world they were going to, there was a promise in it for a future better than to be had here. And whatever trials might await, George would be with them.

No one was going to be left alone. Ever.

For a heart-stopping moment she lost all sense of touch and sound, unable even to feel her own body. She was alone in a nothingness, her vision filled by the white light at the center of the crystal.

And then she heard a woman's voice, faint at first, then growing louder. It spoke in an accent that was difficult to understand, but the tone was calm and deliberate, and there were a few words that kept repeating that came clear:

"George" and "slowly waking."

Then all of a sudden Alizon could feel her body again, and the hands clenching tight at her own. The light in the crystal extinguished itself, wiping the glare from her vision.

The woman's soft speech abruptly turned to a scream.

Alizon blinked and looked about. A dark-haired woman was sitting in a strange chair, her hands slapped over her mouth as if to keep in further screeches. Her wide hazel eyes were jumping from virgin to virgin as they held hands in their circle: from Pippa to Braya to Reyne, Greta, and then herself.

The woman's hands dropped from her mouth as she met Alizon's eyes. A frown of puzzlement creased her brow.

Alizon tilted her head to the side, staring at the

woman, feeling an unaccountable sense of recognition.

"Emoni . . . ?" she asked softly.

The woman's lips parted, her frown deepening, as if searching her memory for a face that should have been there but was not. She shook her head slightly, as if helpless to answer.

"Holy Christ," George said. "It worked!"

Alizon broke her gaze with the woman and turned to George. He was still clasping her and Pippa's hands but was sitting in the same strange type of chair as the woman, wearing clothes she had never seen, and his beard was gone. The dragon tooth was no longer hanging around his neck.

Alizon glanced down, suddenly anxious. Her tapestry was still with her.

"George?" the woman squeaked.

He released their hands and jumped up, sweeping Alizon into a bear hug and lifting her off the floor. "It worked! It worked!"

Alizon was too dazed to answer, but felt a smile begin to stretch across her lips. She *was* here, wherever *here* was. They all were! She started to laugh.

"George?" the woman squeaked again.

The virgins released each other's hands, blinking at the room around them, turning to look at the fire, at the woman, at herself and George. Her joy must have reassured them, because they started to smile, and then they were laughing, too, hugging each other and dancing around.

"George!" the woman cried.

George set Alizon down abruptly and kissed her hard and quick on the lips. He turned her to face the woman, who was standing now, trembling.

"Alizon, I'd like you to meet my sister, Athena." He spoke in a thick accent, like the woman's, but slowly and carefully enough that Alizon could just manage to catch his meaning. "Athena, meet the heart of my heart, Alizon. You sent me to find her, whether you know it or not."

"I . . ." Athena said.

Alizon felt tears start in her eyes. This woman *was* Emoni. Athena had sent George to her, across the boundaries of their worlds, Athena's soul knowing their bond of friendship even if her mind did not.

"Everything is clear to me now. Your little crystal there has powers you have not even guessed at." He held his sister by the shoulders and kissed her forehead. "Thank you."

"I . . . well . . ." Athena looked at them both, then at the virgins, who were examining the room with eager interest. She turned a helpless expression back to George. "I need to put sheets on the guest beds—if they're staying the night."

"I will help you," Alizon said.

"Yes . . . thank you." Athena met her eyes, and then for a brief moment her confusion cleared away. "Alizon."

Epilogue

Two years later

"Dammit!" George said, hanging up the phone.

Alizon looked up from her museum book of medieval art. "What is it?"

She could see his face soften as he looked at her, in the way it always did. She was constantly surprised that he still found her as entrancing as back when they had first met, especially when she looked like she did right now. She was lying on her stomach, on the sofa in the family room, wearing a pair of his boxer shorts and a threadbare T-shirt. Her hair was up in a loose bun, a green Japanese chopstick jammed through it.

Sundays were her declared day of sin and sloth. Whether she was traveling with George or at home, she devoted herself with unflinching hedonism to junk food, lazing about on her beloved sofas, television, and letting her hands roam as often as they pleased over her husband's body.

She took the enjoyment of Sundays almost as seriously as she took Dragon Maiden Tapestries. She and the remaining virgins continued to weave their art, and George had arranged for their work to be sold through both their own Web site and a gallery on a street somewhere called Rodeo Drive. They sold for up to $45,000 apiece, depending on size and detail.

The tapestry that looked so much like George hung in his den, never to be sold. He said that it reminded him to keep his head screwed on straight.

She still wasn't quite sure what he meant by that.

"That was my agent. The studio wants my script, but only if someone younger and better-looking plays my part. Younger and better-looking! Can you believe it? Some candy-ass pretty boy is going to be playing *me.*"

She ducked her head, her shoulders shaking, a snort of laughter slipping out.

"They offered to let me play Milo."

She looked up, and at his disgruntled expression could hold it in no longer. She rolled onto her back, laughing, tears in her eyes.

"You think that's funny?" he asked, leaning over the back of the sofa.

"Yes, my darling, I'm afraid I do. You are becoming an old, old man!"

"I'll show you funny, Ms. Fifteenth Century!" He reached down and tickled her until she squealed.

"Stop it, stop it," she cried.

His hands stilled. Her giggles quieted, and she met his eyes. She wasn't wearing anything under the T-shirt and could feel her breasts full and free beneath the thin white cotton. His warm palms slowly slid up her rib cage to her breasts, his thumbs stroking over the soft curves.

She lifted her arms and dug her fingers into his hair, pulling his face down to hers. Her lips met his with a hunger that a lunch of potato chips and Junior Mints had done nothing to satisfy. He slid over the back of the sofa as her arms tightened around his neck, her lips demanding everything he had. He came to rest atop her, his body pressing hers into the deep cushions, the wakening of his own desire becoming a hard ridge against her belly.

"Uncle George! Aunt Alizon! Come watch, come watch!"

She was pulled out of her lustful fog by Gabrielle, yanking on their sleeves.

"Pippa built a new jump and is going to test it!"

"Oh, Christ!" George said, climbing off her. She was right behind him as he ran out the sliding glass door onto the back deck. "Pippa! Pippa, don't you dare!" he shouted.

The only reply was the revving of a dirtbike engine, floating to them from across the field that edged up to the back lawn.

"Pippa! You listen to me!"

George had bought the virgins horses soon after their arrival, in a misguided attempt to make them feel at home. The virgins had found the contents of the garage much more fascinating than those of the stable, however, and now the only exercise the horses got was galloping around the field trying to escape the off-road madness of virgins in Land Rovers.

Pippa, alone among them all, preferred two wheels to four. What was worse, she had a streak of the daredevil in her that George said reminded him of himself, at her age.

"Pippa!" he yelled again, the twang of a fearful parent in his voice. He had threatened to cut Pippa off from "Xtreme Sports," her favorite television show, if she tried any more stunts like the time she rappelled down one of the towers. Then there had been the sheet-as-parachute disaster, which had required a visit to the emergency room to sew up a gash in her leg from landing in a rhododendron. Presently she was on a campaign for hang-gliding lessons.

George jogged down the wooden stairs in his bare feet, then ran across the lawn. "Pippa! You shut that thing off, you hear me?"

Alizon could see Pippa's new jump from the deck: a ramp of dirt about three feet high that would send her flying over a long Pippa-made mud puddle.

Alizon hadn't told George, but Pippa had already started talking to her about training to become a professional wrestler, a high-flyer like her idol.

"Pippa's on the bike again?" Athena asked, coming to stand beside Alizon at the porch rail. George jokingly referred to his sister as Chief Virgin Wrangler. She had undertaken the basic education of them all, putting them to work on the same texts from which little Gabby learned. She and Alizon had become close friends, both certain that they had known each other in more lifetimes than this one.

Alizon nodded, then glanced at Reyne, Greta, and Braya, who had their purses slung over their shoulders. "Where are you all going?"

"Athena's taking us shopping," Greta said and smiled. The scar from the surgery repairing her harelip was concealed with makeup, and her hair, cut in a chin-brushing bob, had sunny blond highlights in it.

Reyne's plastic surgery and dental work had been more extensive, but the results as successful. No stranger looking at her would suspect that her nose had once been smashed, her teeth broken, or that her eyelid had drooped. She was still shy of her looks, but there was a certain coyness to her now, as men started to notice her and she gained confidence.

George had forbidden any of his single wrestling colleagues to "so much as think about" getting involved with any of his "foreign cousins." He told everyone they were distant relatives from Yugoslavia.

Reyne supplied the rest of the information on their outing in her softly sweet, misleading voice. "Braya has a date."

"Shut up!" Braya said, blushing.

Alizon looked at Braya in surprise. "A date? Where did you meet him?"

She mumbled something.

"One of those online dating services," Athena filled in.

Alizon looked at George's sister in wide-eyed question.

Athena shrugged. "It's hard to meet people these days. I wrote her ad and read the men's out loud."

"Does George know?"

"As if he would understand. He's turned into a mother hen, afraid to let any of you out of his sight. He'd try to send a bodyguard with her."

Alizon smiled. Poor George. It had been mothers overanxious to protect their offspring that had been the catalyst for his arrival at Devil's Mount. Now he himself was living that frantic parental role, trying to keep safe five medieval women in a modern world full of temptations to trouble.

She and the others had been surprised to find out what George did for a living—but not as surprised as he seemed to have expected. Fighting had been entertainment in their time as well, and George's version was just a little more colorful.

It had taken longer for them to understand that George's world was still their own, only six centuries later. He had shown them travel videotapes of modern England, including one that showed Devil's Mount. The fortress had been added to, burned, and rebuilt through the ages and was no longer recognizable, although the causeway across the bay was remarkably the same.

Markesew had become the town of Marazion, and history said the mount had become a pilgrimage destination, the legend of the slaying of the dragon having spread across the country. There was, however, no trace remaining of Belch, or any proof that he had existed.

She wanted to go see Devil's Mount in person, but that would have to wait until George's lawyer managed to convert them all from paperless, illegal aliens to legal residents of the United States, or some such nonsense. She and George wouldn't even be considered legally married until the identity issue was straightened out, despite the ceremony held on this very deck a year and a half past.

The bike engine hit a fever pitch, and Pippa tore into sight from behind a clump of trees, a rainbow of ribbons flying from the plume atop her purple helmet. Yellow plastic guards protected her shoulders, elbows, and knees. Alizon was reminded of the pictures she'd seen of a knight in full armor, charging down the lists.

George stopped his own dash across the field, obviously realizing it was too late to halt the jump.

Pippa hit the ramp, ripped up it, and flew. The front tire of the dirt bike rose up, Pippa standing on the footrests like a rider in stirrups. The rear tire touched down in the end of the puddle, sending up a spray of water. The front wheel came down on dirt, and for a moment it looked like she'd caught the landing just right.

Then the rear wheel slid out sideways, and the bike went over on its side, taking Pippa with it and catching her leg under its weight. The plumed helmet hit dirt.

"Pippa!" George cried, rushing to her. He pulled the bike away and tossed it aside, then huddled down over her. Alizon could not hear what was being said but guessed George was checking her for injuries.

A minute later Pippa was on her feet, helmet off and black starburst hair flaming undeterred. She looked up at the deck and her audience, and even from this distance Alizon could see the grin of triumph on her face. The girl punched her fist into the air.

Gabrielle punched hers into the air in response, and then whistled with her fingers in her mouth as her uncle had taught her. Greta, Braya, and Reyne applauded politely. George stalked behind the daredevil, a dark and harried frown on his brow.

Alizon took his arm when he came up the deck stairs and pulled him away from the others.

"She's giving me gray hairs," George complained. "I found another one this morning."

She wrapped her arms around his waist and laid her head against his chest, hearing the beat of his heart beneath her ear. "Maybe that's why they won't let you play yourself in the movie."

He swatted her on the butt, and Alizon giggled into his shirt.

"She's going to break her neck. What am I going to do with that girl?" he implored.

"Promise her hang-gliding lessons if she behaves."

He was silent for a moment, and then she felt the tension leaving his body. He ran his hands up her back and then pulled the chopstick out of her hair and laid it on the deck rail. Her hair fell in a heavy wave down her back, and he dug his hands into it, tilting up her face.

"What am I going to do with *you?*" he asked.

"I can think of a few things."

"You're a temptress, my Alizon, and I'm no saint."

She kissed him tenderly on the lips. "I never thought you were. But you'll always be my hero."

The Wildest Shore
LISA CACH

Teasing the female passengers about the perils of the sea is great fun, but once Horatio Merivale opens his mouth to laugh at danger, he wishes he'd kept it shut. A storm drags the *Coventry* under, and it is all the East India Company officer can do to rescue a lovely but terrified blonde. Still, the whole escapade seems the start of a marvelous adventure. The dream luring Anne Hazlett from England is grand—a turquiose seascape with a jade-carved island whose beaches beckon. Yet she doesn't expect to arrive on flotsam, be accosted by pirates, or have such an odd entourage. Indeed, the man who saves her is thrilled by their bad luck, calling it "The Hand of Destiny." And looking into her eyes, Horatio promises to see Anne to the wildest shore.

Dorchester Publishing Co., Inc.
P.O. Box 6640
Wayne, PA 19087-8640

_52454-6
$5.99 US/$6.99 CAN

Please add $2.50 for shipping and handling for the first book and $.75 for each additional book. NY and PA residents, add appropriate sales tax. No cash, stamps, or CODs. Canadian orders require $5.00 for shipping and handling and must be paid in U.S. dollars. Prices and availability subject to change. **Payment must accompany all orders.**

Name: _____

Address: _____

City: _____ State: _____ Zip: _____

E-mail: _____

I have enclosed $_____ in payment for the checked book(s).

For more information on these books, check out our website at www.dorchesterpub.com.
____ *Please send me a free catalog.*

❧the
Mermaid of Penperro
LISA CACH

Konstanze never imagined that singing could land someone in such trouble. The disrepute of the stage is nothing compared to the danger of playing a seductress of the sea—or the reckless abandon she feels while doing so. She has come to Penperro to escape her past, to find anonymity among the people of Cornwall, and her inhibitions melt away as she does. But the Cornish are less simple than she expected, and the role she is forced to play is harder. For one thing, her siren song lures to her not only the agent of the crown she's been paid to perplex, but the smuggler who hired her. And in his strong arms she finds everything she's been missing. Suddenly, Konstanze sees the true peril of her situation—not that of losing her honor, but her heart.

___52437-6 $5.50 US/$6.50 CAN

Dorchester Publishing Co., Inc.
P.O. Box 6640
Wayne, PA 19087-8640

Please add $2.50 for shipping and handling for the first book and $.75 for each book thereafter. NY, NYC, and PA residents, please add appropriate sales tax. No cash, stamps, or C.O.D.s. All orders shipped within 6 weeks via postal service book rate. Canadian orders require $2.50 extra postage and must be paid in U.S. dollars through a U.S. banking facility.

Name_____
Address_____
City_____ State_____ Zip_____
I have enclosed $_____ in payment for the checked book(s).
Payment <u>must</u> accompany all orders. ☐ Please send a free catalog.
CHECK OUT OUR WEBSITE! www.dorchesterpub.com

The CHANGELING BRIDE

LISA CACH

In order to procure the cash necessary to rebuild his estate, the Earl of Allsbrook decides to barter his title and his future: He will marry the willful daughter of a wealthy merchant. True, she is pleasing in form and face, and she has an eye for fashion. Still, deep in his heart, Henry wishes for a happy marriage. Wilhelmina March is leery of the importance her brother puts upon marriage, and she certainly never dreams of being wed to an earl in Georgian England—or of the fairy debt that gives her just such an opportunity. But suddenly, with one sweet kiss in a long-ago time and a faraway place, Elle wonders if the much ado is about something after all.

___52342-6 $4.99 US/$5.99 CAN

Dorchester Publishing Co., Inc.
P.O. Box 6640
Wayne, PA 19087-8640

Please add $1.75 for shipping and handling for the first book and $.50 for each book thereafter. NY, NYC, and PA residents, please add appropriate sales tax. No cash, stamps, or C.O.D.s. All orders shipped within 6 weeks via postal service book rate. Canadian orders require $2.00 extra postage and must be paid in U.S. dollars through a U.S. banking facility.

Name_____
Address_____
City_____ State_____ Zip_____
I have enclosed $_____ in payment for the checked book(s).
Payment <u>must</u> accompany all orders. ❑ Please send a free catalog.
      CHECK OUT OUR WEBSITE! www.dorchesterpub.com

Everyone loves a little meddling *help* from Mom ...

A Mother's ~~Day~~ *W*ay

Romance Anthology

♥

Lisa Cach, Susan Grant, Julie Kenner, Lynsay Sands

Is it the king who commands Lord Jonathon to wed, or is it the diabolical scheme of his marriage-minded mama? After escaping her restrictive schooling, Miss Evelina Johnson wants to sow her wild oats. Mrs. Johnson plants different ideas. Andie never expects the man of her dreams to fall from the sky—but when he does, her mother will make sure the earth moves! Jennifer Martin has always wanted to marry the man she loves, but her mom knows the only ones worth having are superheroes. Whether you're a medieval lord or a marketing liaison, whether you're from Bath or Betelgeuse, it never hurts to have some help with your love life. Come see why a little meddling can be a wonderful thing—and why every day should be Mother's way.

___52471-6 $5.99 US/$7.99 CAN

Dorchester Publishing Co., Inc.
P.O. Box 6640
Wayne, PA 19087-8640

Please add $2.50 for shipping and handling for the first book and $0.75 for each additional book. NY and PA residents, add appropriate sales tax. No cash, stamps, or C.O.D.s. All Canadian orders require $5.00 for shipping and handling and must be paid in U.S. dollars. Prices and availability subject to change. **Payment must accompany all orders.**

Name	
Address	
City	State _____ Zip
E-mail	

I have enclosed $_____ in payment for the checked book(s).
❏Please send me a free catalog.
CHECK OUT OUR WEBSITE at www.dorchesterpub.com!

LEISURE BOOKS PROUDLY PRESENTS ITS
FIRST HARDCOVER ROMANCE!

Wish List

A sparkling holiday anthology
from some of today's
hottest authors.

Remember, this year
the very best gifts
in Romance come from:

LISA KLEYPAS

". . . knows how to make a reader's dreams come true."
—*Romantic Times*

LISA CACH

"An author of ingenuity . . . [with] a uniquely entertaining voice."
—*The Romance Reader*

CLAUDIA DAIN

"An author with an erotic touch and a bright future!"
—*Romantic Times*

LYNSAY SANDS

". . . writes books that make you laugh and turn up the air-conditioning!"
—*Romantic Times*

AVAILABLE NOW!

Dorchester Publishing Co., Inc.
P.O. Box 6640
Wayne, PA 19087-8640   _4931-7 $16.00 US/$25.95 CAN

Please add $4.00 for shipping and handling for the first book and $.75 for each book thereafter. NY and PA residents, please add appropriate sales tax. No cash, stamps, or C.O.D.s. All orders shipped within 6 weeks via postal service book rate. Canadian orders require $2.00 extra postage and must be paid in U.S. dollars through a U.S. banking facility.

Name_____
Address_____
City_____ State_____ Zip_____
I have enclosed $_____ in payment for the checked book(s).
Payment <u>must</u> accompany all orders. ❑ Please send a free catalog.
CHECK OUT OUR WEBSITE! www.dorchesterpub.com

Seduction By CHOCOLATE

Nina Bangs, ♥ Lisa Cach, Thea Devine, ♥ Penelope Neri

Sweet Anticipation . . . More alluring than Aphrodite, more irresistible than Romeo, the power of this sensuous seductress is renowned. It teases the senses, tempting even the most staid; it inspires wantonness, demanding surrender. Whether savored or devoured, one languishes under its tantalizing spell. To sample it is to crave it. To taste it is to yearn for it. Habit-forming, mouth-watering, sinfully decadent, what promises to sate the hungers of the flesh more? Four couples whet their appetites to discover that seduction by chocolate feeds a growing desire and leads to only one conclusion: Nothing is more delectable than love.

___4667-9 $5.50 US/$6.50 CAN

Dorchester Publishing Co., Inc.
P.O. Box 6640
Wayne, PA 19087-8640

Please add $1.75 for shipping and handling for the first book and $.50 for each book thereafter. NY, NYC, and PA residents, please add appropriate sales tax. No cash, stamps, or C.O.D.s. All orders shipped within 6 weeks via postal service book rate. Canadian orders require $2.00 extra postage and must be paid in U.S. dollars through a U.S. banking facility.

Name_____
Address_____
City_____State_____Zip_____
I have enclosed $_____ in payment for the checked book(s).
Payment <u>must</u> accompany all orders. ☐ Please send a free catalog.
CHECK OUT OUR WEBSITE! www.dorchesterpub.com

LYNSAY SANDS
The Reluctant Reformer

Everyone knows of Lady X. The masked courtesan is reputedly a noblewoman fallen on hard times. What Lord James does not know is that she is Lady Margaret Wentworth—the feisty sister of his best friend, who has forced James into an oath of protection. But when James tracks the girl to a house of ill repute, the only explanation is that Maggie is London's most enigmatic wanton.

Snatching her away will be a ticklish business, and after that James will have to ignore her violent protests that she was never the infamous X. He will have to reform the hoyden, while keeping his hands off the luscious goods that the rest of the ton has reputedly sampled. And, with Maggie, hardest of all will be keeping himself from falling in love.

____4974-0 $5.99 US/$7.99 CAN

Dorchester Publishing Co., Inc.
P.O. Box 6640
Wayne, PA 19087-8640

Please add $2.50 for shipping and handling for the first book and $0.75 for each additional book. NY and PA residents, add appropriate sales tax. No cash, stamps, or C.O.D.s. All Canadian orders require $5.00 for shipping and handling and must be paid in U.S. dollars. Prices and availability subject to change. **Payment must accompany all orders**.

Name _____

Address_____

City_____State_____Zip _____

E-mail _____

I have enclosed $_____ in payment for the checked book(s).

❏Please send me a free catalog.

CHECK OUT OUR WEBSITE at www.dorchesterpub.com!

KATIE MACALISTER
NOBLE INTENTIONS

Noble Britton suffered greatly at the hands of his first wife, and he refuses to fall into the same trap again. This time he intends to marry a quiet, biddable woman who will not draw attention to herself or cause scandal. Gillian Leigh's honest manner and spontaneous laughter attract him immediately. It matters little that she is accident-prone; he can provide the structure necessary to guide her. But unconventional to the tips of her half-American toes, his new bride turns the tables on him, wreaking havoc on his orderly life. Perpetually one step behind his beguiling spouse, Noble suffers a banged-up head, a black eye, and a broken nose before he realizes Gillian has healed his soul and proven that their union is no heedless tumble, but the swoon of true love.

____4965-1 $5.99 US/$7.99 CAN

Dorchester Publishing Co., Inc.
P.O. Box 6640
Wayne, PA 19087-8640

Please add $2.50 for shipping and handling for the first book and $0.75 for each additional book. NY and PA residents, add appropriate sales tax. No cash, stamps, or C.O.D.s. All Canadian orders require $5.00 for shipping and handling and must be paid in U.S. dollars. Prices and availability subject to change. **Payment must accompany all orders.**

Name _____
Address _____
City _____ State _____ Zip _____
E-mail _____
I have enclosed $_____ in payment for the checked book(s).
❑Please send me a free catalog.
             CHECK OUT OUR WEBSITE at www.dorchesterpub.com!

ATTENTION
BOOK LOVERS!

Can't get enough of your favorite **ROMANCE**?

Call **1-800-481-9191** to:

✳ order books,

✳ receive a **FREE** catalog,

✳ join our book clubs to **SAVE 20%!**

Open Mon.-Fri. 10 AM-9 PM EST

Visit **<u>www.dorchesterpub.com</u>**
for special offers and inside
information on the authors you love.

We accept Visa, MasterCard or Discover®.
LEISURE BOOKS ♥ LOVE SPELL